HUSTLE

HUSTLE

a novel

JASON SKIPPER

PRESS 53
Winston-Salem

Press 53
PO Box 30314
Winston-Salem, NC 27130

First Edition

A Robin Miura Novel Selection

Cover design by Kevin Morgan Watson and Sara Maher

Cover image Copyright © 2011 by Beat Eisele

Author photo by April Smith

Library of Congress Control Number: 2011928856

The author gratefully acknowledges the editors of the following
publications, where several chapters from this novel first appeared in
slightly different form: *Hotel Amerika* ("Girlfriend in the Lights"); *Crab
Orchard Review* ("Tangled in the Ropes"); *Phoebe* ("Ghosts"); *Cream City
Review* ("Contracts"); *The Redwood Coast Review* ("Acoustic"); *Touchstone*
("Hustle"); *Blue Mesa Review* ("Outlaws," previously titled "Buddy").

This novel was completed with the assistance of an Irving S. Gilmore
Emerging Artist Grant provided by the Arts Council of Greater Kalamazoo.

Printed on acid-free paper
ISBN 978-1-935708-34-6

For my mother,
Kathy Skipper

I

ACOUSTIC

Who can say where want begins?

I wanted my family to be rich. With running cars and our own house. A VCR to watch *Star Wars* and *Xanadu* every day. My mother to stop crying so much, and my father to not leave the house whenever she did cry. I thought if I was famous, I could save us. I was nine years old and would be better than Michael Jackson, or even Elvis. I listened to music all the time and sang when no one was around. *Thriller* had hit the shelves that past December, and by spring I'd worn out two copies. I knew the words to every country song on the jukebox at the bars my father went to. Bands on the radio like Mötley Crüe, Duran Duran, and Run-DMC. Most of my life, I'd followed my mom around the house, singing the Dylan and Carpenters she liked, and I had wanted a guitar almost as long as I'd known want.

One afternoon while I was listening to the radio behind the counter in my father's seafood store, an old man came in carrying a large, worn-out guitar case. He set it against the glass display counter and rang the silver bell for help. My job was to yell for my dad, Wrendon, before customers came in, but I sucked at it. I'd been working there three weeks, since my mother took a job doing data entry for a propane company. Up to then, after school, I'd taken the bus home, where she and I hung out all afternoon. With the radio in the background, we did chores and made dinner. Most nights Wrendon went straight out after work, and she and I ate alone. But now he brought me home and stayed more often. I wanted to keep him happy with this situation, but I could never pay attention. This time, as the old man walked in, I was staring at the case, wondering if the guy was famous. If I should know him. But when I focused on his wrinkled face and torn shirt pocket, I knew he wasn't, and I wondered what he wanted.

The bell was still ringing when Wrendon came through the doorway separating the front of the store from the back, where he did the cleaning. His apron was stained with blood from the fish. His thin hair was patted down, and his hands were wet. He rubbed them across his stomach, shot me a look, and assessed the man. A different sort of irritation flickered across his face. "What can I do for you?" he said, trying to sound patient.

The old man set the case on the counter, popped the rusted brass latches. With shaky hands, he pushed up the lid. Wrendon crossed his arms and peered past the old man, at the door, to see if anyone else was coming, and stepped forward. "How much are you asking?"

I hadn't realized the man was selling it, and Wrendon knew I wanted one. I'd been saving up already.

"Veinticinco," the man said.

"It's not worth twenty-five," Wrendon said.

They spoke for a few minutes. The man in Spanish, my father in English. Sometimes they nodded at me, and I grew anxious, but Wrendon kept his arms folded. Finally, he said, "Get over here," put his hands under my armpits, and lifted me up to the counter. "What do you think? Think you could do something with this?"

The guitar was bulky and tan, the strings rubbed to a dull shine. It was beat up, just like the old man, looking nothing like the shiny, new electrics people played on *Friday Night Videos*. I said. "It's old."

"It's an acoustic," Wrendon said. "Most people start out with these. A lot of folks still play them. Willie Nelson. Johnny Cash."

I hung there limp, my armpits hurting.

"Yes or no," he said. "I'm not going to convince you. What you want costs too much money, and he'll sell for fifteen. That's three week's pay, *if* I keep you."

I waited and stared up at the man, hoping he might pull something else out.

"Yes or no," Wrendon said.

I said, "I'll take it."

The old man's smile was missing a tooth on each side. He clapped his hands. Wrendon said, "All right," and I was excited. He set me down and pulled the case to our side of the counter, laying it on the floor. After going to the register and popping the drawer open, he handed me a crumpled five and ten. "Go pay him."

I walked over and set the money on the counter. The old man took it, folding the bills into his shirt pocket, repeating "Gracias" as he backed out the door. He crossed the parking lot and the highway, holding his hat down.

I went to the stool where I'd been sitting. Wrendon said, "You going to leave this here?" and nudged the case with his boot.

"You want me to play it right now?"

When he laughed, I knew he'd meant to put it in back so customers wouldn't see. He said, "I bet you think you can pick it up like it's nothing."

I shrugged. How hard could it be?

"Everyone thinks that," he said. "Why don't you give it a shot?"

I said, "Right now?"

"It's your guitar," he said. "Why not?" As he spoke, he untied his apron and laid it over the counter.

I walked to the guitar case, kneeled down, and undid the latches. I wasn't sure how to hold it, lifting it by the long part. I climbed back up on the stool, trying to balance it on my lap. "What should I play?"

"You choose," he said.

I figured I should make something up on the spot, just to show him that I could. But the guitar felt like a block. I couldn't work my right arm around the thick part, and when I managed, gripping the skinny part with my left hand and keeping the bigger part up with my right elbow, it steadied, somewhat. Thinking I had it, I lifted my right hand and strummed the strings with my fingertips. This wasn't how other people played, but I figured it was my style.

5

After a second, Wrendon grabbed my wrist midstrum.

"I think it's broken," I said, staring up at the spot where the man had crossed the road, angry about the money I'd lost, knowing we should have waited.

"You have to tune it," Wrendon said.

He walked behind me and tapped my spine. "Sit up straight," he said, and I did. He took his hands and moved the guitar around on my lap, repositioning my arms. "This bottom part is called the body," he said. "The long part is the neck. Just like a person."

I saw what he meant.

"Some folks name their guitars after women," he said. "You got one in mind?"

I said, "I don't know any women," but thought *Olivia Newton John.*

"The point is to treat it like a woman. You can't go banging right away."

He showed me the tuners, and then the frets. "The closer you come to the body," he said, "the higher the notes get. But let's just focus on what we're doing."

He said the top string, played open, should be in the key of E. He found the E by turning the tuner and made me play that string by itself. "That's a note," he said. "But we'll get to those later. Right now, all you need to know is E."

He turned the tuner down until the string flopped loose and said, "Now find the E yourself." As I searched for the note, he made the sound with his voice. I heard the noises against each other until they sounded the same. He said, "You've got it. Now push that string down at the fifth fret. That's the note the next string needs to make when it's played open, without you touching any frets. You've got to listen for the tone just like you did with the open E."

I struggled at first with holding the strings down and turning the tuners, but by the fourth string it was easier. Wrendon showed me how this one was different. "You have to move to the fourth fret. Be extra careful with these last strings, or else you'll pop them."

I tuned the strings, and he loosened them all again. By the time I figured it out, the sun was farther down in the window and the parking lot pavement was darker. My fingertips hurt and my arms ached. But the guitar sounded right. Almost new. Even still, I had thought this would come easier. I said, "How long till I learn songs?"

Wrendon was pulling his apron back on. "Just concentrate on keeping your fingers on the strings," he said, smoothing out the front, "playing up and down the neck." He disappeared behind the doorway. From in back, he said, "How about tonight when we get home, I'll show you some chords? Maybe each week I can trade you songs for pay. And when you come in here after school, I'll start to teach you how to work the counter and clean the fish. Then on Fridays, I'll give you lessons."

"You know songs?" I said.

"Sure," he said. From in back, he started singing Hank Williams.

I thought of coming here more often, learning to do what he did. Our matching aprons. Holding knives and gutting fish on the large cutting board he kept. I heard his knife knocking against it. I almost put the guitar back inside its case. "Can I play a few more minutes?"

The knocking stopped. "Put it away when someone pulls up," he said. "And pay better attention, or else I'm going to have to can you."

I knew he was kidding and said, "All right."

I was alone now with the front of the store to myself. I looked at the beat-up, faded case, spread open on the floor. My case. I plucked the E string three times before doing this again while pressing a finger behind the first fret, then the second. And so on. I followed each string through each note, not knowing yet if one was flat or a major or a minor or whatever. I shut my eyes and followed my worn-out new acoustic from its lowest note to highest. I pressed my ear against its body and felt it hum.

OUTLAWS

The first time I heard the song "Guitars, Cadillacs" by Dwight Yoakam, I was ten and had just taken my place in a string of con artists that stretched back to my grandfather, Buddy. Standing in the back of my father's Dodge utility van, we were heading through the night from Wewahitchka, Florida, to Fort Worth. Buddy sat beside me, duct-taped into a La-Z-Boy. The tape was triple-layered around his ankles, stomach, and arms, but he could still snap his fingers and shake his stringy white hair. He used the tips of his toes to pitch the chair back and forth. Between swallows of watered-down High Life, he threw his head back and hollered out his plans to rock us home.

He was beginning the slow comedown off a three-week bender. Wrendon and I were rescuing him. Still Buddy crooned on, and I sang with him. Our paired strain of out-of-tune voices ringing against the metal walls, loud enough to outdo the blaring music, echoing Yoakam's sentiment that guitars, cadillacs, and hillbilly music were the only things that keep us hanging on. After holding the golden tallboy to Buddy's lips, I stamped my feet, strummed an air guitar, and shook my sweaty hair, belting out the words.

Another flash of car lights whooshed by us.

When Buddy finished one beer and the song started to fade past its closing lines, he waved me to the front of the van and twirled his finger in circles, saying to rewind the tape to its start. "It's the only thing worth hearing," he said.

When I stumbled to the front, Wrendon asked, "How are you boys holding up?"

"Fine," I said, pushing the button on the deck. "But Buddy needs another cold one." I reached inside the Styrofoam cooler that Wrendon kept behind his seat at all times, stocked with Schlitz. Only now his cans were mixed in with Buddy's golden High Life. Propping myself up with my elbows on the arms of the two captain's chairs, I flicked ice off the top and peeled it open. I handed the can to Wrendon, and he chugged half. Wiping his arm across his face, he handed it back. I dipped a plastic cup in the cooler's water and poured the water in the can, repeating this until it was full. I put the lid back on the box and checked the speedometer. Eighty miles per hour. The lit-up road stretched before us. We sailed by state-long rows of pine trees, signs for rest stops and gas stations, long-nosed Peterbilts and snub-faced Mack trucks. The CB was screwed on the dashboard, and Wrendon's Merits sat beside it. I said in my best trucker drawl, "Hey, Road Toad. Got anybody on the horn?"

"Nope, Tadpole," he said. "But I'll holler if I do."

From in back, Buddy said, "Are you drinking all my cold beer? Where's my hillbilly?"

I yelled, "Hold your horses."

Wrendon said, "Make sure his tape is down and he doesn't piss in the chair. If he says he's got to go, hand him the pee jug."

"Ten Four, Road Toad."

"Over and out, Tadpole."

By the time I staggered back to Buddy and the La-Z-Boy, the deep chords and drumbeat of Dwight Yoakam's song had started rolling. The shock of the speakers got my knees shaking. I was working on my own routine of hip gyrations, toe-turning, and running the course of some stage where I could play every instrument at its most important part, always singing, either for Wrendon, who had pulled me out of school without telling my mother, the grandfather I had met the day before when we found him passed out in his river house, or the car behind us with its lights flooding in, blazing me up like a ten-year-old star.

Up until the day before, Buddy's name had never been mentioned. I later found out I had spoken with him once over the phone when I was eight, when Wrendon first owned the store. In a deep, raspy voice, he had asked how old I was and how my dad was doing. I answered his questions and asked if he wanted to talk to my father, but he said, "Nah." When Wrendon asked who called, I told him what happened. He thought for a minute and half-smiled, shaking his head. I asked if he knew who it was, and he said "I know who it was" as he walked into the back. Those days we barely had any business, and the door chime never rang. But two years had passed. We now had dozens of regulars who stopped in every week. Business cards with the store's name—*Saxton's Seafood*—in bold letters, a drawing of a shrimp, and the phone number below *Call for Catering*. Earlier that year he had bought the van used, thinking he would hire weekend help to sell shrimp on the roadside next to flea markets and produce stands. He called it expansion.

Later on, Wrendon would say he wasn't surprised when he got the call that Friday morning from a worried friend of Buddy's, saying he was two steps short of the deep end. The man on the phone explained that Buddy had been diagnosed with emphysema. He'd been on and off the wagon since moving to Wewahitchka a year earlier, after his wife died. But he'd recently hit the throttle when some younger gal nearly drained his checking account. It didn't seem he'd last the month, not at this rate. Though they hadn't talked in ten years, Wrendon immediately hung his orange CLOSED sign in his storefront window, drove straight to James A. Arthur Elementary, and pulled me out of art class to keep him company on the fifteen-hour drive.

Wrendon explained all of this as we pushed through the glass doors and crossed the walkway outside my school, into the crisp fall day. He wore boots, faded jeans, and a light blue polo that still carried the thick smell of ice that filled his store. The sky was clear, the sun bright. He'd left the van parked in the fire lane. I felt like he'd busted me out of jail. I shielded my eyes and said, "Who's Buddy?"

He opened my door and said, "Hop in."

Once we settled on the interstate, Wrendon turned down the radio and rolled up his window, what he did when he wanted to talk about something serious. If he needed me to understand the late-night fights he had with my mother, that he couldn't see why our house stayed so cluttered. "She won't throw out anything," he said. "Ashtrays all over. Extra plates in the kitchen. And all the romance novels she keeps in the closets. Have you counted them? Hundreds. Lining the walls. Stacked to the ceiling. And they're ridiculous. Have you flipped through one?" I had. They were all about sad women getting rescued. But this didn't seem worth fighting about, and I knew there were other reasons. I wanted to stick up for her. He would turn down the radio when he wanted to give advice. "People will always tell you how to be," he said, waving his Schlitz around. "But be your own boss. Never let anyone tell you what to do." I never knew what was coming, and I rolled up my own window, making the van quiet.

"I should start at the beginning," he said. "When I first met him. I never actually knew Buddy until I was your age. Up to that point, he'd been in a Georgia state penitentiary, doing time for con jobs."

I said, "For what?"

"He used to con folks," Wrendon said. "You know. *Con jobs.* He'd go around to different towns he didn't live in, convincing people he owned a roofing company and telling them their roofs were about to cave in. They'd give him the down payment, and he'd cut town."

"Isn't that bad?"

"Of course it's bad," Wrendon said. "But it made shitloads of money. He was on Hoover's most wanted list. He had his picture up in post offices."

I didn't know who Hoover was, but my father said this proudly. "So it's okay?"

Wrendon creased his eyebrows, as if questioning whose kid I was. He waved me off. "Anyhow," he said, "Buddy didn't want anyone seeing him in jail, not until he got released. On that day my mom dressed me in my church suit, and we went. I stood beside

11

the car outside the prison gates in the hot sun. After an hour he showed up. Six foot two with his dark hair slicked back. His slacks so starched that even from where I stood, you could make out the lines. When he came up, the first thing he says to me is 'You're Wrendon, right?' And I nodded. He said, 'I gave you that name. Did your mom tell you that? You're older than I'd remembered. But that's a good thing, I guess. We can skip all that daddy shit. You just call me what my friends do.' He took the keys from my mom and said, 'Let's hit it.' Then he looked at me and said, 'Get your hands out of your pockets. You look like a vagrant.' We loaded up and headed back to Pensacola, where we lived at the time. A year later he and my mom split up. He kept doing con jobs over the years. Last I heard he was married, but I guess that woman died in a car wreck. Up to recently there was some other woman he met at a bar. He has a trailer on a river in Wewahitchka. That's where we're headed." He turned up the radio, and I knew that was it, at least for now.

I turned it down and asked why he and Buddy hadn't talked in so long.

Wrendon cocked his head to the side. "Buddy once said himself that disappointment goes hand-in-hand. 'We all let down folks we love, and sure enough they do the same.' I guess it got to be too much. He's not an easy man to deal with. Does what he wants, when he wants, with little regard for others. Family means nothing."

"So why are we going?"

"Because," Wrendon said, "what kind of son just leaves his dad like that?"

He waited for an answer, but I wasn't sure how to respond. "No kind of son," he said.

I thought of my mother and how we hadn't called to say we were leaving. There were days I missed her, working at the store. I once mentioned this to Wrendon, and he said to get that out of my system. It was close to five o'clock. Most nights, Wrendon and I shut the store down at six. By the time we got home, dinner was already on the table. On Fridays, while we were eating, he would ask if she wanted to go out dancing, and she usually said no, saying she was too tired and wanted to stay home and relax. He would say, "Suit yourself," shower and change into starched jeans and a button-down and kiss her cheek good-bye. She would change into her pajamas, and we would settle in the living room with Monopoly and TV. Or she would read one of her books while I practiced my guitar. I liked when they went out together and didn't mind sitting at home alone. I could turn up the music on the radio in my bedroom and play along with it. When I asked her why she didn't go more often, she said, "I can't run like I used to when I was younger. Plus I hardly know his friends."

"You don't like them?"

"They're fine," she said. "But I'm happy here, sitting with you." I would look at her to see if she was telling the truth, and she was. Most nights we went to bed around ten and slept all night. But some nights, I woke up to them yelling. Usually throwing women's names around. He said she wouldn't have to worry if she came out. She said, "You know why I don't go? Because you leave me sitting alone at the bar."

Laying in bed, I could picture it, and I felt sorry for her.

He said, "Stop it."

"Admit it," she said. "You're ashamed of me."

I cringed, hearing her say this. She always said she was fat and talked about being on a diet. I knew from looking through old photo albums, at pictures from when they were younger, that she had once looked different. Skinny and smiling in the flash of some camera, with bright brown eyes, wearing bright clothes. In the pictures they always sat side-by-side, pressed together. Now they never sat together. Her hair was always a dull brown that matched her eyes. Sometimes the gray roots showed, and even now at thirty-three she had wrinkles by her eyes and her face was always puffy.

I imagined her getting home that night, making dinner and sitting alone at the table with her chin resting on her clasped hands, wondering where in the world we were. It was like Wrendon not to call, but not me. I said, "Do you think Mom will be all right?"

He slapped the steering wheel and said, "How in the hell did I forget?" He gunned the van, grabbed the next exit, and pulled into a gas station. He said, "Wait here," and walked across the dusty parking lot to a pay phone. After talking he went in the store and came out carrying a Styrofoam cooler, bag of ice, case of beer, and a six-pack of Cokes. He climbed in his seat and gave me a large pair of mirror sunglasses with the price tag still dangling from the middle. I'd never owned a pair before, and they matched his. He tossed his orange lighter in my lap and said, "Burn that tag off the center." He started up the van and yelled over the engine, "Your mom said we should treat this like a vacation."

I could hear her concern. We weren't the type to take trips. Wrendon went to his favorite bar, hunted and fished, but that was it. As he steered us back on the road, I put them on. I was happy, drinking Cokes as he drank beers. Pressing up the highway, I listened to truckers' voices crinkle through the CB radio that stayed in my hand, up by my ear. The sun slipped over the windshield, and eventually the world became red lights and headlights, the lights from the dashboard, and the intermittent flame of his lighter. Green road signs we flew past. We talked every so often; radio stations came and faded; the hush of wind slipped through the cracks at the top of our windows that eventually sent me to a shallow sleep.

I woke up startled in the dark. My door swung open, and humidity filled the van. "We're here," Wrendon said, standing outside my door. My face and arms were already layered with thick sweat, my clothes clinging to my body, and I felt swollen. Crickets chirped, and the river was loud behind the house. I said, "Where's Buddy?"

"I got him to bed," Wrendon said, stepping aside. "Now hop out."

I climbed out of my seat and into the yard. Along the edges stood tall pine trees. The lawn was soft. Thin cotton curtains hung in the windows. The air conditioner buzzed and rattled. The house's front door was cracked open, and a yellow light came through. Walking through the front door, I saw that every light in the house was on. Empty beer cans and overfilled ashtrays covered the furniture. On the end tables and arms of the couch. Turned sideways all over the floor. Clear, empty liquor bottles stood on top of the refrigerator and counter. The smell of urine rushed so fast up my nose that I wanted to bolt outside, but Wrendon steered me toward a bedroom.

The room was dark, and the air smelled thin and clean. He

turned the blankets down on the bed, and I climbed in between the cold sheets. "What's going on?" I said.

He stood by the door, about to head back into the living room. "Tomorrow's going to be a long day," he said, "and I want you to get some sleep. I have to straighten some things here. My sense is we're going to leave early."

I pulled the blankets to my chin. "What about the river?"

"Don't forget to say your prayers," he said and shut the door behind him.

He always said this on those nights when he tucked me into bed. Lying there I heard garbage bags flapping and cans banging, and I tried to pray but, like always, fell asleep before I could finish.

I woke up early the next morning when there was hardly any light. I looked for Wrendon, but he wasn't in the bed. I threw off the blankets and climbed out and went to the living room to find him. The windows were rolled open. Cold, moist air came through the wire-mesh screens, filling the house. The ashtrays lay stacked, freshly cleaned in the dish drainer. All of the cans were gone, and the air smelled like Pine-Sol. I glanced out the back windows, past the deck and down at the river. Too big for me to do anything useful with it. I tiptoed past the glass dining room table, to a closed bedroom door, and pushed it open. A man was snoring underneath white blankets in the center of the bed while Wrendon slept on his side on the floor, still fully dressed and using his arm for a pillow. I considered getting him one of my blankets but somehow knew not to take care of him like that, and I tiptoed back to my room.

When I woke again later that morning, I sensed things had changed. Walking back into the living room, I saw the other bedroom's door was open. Through the large front window I saw Wrendon outside, smoking a cigarette beside the van. The sky was burnt orange with a light fog in the air. The two-lane road sat in front of the house, and a car went by. A large, tan chair sat on the ground next to the van's open side doors, and Wrendon was trying to figure out how to fit it inside. I put on my shoes, went out the door and down the wooden porch steps.

As I crossed the dew-glistened lawn, he said, "Help me lift this."

We got the chair inside, and he slid it, thudding over the corrugated metal, to the center. He said, "Hop up there and sit down."

With me in the chair, he went to the driver's seat, positioned himself and looked back at me over his shoulder. He walked to the La-Z-Boy, grabbed its arms, and scooted it around, took his seat again and worked his rearview mirror until his blue eyes shone in it. "Can you see me?"

I said, "Yes."

He said, "Good, now get up."

Following him out, I said, "I guess that chair's for me?"

"It's for Buddy," Wrendon said, already crossing the lawn toward the side of the house. "But first we need to discuss something." We climbed the steps to the back porch, and he pointed toward two wrought-iron chairs. The seats were still wet, the bottoms cold against my legs. I waited as he sat down and lit a fresh Merit. "First things first," he said, "I want to apologize for not sticking around here longer. There's all kinds of fishing in the lake where this river runs, and I intend to bring you back. But here's the deal. We've got some serious business to attend to, and I'm sure it won't be pretty. In fact, it's probably illegal. But Buddy is very sick right now, and we need to get him to Texas. Are you keeping with me?"

I nodded.

"And to do that, we have to make sure he stays in that chair and doesn't put us in any danger."

I said, "How?"

"Well, he could steer us off the road and flip the van over."

"No, I mean how? How do we make sure he stays in the chair?"

"That's what I'm about to tell you," Wrendon said. "I just need to make sure you're okay with this."

I said whatever it was, I'd be okay.

First we needed to clean him up. I filled the bathtub with warm water, and Wrendon dumped in peach shampoo, making bubbles. With a pink washcloth and bar of soap, Wrendon scrubbed Buddy's chest and stomach. Washed his ears and thick yellow toenails, lathered his face with shaving cream and shaved him slowly, shaking the razor in the bathwater. After that Wrendon pried Buddy's mouth open and carefully placed his dentures inside. Setting him down on the toilet, he dried Buddy with a towel and dressed him in a white button-down and brown slacks. He rubbed peppermint Brylcreem through Buddy's hair and combed it back into small lines. At times Buddy murmured, but he was too far gone to stay awake.

Wrendon cradled him and carried him down the steps, to the van. I walked sideways with my arms held out beneath him in case he fell. Finally we set him down in the chair.

Wrendon told me to stay put and disappeared inside the house. A minute later, he was back at the top of the stairs, holding a roll of duct tape. He pulled the door shut and made sure it was locked. I stood between the van's side doors as Wrendon approached, pulling a strip of tape loose with his teeth.

"What are we doing with that?" I said.

"We're saving his life," Wrendon said. "Now grab his shoulders and hold him still."

Buddy woke up later that afternoon in Alabama, screaming, "Goddammit, cut me loose!"

I was holding the CB and jolted upright. Wrendon stayed calm and looked in his rearview mirror. "Oh, you're all right."

"You turn this van around," Buddy yelled.

Wrendon noticed that I was freaked out and patted the arm of my chair. "He's just feeling a little cranky. You know how it is when you first wake up." He turned toward Buddy. "You want a beer?"

"I can't breathe!" Buddy said. "You got my cigarettes?"

"No can do," Wrendon said. "Doctor's orders."

The chair was thumping around. "I don't know what shithead doctor you've been consorting with," Buddy said, "but this ain't right." He started coughing.

Wrendon took a light blue inhaler off the dash and held it out to me. "Give him this. It's his prednisone, to help him with his lungs." Wrendon pointed to the hole at the bottom of the little cylinder. "Put this up to his mouth and push down on the top." He pushed it down and mist came out.

I leaned against my door. "I'm not going back there."

"I mean this," he said, and dropped the inhaler in my lap. "Buddy won't hurt you." Wrendon stuck his arm behind his seat, inside the cooler, and took out a Miller High Life. "Just give him this."

I knew from the serious look on Wrendon's face that I couldn't stay in my chair, so I reluctantly took the can. With the beer in one hand and the inhaler in another, I tried to keep from toppling over in the swaying van as I started toward Buddy. His white hair hung down the sides of his face, and his nostrils flared. "What are you supposed to be?" he said.

Standing before him, I wanted to look tough but had trouble even staying on my feet. "I'm your grandson," I said.

"Bullshit," he said. "And do you know how I know? Because no kin of mine would kidnap his granddad without so much as a hello and how are you, then strap him down to a recliner. Now cut me loose before I break free and whoop your sorry ass."

I felt my face crumple in and my eyes tear up.

Buddy's neck craned forward in disbelief. "Ahh lord, son," he said. "You're going to cry just like that? You hardly know me."

"There's more tape where that came from," Wrendon said, and he tapped the roll on the dash. "You keep talking to Chris like that and I'll use it on your mouth."

Buddy tried to wiggle his bound arms and legs. He flung his hands out, giving up, and shook his head. "Ahh, man." He started to cough and nodded toward the inhaler, his face quickly growing red and the coughs getting more strained. "You've got to shake it up," he said, "or else the shit's no good."

Relieved, I shook the canister and put it to his dry lips. As I pushed the button down, his thin chest sank in. He held his breath while I stood there, and he exhaled a small puff of air. He started coughing again, trying to bring his fist to his mouth, and nodded at the beer. "Give that here," he said, "before I choke to death."

I put the can to his mouth, and he eased back his head. Lines of liquid poured down his chin, collecting on his starched white shirt. My eyes narrowed in amazement as the can got lighter, tilting upward. When it was empty, he swallowed hard and said, "Another."

I'd seen Wrendon drunk before, but he wasn't the type to swear or get mean. Schlitz seemed a part of his hand, like his digital Timex watch or the horseshoe ring he'd won in a pool tournament. The maroon and white cans always sat at the bottom of our refrigerator and in the cooler at the back of his store. Always within his reaching distance. He drank them the same way some people sip iced tea all day. But Buddy was different. He drained them in minutes and said to keep them coming. By his fifth can, he got chattier. Almost cheerful. As much as I wanted to sit in my chair up front, I was in charge of his supply.

As the afternoon drifted, he started telling stories about my father, from when he was younger. Things I'd never heard. At first Wrendon seemed bothered, making pained faces when I came back to get more beer. Later the faces stopped, and he started smiling. Buddy told me about the afternoon he caught Wrendon driving a stolen Mustang. "There I was at a stoplight," Buddy said, "and who do I look over to see," he nodded toward Wrendon, "but my *savior* up there, sitting in a brand-new convertible with one of his slack-jawed friends. I said, 'Wrendon, you take that car back where you got it.' But he was nothing doing. He ducked his head laughing, peeled through that red light and headed west for Mobile. Over there he knew some hood who tore down cars and sold them off. Turned out he had a racket going. Just ask him sometime what he did with all the money."

On my next beer run, I did.

Wrendon said, "One time I bought him a brand-new Buick."

"You did," Buddy yelled, suddenly remembering. "And that heap of junk leaked oil all over my driveway." He turned to me. "I figured he stole that beater too, probably off some old widow. Oh, he was a decent enough car thief. But I tell you one thing." Buddy raised his eyebrows, pointing his finger up toward Wrendon. "Your dad was one of the most pathetic cons I've ever seen. Couldn't talk his way out of an open field." Buddy rocked his chair and eyed me. "He ever mention doing the roofing jobs?"

I shook my head.

Wrendon turned down the radio. "Hey, Buddy. I think Chris has heard enough."

Buddy whispered, "You want to hear it?"

I said, "Yes."

He explained how my father got into the roofing schemes, that Wrendon would dress up in a blue suit and go around to poor neighborhoods in the summer, claiming to be an investment realtor. He would tell the homeowners he was interested in their run-down property, and he was willing to pay thousands more than the place was worth. But he'd noticed this one little spot on the roof, and if they could just get that fixed, they'd be in business. When the owners said they didn't know any roofers, Wrendon said he knew a guy who'd do it for nothing.

Buddy came to do the job. The repairs always started small, patching up a spot or two. Then he pointed out the sheeting beneath the roof was also rotting, and that would need to be fixed. It would cost extra, but not much. Or, he'd say, he could just cover it up and not say anything to the realtor. "If you want to slide me a few more bucks," Buddy said. "They'll never know the difference. Hell, you're selling the place off anyway."

Wrendon came back out with a new roofer once the job was done, to say they'd figured out Buddy and the homeowner's scheme. Wrendon would say that Buddy had tried to set up similar deals with others, but this one person—the person they were dealing with right now—was the only one to go for it. And Wrendon would be damned if he bought a house off someone trying to screw him over.

Eventually they were arrested, and Buddy had to stay in jail. Obviously, the judge said, the earlier time in Georgia had done no good. Because Wrendon's record was clean and he had a kid on the way, he got probation. That kid was me.

"We got busted," Buddy said, "because your daddy started getting squirrelly around the people we were scamming. There was a fifty-year-old woman who figured out what was happening. She called the law on him, and it turns out he was walking around with the number to our motel in his pocket, scribbled on a piece of paper."

"We got arrested," Wrendon said, "because Buddy started tacking on new scams. The plan in the beginning was to get some sort of deposit and cut town. None of this shit about rotting roofs."

They tried to act annoyed, but they liked telling the story. As we drove on, I kept picturing Buddy and my father tricking people, dressed in their suits and roofing clothes, leaving towns with suitcases full of cash. All my life Wrendon had simply been some guy who sold fish. But now he seemed different, like a mobster or something out of a movie.

Around eight that night we pulled into a convenience store for gas. The fluorescent lights hummed white over the pumps. Buddy's head kept falling to his chin and he sounded half-asleep, but he said to grab more High Life.

Outside the van, the air was thick with gnats and smelled like oil. The store's front was all glass, lit up bright, with a woman leaned against the counter, eyeing her nails. I asked Wrendon where we were.

"Shreveport," he said. "Just a few more hours to go." He set the gas pump on automatic. "I'm going to call your mom. While I do that, why don't you drain out the beer cooler."

I said okay and opened the van's side doors and pulled the cooler out, tipping it over. As the water drained, I paced the cement, then looked up and saw the woman behind the front counter holding a phone to her face, wide-eyed and frantic, staring at the van like it was on fire. I spun around to see what she saw. Framed in the doorway, Buddy leaned to the side of the chair, the shiny tape wrapped around his chest and golden cans piled at his feet. His head hung slack, and he looked dead.

She hung up and stared at the street, waiting for somebody to pull in.

I slammed the doors and ran across the gravel parking lot to Wrendon. "We need to go," I said.

He pressed the phone against his chest and said, "What are you talking about?"

"The woman at the counter," I said. "She was looking in the van when I was taking out the cooler. She must have seen Buddy and called the police."

"Are you sure?"

"We need to leave right now."

Wrendon put the phone to his ear. "I've got to go," he said and hung up. He thought for a second and started toward the store. I asked what he was doing. "It's probably nothing," he said. He tried to seem calm, but he still hurried.

Inside the store, three Slushee machines rattled and a clear plastic box full of rotating hot dogs blew steam out the top. Wrendon took a pack of spearmint gum from a small stand on the counter, set it down on top of a twenty and slid it toward her. The woman stood facing us with her back pressed to the cigarette rack. She said, "Is that it?"

Wrendon said, "This and the gas." She stood away from the counter, still eyeing the road. "We're kind of in a rush," Wrendon said. "Getting my dad home. He's sick."

She seemed unconvinced but came forward, quickly pressing buttons on the register and drawing change from the till.

As we walked out, Wrendon picked up his pace. He said, "Dammit," and started to jog.

We jumped in the van and sped away, with the lights slipping over the windshield. The darkness returned as we drove down the service road. I smiled at Wrendon, looked back at Buddy, and saw the squad car in the back window. Its blue and red lights started to spin. Wrendon calmly steered us onto the shoulder and unwrapped the gum. I wanted to jump in back and rip off Buddy's tape, but I knew the cop would see me through the rear window. I looked at Wrendon, imagined us getting handcuffed and thrown behind bars. "Are we going to get arrested?" I said.

"Just sit tight," he said, sliding a stick of gum into his mouth. "I'll do the talking."

"The hell you will," Buddy said.

Now I was sure we would go to jail.

The state trooper appeared in the window. With his wide-brimmed hat, he shone a huge black flashlight in Wrendon's face and over me. "How are you folks doing?"

Wrendon said, "All right."

The trooper asked my father for his license and registration, and put the light on Buddy. Because his arms were strapped down, he could only squint. I waited for him to tell the trooper how we broke into his house, kidnapped him, and taped him down. That he wanted out of the chair this fucking instant. The trooper said, "What in the world?"

Wrendon said, "Is there a problem?"

The trooper looked at my father like it was the craziest question he'd ever heard. "Aside from this vehicle smelling like a beer can, and the fact that you have an elderly man taped to a recliner in the back of your van?" He shook his head. "There's not a problem." He stepped away from the door. "Would you mind coming out here so we can talk?"

Wrendon groaned lightly, popped the door open, and they walked behind the van. Through the rear window I saw them standing in the squad car's headlights. Wrendon held out his arms, raised one leg and brought his right hand to his face. He teetered along a white line, heel to toe. They stood and talked a while longer. After a few more minutes, they returned. Wrendon reached in one of the suitcases behind his seat and pulled out Buddy's leather wallet. Sliding the license out, he said, "See? We've got the same last name. The same big ears. And, like I said, that beer you smell is what we're giving him. Otherwise he might hemorrhage."

"What about the tape?"

Wrendon was about to say something when Buddy cleared his throat. Here it comes, I thought. "It's a game," Buddy yelled. "The young'un here is a jackass for Indians. He got a wild hair with the tape is all. Come show him, Chris. Come show him so we can go."

The trooper and Wrendon stood staring at me, waiting. My father tilted his head. "Go show the man."

Hesitant, I climbed out of the chair and walked to Buddy, the light now on us. Feeling my hands sweat, I swallowed. Unsure how to begin. I thought of every Indian movie I'd seen. Where the braves circled stagecoaches, swinging tomahawks, fighting with cowboys. I started to pad my feet, imagined wearing moccasins and a huge, feathered headdress.

Buddy yelled, "Oh, please! Comanche man! For the love of God, don't hurt me!"

I patted my hand against my mouth and chanted, "Woo-woo-woo-woo-woo-woo-woo-woo."

Buddy yelled, "Somebody! Save me!"

I circled my grandfather with the floor bouncing underneath my feet. After a while I got into it, throwing in spins and different cries. Lifting my arms like I held a tomahawk. Taunting Buddy by standing in front of him, pointing my fingers in his face. He kept hollering, acting scared.

"Okay, okay," the trooper said. "I get it. Now you can quit." It took a moment for me to stop, sweaty and panting. "I just don't think all that duct tape is necessary."

"That's what I told him," Buddy said, "but the kid's so damn conniving. He gets something in his head and there's no breaking it. I agreed to one layer, but he kept at it. His daddy couldn't do much, sitting up there."

The trooper said in a firm voice, "Is this true?"

I hated lying and cracked easily, but he was waiting. I imagined myself on TV, in a movie, or with Buddy and Wrendon out on some job. I pouted my lip, looked at the floor, and scuffed my foot. "Shucks," I said. "I was just having fun is all."

"Fun or no," the trooper said. "It's pure and simple consideration."

"Yeah, I guess so," I said. I looked at Buddy. "I'm really sorry."

He winked at me.

A staticky voice came over the walkie-talkie at the trooper's hip. He picked it up, wheeled around and spoke for a moment. When he came back he said, "There wasn't any report of a traffic violation, but I suggest you boys find yourselves a motel room for the night."

Wrendon took his license back and said, "Will do."

As the trooper walked away, Wrendon climbed in and gripped the steering wheel, suddenly relieved. He said, "Shit, that was close." He looked at me and said, "You did good."

I felt proud. I started to leave Buddy's side to walk back up to the front, but Buddy grabbed hold of my wrist. "Stay here until this jackass turns around and shuts his lights off."

Together we watched until the squad car sped off the other

direction. Buddy spun the chair back toward the front. "Next exit we come to," he said, "don't forget to get my beer."

At the next gas station, Wrendon returned with more beer, unwrapping a cassette. He was tired of fussing around with the radio, he said. We only played the whole tape once. Typical country, most of the songs were trucks and divorce, liquor and tears. But something about Yoakam's song about guitars, nice cars, and hillbillies struck Buddy. He was the first to start singing, and I joined in. We started soft but got louder, until we were yelling. At one point, as the song started to fade into its final lines about hanging on, Buddy said, "Christopher, you always remember this song. Remember how little you need to get by."

I let Buddy try on my sunglasses at one point. We were all in a good mood, having just escaped the law. I felt strange without them on, having become a part of my routine. But he wanted to give them what he called a whirl. The mirrored lenses looked funny against his bony cheeks and big ears, but he still snapped his fingers and shook his head, flashing his smile. My cheeks hurt from laughing so much, and I thought Wrendon was singing with us. But when I glanced up front to see, I had to stop. He wasn't singing, only gripping the wheel and staring intently through the windshield, past the lights and farther down the road than I could see.

CONTRACTS

The first week after getting back from Florida was the roughest. Wrendon put Buddy in my room and bought a doorknob we could lock from outside, and I slept on the couch. Buddy became a different person, often banging on the door, sometimes furious and sometimes crying, apologizing for what he'd done wrong. The door only came open when Wrendon went inside to switch out the piss jug and when my mother took in a tray of tomato soup and small stack of white bread for him to eat. I felt sorry for him, but Wrendon said this was necessary. Later that week, while I was at school and my parents were at work, Buddy figured out the door. We lived in a small house, rented and on a two-lane highway, surrounded by pawnshops and liquor stores. He dug my father's prized pool cue from his closet, pawned it, and bought a bottle of Maker's Mark. I came home that afternoon and found him passed out at the dining room table with his jeans soaked, and he wouldn't wake up. I called Wrendon at the shop, crying and saying to come home. I thought Buddy was dying.

That night my mother told Wrendon he needed to take care of this. He couldn't keep some strange man penned up inside my room. Wrendon hired a friend to work the shop and stayed home for the next two weeks, until Buddy's rants stopped. Until he slept a full night and said to at least give him a dinky fucking radio to help pass the time. Instead of going to the store, I had to come straight home from school, call Wrendon, and say that Buddy was fine. All afternoon, he sat on the living room recliner with his hair combed straight back, wearing a short sleeve button-down and jeans. His jaw stayed set and angry, but he didn't outwardly express it. The remote sat at his fingertips, and he stared steadily at the TV. He wouldn't speak and took his meals in my bedroom, staying there all night. My house had always been kind of sad, except when my mother and I hung out. But now it was crowded with this unsettled anger. Buddy's for being pent up, my mother's for being put out, and mine for losing both my afternoons with my mother and my job at the store. I hated him being there and wanted him gone.

Wrendon promised, once Buddy could be trusted, I could go back to work. But even after Buddy started to straighten out, Wrendon said to wait a while. I knew there were other reasons. More often he was headed out to his favorite bar, Greener Acres, after closing up the store. He said he didn't want to drink beer at home in front of Buddy, but he stayed gone long after we all went to sleep.

One afternoon in February, when I got home from school, Buddy looked up at me from his chair and said, "How about we get some air?" His face was fuller now, and his eyes were clear. I said we should check with Wrendon, but Buddy was already halfway out the door. "Just put up your stuff," he said. I knew I'd get in trouble if I let him go alone.

Together we walked along the busy highway to a Dairy Queen, and once we got there he bought us each an ice cream cone. I had no clue where he got the money. The plastic booths were empty, and we sat by the large tinted window, looking out at the gray day. As we ate, he told me about growing up in Florida, how his daddy was a poker player and got shot in a card game, was hauled off and never brought back. Buddy had to cut out early to make his way. There were steady jobs, but those, he said, were for suckers who lacked ingenuity. Next he talked about women. My grandmother who had divorced him and the second wife he had lost. Finally, there was the woman who almost did him in that year. This wasn't his first time to dry out, but it was the meanest. "And I'll be damned," he said, "if I go through this bullshit again."

It was his way, I could tell, of apologizing. For taking my room and for the afternoon I found him at the table.

He finished the ice cream and wrapped the cone inside a napkin. Palmed it flat. He shook his inhaler, took a hit, leaned back and looked me over. "So how about you? You got a girlfriend or what?"

Over the next few months, he put on more weight. We went to Dairy Queen so much they called us regulars. When we came home, my mother had the table set with four plates and four sets of silverware, though it was usually just us three. Buddy and I grinned at each other, pushing the food around with our forks, our stomachs full of hamburgers and fries. Until one day when she finally said, "Do you think I like making all this food for myself?"

After that when we went out to Dairy Queen, Buddy only bought us Cokes. Or he made sure to bring home a bag of burger and fries for her.

Most nights I was asleep when Wrendon got home. Sometimes I managed to stay up long enough to tell him good night. Once I asked when I could start back at the store, and he said early summer, when Buddy headed back to Florida.

Every so often, on those nights, he'd say to keep that Sunday clear to go fishing. But those Sunday mornings, I would catch him sitting on the edge of his bed as he slipped on his boots, getting ready to leave. When I asked if we were still going to the lake, he searched the carpet, unsure of what I was talking about. I reminded him, and he apologized, saying he needed to head to the store after all, to clean out the deep-freeze or fix the walk-in. But I knew he spent most of the day playing pool.

By midspring my mom was letting Buddy drive her brown 1978 Bonneville, and on those Sundays he took me out to Village Creek. There was a tire swing and a reservoir where the water got deep. Wrendon had taught me how to swim there two years before, when I was eight. When Buddy and I went, he sat in an aluminum lawn chair on the grass, reading a paperback western or taking a nap, tilting his head back in the sun. We never stayed long before I got bored with swimming alone, and more often I just stayed home and practiced guitar. There were times Wrendon did make good on his plans and we went fishing. Just enough to make me trust him.

I turned eleven in late May. That week, my father called to ask a favor. He'd been contracted to cater a party and needed eighty pounds of midsized shrimp headed. If I did this, he would take the weekend off and we'd camp out at the lake. My birthday present. He said I could play hooky from school on Friday and spend that morning heading the shrimp. He'd close up early that afternoon and help me finish whatever was left. I insisted Buddy go, and Wrendon said sure.

Buddy agreed to help me out. We got up that morning, went to the backyard and got started. We sat on lawn chairs under the branches of an oak tree. I wore new swim trunks that my mom had bought me for the trip. We kept the cooler of whole-bodied shrimp to our left, a cooler of headed shrimp between us, and a garbage bag for the heads to our right. The small radio that Buddy had gotten for his room sat beside us on the ground, playing WBAP Country through the small tinny speaker. An orange extension cord ran from the radio to the house, inside the screen door. Sometimes a little breeze pushed it open and slammed it shut, a slapping sound. And each time I glanced over.

Just after twelve, Buddy said, "What time'd he say?"

"Around noon," I said. "Or just after."

"Maybe he got tied up."

"Depends on what you mean by tied up," I said.

The door slammed shut again.

One o'clock passed, and we were halfway done. I went to the phone in the hallway, the only working phone in our house, to see if the answering machine's red light was blinking, and it was. I pressed the button. Wrendon's voice came through. "It's me," he said. "I got the date of that woman's party wrong. She doesn't need the shrimp until tomorrow. I'm still planning to come by and get you though, and we're going to run them by her house this afternoon, if I can reach her."

I stood in the hallway and played it again, hearing a jukebox in the background.

Another hour slipped by, and then another. We worked slower, and my fingertips hurt. Every so often I stood up to stretch my legs and pace the backyard barefoot, finding the cooler spots of dirt between the prickly grass. I walked to the large inner tube I'd blown up and set against the house's brown siding that morning, and I kicked it softly to make sure it wasn't leaking air.

The night before, I had lain in bed, picturing the trip. Us on the lake, with him on the dock, fishing while I swam. I thought about my trick with the inner tube. How I'd stand up on it, steadying my legs and keeping my balance, pinching the rubber with my toes until my back was straight. Then I'd jump and do a somersault into the water. After I came back up, I'd ask Wrendon if he'd seen, and he'd say it was perfect.

I started back for the chairs and looked up at the sky, thinking, *There's still some daylight left.*

The orange sun sank behind Buddy's shoulder. By four, the shrimp were done and we were sitting in our chairs, a cool breeze now on the air. I said, "Why does he even ask if he doesn't want to go?"

"I think he wants to," Buddy said, but left it at that. "Maybe tomorrow you and I can head someplace. Not that old creek, but somewhere better. Wherever you want."

I stood and shook the pain from my knuckles, staring down at all we'd done, feeling cheated. I grabbed the garbage bag of heads, warm from sitting in the sun, and dumped them over the headed bodies, emptying the sack until it flapped in the wind. I let it go and watched it blow across the yard. All I wanted was for Wrendon to be sorry. I stared down at the dried-up shells. Their beady eyes, spiny prongs, and long whiskers. The rotten smell shoved up from the box, and black flies were already swarming. I expected Buddy to tell me to pick the heads out right away, before they spoiled the shrimp. Instead he sat back in his chair and used his foot to shut the lid. That night, while I pretended to sleep on the couch, I heard them arguing in the dining room, Buddy saying he was leaving and I should start back at the store. But now I knew I didn't want to. Was sure I never would again.

GIRLFRIEND IN THE LIGHTS

The first time I heard Theresa's name, a man was shouting it outside my house in the middle of the night. Nearly a year after Buddy had left, and one month after my twelfth birthday. In June, late one Saturday, I sat up in bed to the sound of some man saying, "Theresa! Get your scrawny ass out here!" My room was dark, and his yells rattled the windows. Living along the highway, sometimes things like this happened, where drunks wandered off the road into our yard and walked around, peering inside. They rarely spoke, and no one stuck around for long. But I could tell from the anger in his voice he wasn't leaving.

I looked out my back window. Behind the house lay a field and a small road. The thought of trying to escape scared me more than staying in bed. My parents were out at Greener Acres, the number tacked to the fridge. After Buddy had taken off, we'd turned around the doorknob to my room so I could lock it from inside when they went out, but I always forgot. At any second I knew this man would be inside and searching every corner. As he yelled again and banged on the door, I wondered if maybe some person named Theresa was actually hiding in the bushes or if she'd somehow gotten in through a window and was sitting on the chair in the living room, sweating and watching the door in the dark. He pounded harder, saying, "Out here right now."

Scared but wanting to see who this was, I pulled the thin sheets off my legs and crawled to the front window. Pushing the white

31

curtains aside and keeping most of my head beneath the sill, I could make out the white columns supporting the roof on the porch. The man paced back and forth, down the steps and into the yard. There I saw my dad's van was already parked in the driveway, that my parents were home and the living room light was on.

I relaxed and lifted my head, saw the man more fully, with his T-shirt half-untucked and hair a mess. He dropped his hands to his hips, shook his head, and spat on the ground. "You coming out here or what?" He spoke to the air as if to her. "Or do I have to knock the goddamn door down?"

A moment later the porch light turned on, and the man dropped his shoulders. Now I could see his bloody mouth and swollen eye. He combed his hair to the side with his fingers, as if this might be her coming out. I watched the door and waited for her to appear. This woman worth all the yelling. The door inched open, and my father, still wearing the black jacket and jeans he'd left in earlier, squeezed through, quickly pressing it closed behind him. His voice was firm as he nodded beyond the man's shoulder, saying, "I want you off my property now."

"Or you'll do what? Call the goddamn police?"

"My son's asleep, Dusty. And the landlady's next door. You want her calling the fucking law? Getting them out here, after what you did at the bar? Laying out that girl in front of everyone, right in the middle of the dance floor?"

I recognized Dusty's name but hadn't seen him before. He called the house every so often, never saying hello or asking if Wrendon was home, only saying to put him on. "Just put her out here," Dusty said, "and we'll go."

I could hear people in the living room. My mother's voice and some other woman's. I stood and quietly opened my door, walked down the hall, past the phone, to the living room. Everything was bright like a lightbulb flash. The television was off, and the dining room was lit up. My mom and Theresa sat on the edge of our green couch, staring out the window at the men arguing on the porch.

Theresa held a blood-spotted towel to her mouth and a bag of frozen peas to her right eye. Her blonde hair, parted down the center, was tied back in a loose ponytail. The hem of her flower-printed dress came to her knees. Her faded denim jacket was buttoned to her throat, the collar frayed. My mother wore her silk purple blouse, white slacks, and high heels. She rubbed Theresa's back and, in a tone she used on me when I was upset, said, "It's all right, hon'. Wrendon will take care of this."

Theresa relaxed the hand holding the frozen peas. The skin around her face was already starting to bruise. Still, I was shocked at how pretty she was, that she was in my house.

I said, "What happened?"

My mother said, "Nothing. Just go back to sleep."

I stood waiting.

"Just a fight," she said. "Get what you came for and go to sleep."

The knob of the front door jiggled, and everyone jumped. Through the window I saw Wrendon pull Dusty from the door, trying to get him off the porch. But he wouldn't budge. He stood with his arms spread, yelling again, loud enough to shake the panes. "Goddammit, Theresa, I said I was sorry. Can't we forget the whole thing and go home?"

Theresa yelled, "Why? So you can punch me in the face again, you fucker?" The bag of peas smacked the door and slid down, leaving a long, wet line. She half stood as she yelled, her eyes wide and strained.

Dusty tried to push past my father, and when he couldn't, he got in Wrendon's face. "You're just as much to blame for this. I've seen how you stare at her, making her think she can act that way. You're no better than anyone else."

My father regained his balance by grabbing one of the porch columns. I'd never seen someone shove him, and I felt my forehead wrinkle. His eyes leveled with mine, and I realized how this would go. He turned to Dusty and said, "All right. We've had enough." Grabbing Dusty's collar, he walked him backward off the porch and wheeled him around in the gravel driveway.

"Sweetie," my mother said to me. "Go turn off that light."

I walked to the switch beside the window. In the yard, Wrendon held Dusty's collar and punched his face. I flipped the light off and they were gone.

My mother told Theresa, "You know you're welcome to stay the night. Then you can call him in the morning, when he's sober."

"But I was hoping—" Theresa said, and she waited. "This isn't the first time. And I'm afraid of what he'll do if I go back. Do you remember us driving over here? After the bar? When Wrendon said I could stay a while?"

My mom looked down at the carpet.

Theresa said, "Just a week or so. I promise. Up until I get a job and find a place."

My mother took a deep breath, and her shoulders dropped, unable to fight this. She didn't want Theresa here, but I didn't know why. When my mother saw me, her face got red. "Why are you still standing there?"

Theresa smiled at me tight-lipped, like she was sorry. I smiled back, turned, and left.

In my room my father's headlights swept over the wall as the driveway's gravel turned. For a while I imagined her face, her pretty eyes and raspy voice. Her blonde hair and skinny legs. Her bony knees and that smile.

The next morning I woke up in my nylon sleeping bag on the floor of my room. Theresa lay in my twin bed, beneath my blue blankets. I remembered sometime in the night when my parents had tried to wake me. Theresa had whispered she was fine to sleep on the couch, but my mom said no.

I sat up and crossed my legs, rubbing my eyes and staring at her. She still wore the denim jacket, with her hands stuffed inside the sleeves and her chewed-up fingernails curled over the frayed cuffs. Her blue eyeshadow glittered, and her lips were glossy pink. My room smelled like a flower torn and turned inside out. Suddenly her eyes blinked open, looking around until they settled on me. She pushed herself up slowly until she was also sitting cross-legged. "Morning, kiddo," she said. She stretched her arms and yawned. Her right eye was still swollen, and she smiled like she'd forgotten, or else didn't care. Sunlight poured through the window behind her.

She smoothed the blankets around her legs. "I guess I stole your bed."

"It's no big deal," I said. "Are you staying here?"

"For a while, I think," she said. "You saw last night." She picked at the blanket. "I offered to crash on the couch, but your mom said this was better. I guess she has some sleeping problems and sometimes needs to stay out there."

My mom slept fine, and never on the couch. Since Buddy had taken off the year before, nobody slept out there. I said, "I don't mind. Friends sleep over sometimes."

She looked around my room, taking it in. Posters of bands like Iron Maiden and Kiss, my acoustic in the corner by the closet. On the floor, along half of an entire wall, I had LPs propped up with my portable record player. The collection had started with some Beatles albums my mom handed down and grew as she took me to thrift stores where they sold for a quarter. I felt lucky when I found something by a band on the radio or something I heard on the jukebox. But if those weren't available, I bought anything that looked interesting. Heavy metal bands with suggestive song titles. Country albums with guys playing guitars on porches. Punk records that looked like the band had made the albums in their basements. If the girl on the cover was pretty but had a kind of sadness in her face, I bought her record. I sometimes picked with my eyes closed, wanting anything different that I could say I discovered. They usually had faded covers, cottony edges. I listened to each of them with my large headphones on, to hear every instrument and change. I pretended to follow along on my guitar as best as I could. My father joked about the collection, saying they reminded him of my mom's romance novels. I didn't mind. If anything, it only helped me understand why she kept them around.

Theresa said, "Fucking-A, kid. How many records have you got?"

"Ninety-three," I said proudly.

She pointed to my Kiss *Destroyer* poster, with the guys in all their makeup, leather clothes, and dragon boots, smashing through a brick wall. "I saw them once," she said, "at the Cotton Bowl. My uncle took me." She looked down at me. "Is that what you want? To be a rock star?"

I said, "I think so," my face turning warm.

"Don't be embarrassed, dude. Embrace it." She raised her fist and held up two fingers on each end. "Say, 'Fuck yeah.'"

I raised my fist.

I thought of every girl I had a crush on who called me a dork. There was Toni Corland with her straight blonde hair and Angela Range, the freckled redhead. Instead of playing football during recess or after lunch, I read books and listened to music on my Walkman. I wondered what they would think to see this girl in my room, saying *fuck yeah*. And I thought of the guy they liked—Stevie Ruttles—who had been held back one grade. He had a rattail and a dirt bike, and he sometimes said that I was cool but other times, when people were around, called me a faggot. I knew Theresa would agree he was a dick, especially if she saw his stupid haircut. And all the girls would think I was cool, to see me with her.

I heard my parents, pots and pans. Smelled bacon from the kitchen. I said, "I think they're making breakfast."

Pushing the blankets off her legs and putting her bare feet on the floor, she said, "Good, because I am freaking starving."

School had let out for the summer, and I'd been spending the days at home. Every morning Wrendon headed out by seven to open the store, and my mom took off right afterward for the propane company. I'd gone without babysitters since learning to work the buttons on the microwave and TV remote, but Theresa had to earn her keep in some way. My parents asked her to watch over me to make sure I didn't pull last summer's idiot moves. Once Buddy had left and I wasn't working the store, I got bored at the house. There was the day I emptied a can of carpet cleaner behind the stove, just to see how it would look. The day I turned our sun tea jar into an ant farm, and the time I learned to make french fries and got grease all over the floor. It took two weeks to get it clean enough so nobody would fall.

I knew Theresa couldn't go back to waitressing at the bar, where Dusty could get her. And she held off finding a job because of her eye. So far as friends and family she could stay with, there were none. My father only asked she keep the house clean and prevent me from blowing it up. They also told her to keep me clear of the vacuum cleaner, lawnmower, and weed trimmer. For some reason if I used anything like this, it broke immediately.

That first week, Theresa and I slept every morning until ten. We got up and watched black-and-white reruns like *Leave It to Beaver*, *The Munsters*, and *The Beverly Hillbillies*, sitting on the couch and eating cereal, with the boxes and milk on the coffee table. After that, we got dressed and went to the kitchen table, took the three dollars my mother had left for spending money, and started up the highway. People slowed as they drove past us, mostly men eyeing Theresa. I was proud to walk beside her. At pawnshops and second-hand stores, we stopped to check for records. She picked some out for me, Melanie Safka and Janis Joplin at ten cents apiece, and we continued, with me carrying them underneath my arm, a mile further to Mr. M's convenience store.

The door rang as we pushed through. The store was air-conditioned, and the floor was checkered in black and white squares. Cold glass cases lined the walls, full of ice cream bars, burritos, and pizzas. Aisles overflowed with chips and candy. While Theresa got a *Star Telegram* and a pack of Kool Light menthols, I grabbed a Snickers and a root beer. Checking out at the register, the guy stared at Theresa's breasts the whole time. Until Wednesday. That afternoon she waved her hands in front of his face and said, "Hey dude, you want to take a picture of them or what?"

When we reached the road, she said, "Now maybe he'll cool that shit out." She packed her cigarettes against her palm. "I can't believe he's even doing that, especially with this fucking eye." She unwrapped the pack and tapped one out. "He probably thinks that *because* I've got this eye he can do that." She swiped a match and inhaled deeply, tossing it to the dirt. "Don't ever pull that shit," she said. "On any girl."

She seemed mad, and I said, "I won't."

"Because it gets you fucking nada." Strands of blonde hair blew over her face. "What you do," she said, relaxing and wrapping the hair behind her ear, "is you look here." She pointed to her brown eyes. "And you'll get these"—she waved her hand over her breasts—"all you want." I glanced them over. I looked at her eyes, where she was waiting. She said, "Got it?" and I nodded. "Yes."

37

At home we shut the windows and cranked the living room window unit to high, where my mom never put it. After I put on one of the records, we made peanut butter and banana sandwiches and grabbed bags of chips. Heading back to the cold living room to watch *The Price is Right* and *Court TV*, she spread the newspaper on the carpet and set an emerald-green ashtray in the corner. She lay across the classifieds on her stomach, smoking and using a red pen to circle the boxes. I asked what kind of job she wanted. She said she wasn't sure. Computers freaked her out. Hell no to data entry or punching stupid-assed buttons. She was a people person, but the wrong sort of people worked her nerves. Sitting at a desk made her knees hurt. "I only want what everyone else wants," she said. "Something that pays shitloads and requires zero skills. Or some rich boy who'll put up with me."

I knew she was kidding, but I got jealous at the thought. I said, "Really?"

With her eyes down on the ads, she dangled her flip-flop off her toes. "He's out there somewhere," she said. "I just need to believe." Then she circled something.

When she finished, she folded the paper into thirds and left it on the corner of the kitchen table where my mother set her purse and keys every night. When she got home from work, she picked it up and glanced it over. Those nights, while the three of us ate dinner, she'd ask Theresa if she found some possibilities. Theresa said she was excited about a few and hoped they'd last until the swelling went away. My mother said, "Are you icing it?"

Theresa said, "Yes."

Since she'd flung the peas at the door, I had never seen her ice it.

In the middle of dinner, at six-thirty, Dusty's calls started. As the phone rang out, Theresa slowly sat up, gripping the sides of her chair and looking at my mother. When my mom stood to get it, Theresa said, "Just say I'm gone."

My mother hated lying to people almost as much as I did, and she was annoyed at the situation, that it happened every night. She answered and talked for a while, getting tied up. She said Theresa wasn't home, didn't know where she was, and hadn't seen who she'd left with. Just some girl. She agreed to pass on his message and stood there listening while he talked for ten more minutes. She promised and promised again. Irritated and drained, she sat back down and picked up her fork. Ten minutes later the phone rang again. My mother told Theresa to take it.

"Is it cool to go in the bathroom?"

"It's cool to go wherever you want. Just go get it."

Theresa left her plate of half-eaten food. Out in the hall she'd say, "Hello?" Listen a moment and say, "Dude, what the fuck?" The bathroom door creaked shut behind her, and my mother pressed her fingers to her temples, saying, "He'd quit if she just stopped playing with him."

"Why would she play with him?" I said.

"Because that's all girls like her know."

This wasn't true. She wasn't playing. Within half an hour Theresa would be crying, but she stayed on the line anyway. Sometimes the calls only lasted an hour. More often they stretched longer, up to the time I went to bed. We had to knock to use the bathroom. She'd step outside and nod us in and go back in when we were finished, mouthing, "Sorry." I said it was fine, but it wasn't. I passed the bathroom every so often so I could hear. I'd sneak looks through the crack in the door where the phone cord went in. She sat cross-legged on the floor, leaning against the toilet and facing the tub. Sometimes they talked, but mainly they argued, with her explaining why it was over. Most calls consisted of her trying to hang up. Hours passed when all she said was, "Dusty, I'm hanging up now. Dude, I'm hanging up."

Mostly she would sniffle and listen to what he was yelling. As she cried I wanted to be on the giving end of her line and instead of being mean tell her things to make her smile. Hours passed and I kept walking by the door until my mom said, "Cut it out."

Then there were the nights. Long after my mom and I went to sleep, I would wake to find my bed empty. Out the window, I saw Theresa was sitting on the porch, smoking alone in the dark with her legs stretched down the two steps. I saw the smoke, the way the cherry from her cigarette dimmed and brightened and flipped out into the yard. The moon lit up the smooth and hard parts of her face. She lit one right after the other, bringing her lighter up to her face. Some nights I fell asleep staring at her, and the next morning I woke on the floor with my room smelling like my father's Old Spice. Theresa sleeping on her side, her hands between her cheek and the pillow.

That next Monday, Wrendon came home in time for dinner, carrying a bucket of fried chicken. Theresa and I sat across from each other, making jokes about the guy at Mr. M's.

Wrendon said, "How long have you two been dating?"

We stopped laughing, and I suddenly felt like a child.

"I don't know," Theresa said, meeting my eyes so I couldn't turn away. "I could do worse. What do you think?"

I tried not to smile.

My mother rolled her eyes, and the telephone rang. She turned to Wrendon and said, "Guess who that is."

Wrendon put down his chicken, wiped his hands on his napkin, looked at Theresa, and stood up. He left the room and picked up the phone. They talked for a moment. He said, "Call again and the next time I see you, I'll knock your head off."

He came back and took his seat. "From now on just lift the phone, hang it up, and leave it off the hook."

"You know I don't like to do that," my mother said. "What if you get in trouble?"

"I'll get out of it," he said.

Theresa tried not to glance at Wrendon out of the corner of her eyes. But she did, and she was glowing. Whatever joke we'd had earlier was forgotten, and I wished I could do something to get that look.

After that night, whenever Dusty called, my mother followed Wrendon's instructions. I was glad because it meant Theresa wasn't crying. On those nights the three of us stayed in the living room together, watching television while my mom read. Some nights Theresa and I sat on the porch in lawn chairs. I played records in my room and opened the window so we could hear and sing along. She never made comments about my voice, like Wrendon did. He said it was broken, and when I told her, she said, "Broken?" like it was the dumbest thing on the planet.

I hoped the music made her feel better like it did me whenever something bad at home or school happened. We stayed outside until the sky was dark and mosquitoes started in.

That second week, when she started interviewing for jobs, I stayed home missing her. The sandwiches and chips were not the same, and our shows weren't half as funny. Theresa did and said what she wanted. Cussed with fluency at the television as she traveled through stations. I was in love as much as twelve years allow. Old enough to feel sex in me but too young to know what to do with it. Bored, I used an X-Acto from my model set to spell out our names on the inside of my desk drawer. *Chris + Theresa. Theresa Saxton. C + T* on my acoustic. Hoping she might see it but scared of what she might say. As I did this, I thought about us running away together. She used to claim trouble found her wherever she went. I thought that someday she would come to see me play at the Cotton Bowl. I would spot her in the crowd, pull her up onto the stage and into a cooler life where she'd never need anyone but me to save her.

When I heard the house's front door open and close, I'd find her standing directly in front of the television, using the remote. I asked her how the interview went, and she'd say, "Sucked." On those nights, when my mom asked the same question, Theresa said, "Awesome." Over that second week my mother's eyes started to bag more than usual. She had in fact begun to sleep on the couch. Theresa started climbing out my window to go outside. One day I asked her about it, and she said she didn't want to bug anyone.

"You could smoke in my room. My parents smoke everywhere."

"I'd feel too guilty," she said. "But do me a favor and don't tell your mom about me sitting out there."

I said, "Why not?"

"Because she doesn't need to know," Theresa said. "I think she's already annoyed with having me here."

I said, "Okay," and kept our secret.

Theresa had an interview on Thursday afternoon. It shouldn't have taken so long, but she stayed gone for a few hours. I spent the day wandering the house. Around two I decided to pull some of my mom's books from their stacks in the closets to build forts for my G.I. Joes, Star Wars figures, and He-Men. This was fine for a while, but I got bored. So I decided to take the men out into the yard and set them on fire.

Out in the front yard I dug up a mound of dirt with a kitchen spoon and shaped it into a circle with a clearing in the center. I stuck the plastic men inside the mound with their grimacing faces sticking out toward the clearing. On top of that clearing I placed dry straws of grass and some leaves off a rose bush. I didn't have matches, so I aimed a magnifying glass and its small dot of sunlight at the leaves. I glanced up at the highway hoping Theresa would appear. I dreamed of everything catching in a small mushroom cloud of explosion as she walked up. Then she'd know I could be dangerous. I stayed on my knees, trying to keep my hand steady.

When Theresa caught my eye, she was walking toward the house along the edge of the highway, eating an orange Creamsicle that matched her orange-and-white-striped shirt. The shirt hung above her bellybutton, and her black jeans gripped the rest of her like a loose fist. As usual she was miles from it all, studying her feet. The way her painted toes poked through her flip-flops. She passed the mailbox and turned down into the driveway where I sat. I focused on the white dot, praying it would catch.

But it didn't, and Theresa stopped. She smelled like cigarettes and the orange syrup that covered her knuckles. She bent down and said, "How much do you really want this to happen?"

More than anything.

She shook the sticky muck from her fingers and said, "Don't you have a lighter? I thought all boys had lighters."

I said, "No," and looked at the house.

"You'd better not take one of your mom's," Theresa said. "You think she won't notice, and she won't until she's lost her last one. After that, she'll go looking. First your pants pockets, then everywhere. Eventually she'll figure out the spot where you hide everything. And you don't want that. Besides you shouldn't be burning your toys."

I said, "Why not?"

"Because all boys burn toys." She stood and threw a shadow over everything. "Come inside with me." She held her hand out.

I took it, lacing my fingers inside hers.

We walked in the house and sat on the couch. She picked the remote off the coffee table. Sitting back, she set her shoulder against mine, rested her wrist on my knee and turned on the TV. I thought I smelled beer. "Where was your interview?"

"Some furniture dealership. They wanted me to answer a phone and sit at a desk. That kind of shit."

Theresa's hand stayed where it was. I nudged my shoulder deeper between the couch cushion and her arm. She found *Oprah*, put the remote down, and rested her head on mine. "Now this is the stuff," she said. "Watching these crazy fuckers and hanging out with you." When *Oprah* ended and the news came on, Theresa said, "Boring!" and switched it over to *Voltron*. It was a rerun and she sighed. "Do you draw? I know you play your guitar a lot. But do you draw?"

"Like with a pencil?"

"Like with paper," she said. "I want to teach you something."

I went to my bedroom and opened my desk and found a pencil and spiral notepad.

When I got back she was already sitting cross-legged on the living room floor. She pointed, and I sat in front of her, our knees touching. I turned to look at the TV, but she guided my chin back with her hand. "I'm going to draw your face," she said. For a moment she leaned forward. So close she could have kissed me. I closed my eyes.

"Keep them open," she said, sitting back. "You have to start with the eyes. The face is entirely framed around them. A simple fact. If you ever want to know whether someone is lying all you need to do is look here." She pointed a finger at her cheekbone. It was still red, but only a small crescent-shaped line. She went back to drawing.

I said, "How?"

"You ask the question outright and watch to see if it twitches," she said. "Like for instance, here's a question. 'Will you be calling me about this job?' Or 'Will you be calling about this apartment?'

I've had to ask those a few times lately. And there are others, like 'Do you love me?'" She kept staring into my face, sketching my picture. She paused and thought and went on, her voice softer and trailing off. "'Do you think of me when I'm gone?'"

That question hit me hard, and right away Theresa stopped. She turned her head off to the side with a surprised look on her face, and she smiled. Now she knew the truth, but I didn't care. I was glad. She started to say something but didn't and stayed quiet a moment. She said, "Someday, sugar, you're going to knock some girl's socks off."

I wanted to knock her socks off. "If you want," I said, "I'll draw you next."

"I don't think so," she said. "I don't need you hanging on to a picture of me like this."

"The swelling's almost gone," I said. "Not that it mattered."

She cocked her head. "I bet you see past all my flaws. Don't you?"

"You don't have any," I said.

"Sugar, I've got tons," she said. "Even if you don't see them, I promise they're there."

That night I struggled to stay awake after Theresa went outside. I propped my elbows on the windowsill. My dry eyes burned, and I was sleepy. I was reminded of those nights the year before, when I would sit up waiting for Wrendon, to run through our days, say good night, and hear him make promises he rarely saw through. But right now Theresa was as close to being my girlfriend as I knew she'd ever be, and I wanted to be around her as much as possible.

I saw the highway blink in quick flashes, light and dark. I thought it was lightning but realized somebody was flashing their headlights, getting brighter as they approached. I could make out the car wash place and lawn mower repair shop across the street. Theresa took a long, hard drag and stood up, stamping her cigarette. My father's white van pulled to the side of the road but not in our driveway. Instead he stopped by the mailbox, facing the yard. The lights stayed on, and by now Theresa was in them. Long hair and hips swinging. She disappeared into the passenger's side, and they left.

I tried to stay up until they got back, just to know that I could. But in the morning I was back on the floor and Theresa was sleeping in my bed. I wondered if last night was real or if I'd dreamed it. If she had in fact been faithful to me. I decided he was talking to her about her day, like friends do, and didn't want to wake my mom.

That next night my mom, Theresa, and I sat at the kitchen table. The front door was open to let in a breeze, and the house smelled like the honeysuckle that hung on the front porch. We ate spaghetti off paper plates and drank iced tea. No one said much until my mother told Theresa that her mom had called the office that afternoon, saying she could move home.

Theresa said, "No fucking way."

My mother said, "You obviously don't have the money for an apartment, and we can't afford to keep you here. You must be so uncomfortable sitting around with Chris all day. It seems right to get back with your own family."

Theresa leaned over her plate. "I talked to her about it last week. She said the minute I get home, she's sending me straight back to Dusty. In her eyes this is my fault for what she calls misbehaving. She thinks I need to try harder."

"Maybe she has a point," my mother said. "You're a grown woman. You need your own things. And Dusty keeps calling here, saying he's sorry. You have to see that people change. They make mistakes. Situations get messed up, fall apart, and you make something out of the pieces. Something a whole lot better. But first you have to sort them out and get it together."

"You saw what he did to me," Theresa said. "If that's what you mean by making mistakes. I can't go back to that, and I can't live on the street." She stirred her food. "It's not like I'm not trying. I just need another week. I talked it over with Wrendon, and he said he understood. Said to take the time I needed. I figured you knew. This is all a surprise to hear."

My mother pushed her plate forward, untouched. "Can I ask you something personal?" she said. "Did you and Dusty ever talk marriage?"

"Not sober," Theresa said.

My mother said, "I never pictured myself marrying Wrendon either. Back when he and I first met up in Iowa, I was nineteen years old. I used to waitress at a pizza place in the town where I grew up. He'd been living there two years. I was different then. I didn't work fifty hours every week. Before Chris. I'd grown up in a good home with good folks. Both worked in the same factory for over forty years, bottling milk. But when I was sixteen, my dad died of a heart attack. For two years my mom hardly spoke, and after that I met Wrendon." She looked at Theresa. "He hasn't told you this, has he?"

Theresa didn't talk, just kept her head down. I had never heard the story, and I wondered why my mother was telling it now. She seemed to have forgotten I was even at the table, and I almost felt like I should get up and leave.

"He ran around with all kinds of girls," my mother continued. "Whatever they were, I was the opposite. I was mousy with brown hair, didn't talk unless spoken to. Hardly any makeup. But all of a sudden, one day he comes in by himself and asks me out. I said no. I didn't want to be one of those girls he ran around with. I didn't have the thick skin for it, to get picked up and dropped. But he kept asking, saying to give him a shot, and I finally gave in. We started dating. I liked him because he was funny and he was smart. He said he liked me *because* I was the opposite of those other girls. I know what that means now. Do you know what that means?"

Theresa shook her head, but I could tell she knew.

"Five months into it, my mom died. Heart attack, too. Just gone," my mother said. "I tried to live in that house by myself, but I couldn't. Wrendon knew this, and he asked me to marry him. Don't think we weren't nervous. Him about settling down. Me about settling with him. I said yes, and we went straight to the courthouse. A Monday morning. After that, we stayed in town a few months, living in my parents' house. But we knew we needed to leave. Start fresh in a different place. Become a married couple all on our own." She stopped and thought for a moment. "So we moved here to Texas. There was oil work for him, and I could get a job. I hoped he would change when he got here, and he has. He's not so bad as he once was. He has his business. Doesn't drink like he used to. I can put up with a few things." She nodded. "We've been through a lot together. Thirteen years. We have a son. Things aren't perfect, I know. But they aren't so flimsy as they appear. As you might think."

Theresa pressed her arms against the table, pinching her hands. She was trying to make a decision, and she decided. "All I need is one more week," she said. "That's it."

My mother took her plate to the garbage. "I have something I need to show you. Something I found when I came home today, in the driveway."

She passed through the dining room. Her face and neck were splotched red. I heard her go to the bedroom. Theresa and I stared at each other across the table. She looked like a kid in trouble. My mother said, "Theresa, get out here."

At first she stayed put. Her shoulders stiff, tapping her fingernails on the table. My mother called for her again, this time louder. Theresa flinched and said, "Shit," under her breath. I now knew she was really in trouble. She stood and went to the living room.

I followed her.

My mother was standing by the front door, holding a small square piece of foil. "You need to explain this."

Theresa's eyes widened, and her hand came to her mouth. "I don't know what that is," she said. "I mean, I know what that is. But why are you asking me?"

"Don't you think I have ears?" my mother said. "That I have eyes?"

I said, "What is it?"

She said, "Go to your room until I say to come out."

I remembered the pile of toys I had left in the yard the day before. I thought Theresa was in trouble for what I'd done. I said it wasn't her fault.

My mother said, "Go!"

Theresa was staring at the driveway.

I went to my room and sat on my bed. I couldn't hear much, but Theresa said trash like this blows up from the road all the time. My mother said, "Not at my house. Condom wrappers don't just appear."

Theresa said maybe I left it there.

My mother gave her an ultimatum. She could either call Dusty, her mother, or walk. But she sure as hell couldn't call my dad or stay here.

I heard her pick up the phone in the hallway and say, "Mama? Hey, it's me." The bathroom door creaked shut.

Minutes later Theresa came in my room carrying a brown paper sack. She picked her clothes up from her pile in the closet and started throwing them in the bag. Already I missed her and wanted to say we could go together. But she was this beautiful older girl about to walk out of my life, and I was a boy stuck in my parent's house. She never questioned what I did but would answer any question. I said, "Theresa."

She glanced up and stopped putting her clothes in the sack.

I said, "What's a condom?"

She set the bag down, walked over, and sat on my bed. It squeaked beneath us. Everything in my room was blue from the oncoming night. She thought for a moment, stood and closed my door. She kneeled in front of me and placed her hands on my knees. Mascara was smeared beneath her eyes, but she smiled in a way I'd only seen in some of my father's magazines. She said, "Let me tell you."

Theresa explained everything. Their uses. When they're necessary and when they're not. As she spoke, she pressed her fingers into my knees, sometimes tracing them up my leg. One word was replaced by another. She used every phrase and expression—sometimes two or three for the same thing. She had all kinds of words: a guy's *thing* became a *penis*, and a *dick* became a *cock*. A girl's *pussy* became her *vagina*, and her *business*. The lists went on.

At times she stopped and asked, "Do you know what that is?"

Sometimes I nodded and other times did not. Eventually I stopped nodding altogether. She took my right hand in hers and guided me across her body, stopping at her breasts and on top of her skirt where she was warmer. Sometimes she pointed to parts of me. I throbbed as she massaged my palms and kept talking. In the dark I could barely see her face, but her touch stayed after her hand was gone. Her voice was like none I'd heard in my life. Not a teacher's, not my mother's. Soft but direct. I waited until she was done, until her hands relaxed and I knew she was finished, before telling her I'd always thought *condoms* were called *rubbers*. I'd seen one a year before when Toni Corland brought it to school and blew it up on the playground.

Theresa sat back and said, "Really?"

"Even still," I said, "I didn't know what they were for. Not all that."

"Well, good," she said. "Now you do."

"Why was it in the driveway?"

"To be honest," she said, standing up, "I have no fucking clue. Maybe your mom."

"Why would she do that?"

"Because she's smart," Theresa said. "If I were her I would have done the same thing, or something like it. Or most likely I'd have beat my ass without a word."

"Why'd you say I put it there?"

She thought for a moment and arrived at what would suffice. "Desperate people say stupid shit."

A rusted yellow station wagon pulled up in the driveway. My mother called for Theresa. Before she left, she held my chin, kissed my lips and stepped back.

"Be good, Chris," she said.

I watched through my window as she stepped out the front door, down the steps, and got in the car, staring forward from the passenger's side. Not looking at anything.

That night my mother didn't call Wrendon at the bar to say what she'd found in our yard or that Theresa had left. Instead she called Dusty and said where he could find her. I stayed up one more time to see what would happen. Around midnight, my father eased into the driveway and gave the sign he'd given before. He waited and flashed the lights again. When no one came, he pulled up closer, all the way in, with the headlights on. And sitting there on the front porch, instead of Theresa, was my mother. Leaning against one of the white columns, wearing her nightgown with her hair up and arms crossed over her chest. Asleep and waiting for her husband to finally get home.

TANGLED IN THE ROPES

That next summer, Buddy and I were sitting on the large bench seat in the van with our feet set on top of the Igloo coolers laid between us and the van's open side doors. Thunder cracked and raindrops hit the lids, and Buddy said we should get at it. He climbed over the coolers, got out of the van, and I followed. The sky turned from blue to gray in the time it takes to snap and smooth a blanket. In the field across the highway, the wind pushed the tall grass to the right. Cars started flipping their headlights on, and rain began to fall. The air smelled like dust and felt like spring, but it was late August, and I hurried to keep up with him.

He had come back that winter, drunk again. In the past two years he and my father rarely spoke. But, in February, Buddy called to say that he was in trouble. Wrendon drove out east alone, and when they pulled up in the driveway, Buddy stepped out of the van. Chest thinned, body sunken, and head down, worse than before. His every word was strained like he was sick of explaining. He wouldn't look at me, hardly spoke. Just waved his hand, as much to say hello as leave him alone.

Wrendon knew that Buddy needed to keep busy. I was thirteen now and had my own friends. I spent weekends at friends' houses, riding bikes and playing guitars, and this often left Buddy at home alone with my mother. On weekends during the springs and summers my father usually had someone set up the van outside a large flea market in Grand Prairie called Trader's Village, selling three sizes of shrimp. Popcorn, mediums, and jumbos. That April, he asked Buddy to take over.

I could go if I wanted, and every so often I went. I liked hearing Buddy's stories and watching him work people. When they first pulled up, he would peer inside their cars and predict the size of shrimp they'd buy. As they approached he said, "How you folks doing?" and sized them up further. While he opened the coolers and talked about the shrimp, his voice was deep and certain. Fast and smooth. Nothing like mine, always hesitant and stammering. He talked as though he'd known them for years, speaking to their interests—fishing, gardening, baseball, cars—even though they were complete strangers. Early on I sat on the seat and watched him, and every so often I took customers and practiced his lines. Usually I dealt with women and older people. Buddy was better with men. They were too pushy and wanted everything half-priced. He said I didn't have quite the stamina to haggle. Wrendon liked to say that Buddy could sell bubbles to a fish, while I couldn't push cut-rate air on a drowning man.

When I went, I got paid fifteen dollars a day. That year I was saving up for a new guitar, a Gibson SG, the same model Pete Townshend from The Who and Ian MacKaye from Minor Threat played. Theresa had once said it was the most badass guitar on the planet. They often appeared in the pawnshops around the house, and I was saving every cent. Kept my money in a cigar box under my bed.

When school let out that summer, I no longer got to choose whether or not to go with Buddy. Wrendon said, now that school was out, I could see my friends during the week. "You're old enough to start helping out," he said. More often he and Buddy talked about me taking over in September, once school started back up and Buddy left. Wrendon wanted to keep the truck open all the way through fall. They decided I needed to learn how to hustle, to pay attention to people's bodies before they spoke. Buddy said it was a power, to know people well enough to say what you wanted to get your way. But I knew it meant sometimes pushing them into things they didn't need and couldn't afford. Saying lies to make a sale. Buddy said they wouldn't have stopped unless they were interested, and my job was to figure out what they wanted and speak to that. "Deep down, people want to believe you," he'd say, "and that makes it easy. Most times, all you have to know is, *What does this person want to hear?* Not what do you want to tell them. That's where most people mess up." He said it was the one thing he could offer. By this I knew, like Wrendon knew, that when he headed out this time, he wasn't coming back.

Rain came heavy on our clothes, and we were soaked within seconds. The wind pushed Buddy's white hair up. I followed him to where we'd pitched the signs that morning in the dirt beside the road. Signs with metal stakes that once advertised apartments. Before we stole them, painted them white, and wrote in red letters: *FRESH SHRIMP, TODAY ONLY, 5LB* FOR *$20.00.* We hauled the signs back through the mud and puddles to the van and leaned them against the rear bumper. Buddy swung the two doors open. I hopped inside and spun around as he lifted them with their pointed ends leading. Mud was clumped on the sharp metal stakes, and I reached to grab them in a cleaner spot.

"Hurry up, Chris," he said. "This shit's pouring."

I said, "Yes, sir." But instead of grabbing them, I jumped out and took the signs from his hands and banged the stakes against the bumper. "So it doesn't get all over the floors," I said. "Customers will see it, and I'll be the one who has to clean it up later."

Buddy nodded and pushed me on, saying, "Go."

When we were done, I followed him inside and slammed the doors shut. Rain fell against the roof, and we collapsed in the two front seats. Closed up, the van seemed darker and smaller. The small signs laid flat on the coolers. We were trying to catch our breath. Buddy started coughing and grabbed his inhaler off the dash, put it to his lips, and breathed in. He held it out to me, but I shook my head.

"It's good stuff," he said.

I figured he felt bad for jumping me earlier. I reached under my seat and found an old hand towel, wiped my hands and offered it up.

Buddy shook his head. "No thanks." He wiped his threadbare handkerchief over his cheeks and forehead. Once he was settled, he took a comb from his back pocket and drew it through his hair, sending the peppermint scent of Brylcreem through the muggy closed-in space. He looked in the rearview mirror and said, "Yes, sir. Yes, sir," smacked my thigh with the comb, and put it back in his pocket. "Fella's got to keep looking good in case some cute gal comes up."

I knew no one was coming up. Through the rain-dotted windshield, cars zipped by. Everyone escaping Trader's Village because of the weather. It made sense for us to leave too. The signs were put up, and we were simply some white van parked by the road. But I knew if I asked he'd get annoyed, saying the rain would swing by. Even if it didn't, we had the vendors still inside to consider. Some were regulars, and they'd be closing down their shops. Leaving now meant throwing out good shrimp, enough to make up our day's paycheck. And I'd hear no end of it from Wrendon. We'd walk into Greener Acres, a dark place with lights above the bar, pool tables, and a stage, to meet up with him, and he'd look at me from a pool table, knowing right away I had shrimp left. He'd drop his head and say, "Tell me you sold out," just to make me admit I hadn't.

"Might as well get comfortable," Buddy said. He repeated his typical Sunday afternoon saying. "Maybe someone'll come along in a Caddy and clean us out."

I said, "Fat chance."

Buddy said, "You can't have that attitude and run this van by yourself. Not once I'm gone."

I wondered if he meant gone this summer or gone forever. "I haven't said whether or not I'm taking over once school starts. Wrendon has done all right hiring extra help. Then you guys won't have to worry about me speaking louder, and I won't have to hear about it whenever I don't sell out. All I want is to get my guitar, and I'm almost there."

"Don't be so selfish," Buddy said. "You're old enough, and you've come far this summer. You should be happy. It's time you show you understand responsibility and that I haven't been wasting my breath these past few months. It's time you show there's more to you than daydreams about guitars and listening to music by druggies dressed like two-dollar hookers." He pointed to my copy of *Rolling Stone* on the dash. On the cover was Mötley Crüe, promoting their album *Girls, Girls, Girls.* The tour where Tommy Lee's drum kit lifted up over the crowd, doing somersaults during his solo. In the picture they all wore spandex and makeup, with primped hair. Nikki Sixx was blowing a kiss. This did not help me at all.

The first time I'd brought up the guitar with my father was on a Sunday night in June. As with every time I showed up, we sat across from each other at a table in the corner of the bar. He wore his red ball cap that read *Saxton's Seafood.* "This is the third week in a row that you've come in here with shrimp left over," he said. "What exactly is wrong with you?"

"We stayed until it was dark and the place was emptied out. Just like you said."

He stopped grinding his teeth after a few more beers, staring down at the spiral notebook where the day's sales were tallied. He asked what I intended to do with my money, and I told him about the SG, that I would have enough by the end of August. He asked what it looked like, and I drew a picture in the notebook. I felt smart for saving up and thought he would be glad for me. With a finger he traced the shape of its body, the way it rounded at the bottom and came up to two points before dipping toward the neck.

"It looks like a devil's head," he said, and pushed the notebook away. "Why don't you like the one you've got?"

"I got it four years ago," I said. "When I was nine. I'm better than that. And all the tuners are stuck. I have to use pliers to turn them. Besides, I'll never make it with a guitar like that."

"You'll never do shit," he said, "if you keep talking so low. People have to strain to hear you out there. I've seen you in action, Lightning, and you're awful. That's why you keep coming back with so much shrimp."

I looked at the drawing, the sketchy lines. Nothing like the real thing.

"You should be saving up your money for new school supplies and clothes," he said. "After you stay on this summer, you could start saving for that racket-machine. You'd have all kinds of dough."

I'd never thought of him saying how I could spend my money, and I got worried. "We've been through this," I said. "I barely have time for myself once school starts. I'd never do anything but school and that truck. No time for friends on the weekends. No time for anything but that. Besides, what if someone comes along with a gun or a knife?"

"Now you're sounding like your mother," he said. "Buddy's told you and I've told you. Money's leaner and I can't afford all the extras you need, much less paying for outside help."

I thought of all the money he blew at the bar. That's where all my help would go.

"You'd like running the truck yourself," he said. "It'd be like having your own business. You'd be your own boss."

"The last thing I want is my own shrimp business," I said. "You're the only Saxton in Saxton's Seafood. I can't stand the smell of it, the cold water, or hauling those coolers in and out of the van. I especially hate sitting there all weekend. Not for fifteen bucks a day."

Wrendon thought for a moment and tapped the notebook. "Show me you can do better," he said. "That you can sell out consistently, and we'll talk about upping your pay. Before you know it, you'll have enough for that guitar. Or any guitar you want."

I stared out across the smoky bar, feeling I was getting tied down to something I didn't want. I said, "No way."

He turned in his chair toward the TV. "Once you get a hustle going and start making more money, you'll be surprised. Just wait and see. I'm depending on you for this. We both know the situation with Buddy, and it's important you pay attention to what he tells you."

I did pay attention. Not because I wanted to take over but because of the compliments Buddy gave me when I pulled a sale. The more I put into it, the sooner we sold out. And the sooner we sold out, the sooner I went home. Each weekend I got better. I spoke up, worked on my lines, and gauged people by their appearances. Buddy taught me that shoes said almost everything. Ostrich skin boots meant I could push the jumbos. Regular cowhide and go for the little ones. Leather slip-ons meant the mediums. Sneakers depended on the brand name and how new they seemed. If you were wearing old shoes with dirty laces, I knew you wouldn't pay eight bucks a pound on jumbos. I'd push the little ones.

But today no one was stopping. We sat in the seats, and I was restless. I'd already eaten my hamburger and chips and practically memorized the issue of *Rolling Stone*. I sat back and stared at the rain on the windshield, wishing I hadn't forgotten my Walkman. The van's battery drained whenever I used its radio, and Buddy couldn't stand the music. A couple of times I had brought my acoustic, but it bothered Wrendon to think of me playing it when a customer walked up.

Although Buddy's eyes were shut, I could tell he wasn't sleeping. He rubbed his thumb in and out of his knuckles, the space where he'd once held his Winstons. I knew he missed them, missed a lot of things. His fingers were thin and thick veined and marked with liver spots. I took a pencil out of the glove box and the notebook off the dashboard, turned to a clean sheet and drew three sets of six parallel lines on the paper. I tried to get the patter of rain out of my head and recall the song I'd been thinking through earlier. I couldn't read music, so I wrote down the fret-number on top of the line that stood for a string.

Without opening his eyes, Buddy asked, "Got one of your tunes going?"

I flipped the notebook over on my lap so he couldn't see.

"Best name this one 'The Shrimper Man's Blues,'" he said. "Or 'Can't Make a Nickel to Save My Sorry Ass.'"

I started to put the notebook on the dash when he leaned forward and turned the page to that day's sales. The date was at the top, and the different sizes of shrimp were separated into columns, with slashes in each column standing for pounds we'd sold. He pointed. "First, take care of that. Figure your sales and add up your dough to make sure everything's squared. We started today with sixty pounds of little ones, twenty midlands, and twenty-five jumbos."

At least it was something to do, and he was right. I needed to know how much was left in case I wanted to start cutting deals. After adding up the columns, I told him we were down to seven and a half pounds of the small shrimp, two of the mediums, and three of the large ones. It seemed so little, and all we needed was two or three more stops. But now the cars were more spaced out, and minutes passed between each. "Without this rain, we'd be home," I said.

The rain came harder, as if it had heard me. Water layered the windshield, and I decided not to work on the song anymore. Trying to imagine the sound without the guitar was pointless and I would only get more irritated. Instead I lay my head against the back of the seat and listened to the rain fall on the roof.

Falling asleep inside the van was stupid and irresponsible, and I sat upright, scared we'd just been ripped off. The sky was still gray, the rain still drizzling. There was a tap on my window, and I turned around. A Hispanic man was staring in, with an orange and beige truck behind him. He wore a straw cowboy hat and striped button-down open to his tanned chest. He said something I couldn't hear through the glass. I rolled the window down half an inch. He said, "Are you guys still open?"

I figured Buddy would take this, knowing he would make the sale. He cleared his throat and said, "Yes, sir. Yes, sir. Long as we're here, we're always open." He climbed over the signs and coolers to reach the bench and set the hanging scales on a hook in the ceiling. He said, "Chris, help me out with this."

After pushing the signs toward the back, I opened the doors and scooted the coolers away from the bench. Rain came inside and hit the lids. The man bellied up and tilted his hat back on his head. "Afternoon," he said.

"How are you doing?" Buddy said.

The man motioned to the coolers and said, "Show me what you've got."

"Well let me see here," Buddy said. He opened the cooler to his far right and the thick smell filled the van. "These are the shrimp we've got on sale today. Five pounds for twenty bucks. Otherwise they're five per pound." He reached inside and took out a handful, letting the smaller ones fall and keeping the big ones in his fingers.

"You ain't headed them?" the man said.

"No time to head them," Buddy said. "These bad boys were swimming in the Gulf of Mexico yesterday. We've got a driver that hauls them up from the coast every morning. Cost is figured and I always throw in extra."

The man nodded toward the next cooler.

Buddy moved to it. "These are bigger," he said, lifting the lid. "You get twenty-five per pound. Thick and meaty, they're best for frying but good for anything. $6.99."

The customer's eyes followed Buddy as he opened the cooler of jumbos, but his hand stayed on the box with the smallest shrimp. Watching his fingers tap the lid, I knew he wouldn't go with the big ones. His boots were worn leather and muddy at the soles. His jeans tucked inside them. As Buddy finished, the man said, "Too much," waving his hand over the big ones. I was glad to be right. He tapped the cooler where his hand had stayed. "How about these bad boys? Can you do three for twelve?"

Buddy checked his watch. "Too early, my friend. We haven't made enough to buy the young'un here dinner."

The two men looked at me, and I waved.

"You'll be here later?" the man said, bringing his hat back down.

"Not if I can help it," Buddy said. "I ain't got much left."

"I see."

"Three for fifteen you may as well get five for twenty."

The man considered it.

Buddy said, "It won't take two seconds to weigh them up. Get you out of this rain and headed home with what you came for."

"All them heads, and this rain. You can do three for twelve."

"Nope." The lid fell. "How many are you feeding?"

The man gestured over his shoulder with his thumb and said, "My wife and our boy."

"What will she eat? You and your son can probably go through three pounds yourselves."

"He's only two and a half."

"Three pounds ain't nothing. Five will feed a family, and you can't beat that deal. Got some left over, just freeze them. These ain't been frozen. Consider it an extra pound or so for free. You can thaw them out and eat them by yourself."

The man stared at the ground, rubbing his chin. Just when I thought he would say no, he reached for his wallet.

While Buddy filled the scales, I looked at the pickup. In the cab, a dark-haired woman was playing with their small boy. He stood on her lap, and she held his hands for balance. Buddy said, "Thank you," as the man walked away, stepping over puddles with the paper sack in his hand. The woman set the boy down between them as the man tried to explain something. She glared forward, and I could easily imagine her, before they stopped, saying to only buy three pounds. That way they could get vegetables on their way home.

"They won't finish five pounds by themselves," I said.

"Not our job to make pals," Buddy said, pulling the notebook off the dash. "That man just paid your wages. Don't forget it. And I know he'll be back. He's been here before. We went through this routine the last time he stopped. Except he was with a few of his buddies, drinking Budweisers. People think we don't remember."

I nodded and watched as the truck pulled onto the glimmering road.

That past July, Wrendon and I sat across from each other at the same square table. Buddy's cough was getting worse, and he had opted to drive the van home, leaving me at the bar with Wrendon. Looking down at the notebook, he ran his finger over the page with that day's sales. A few pounds were left over, and he'd somehow figured out my scheme of tossing in a few extra shrimp here and there. That day I'd given away too much. He asked why I did it, and I said it kept them coming back.

"For free shrimp?" he said. "I thought you were smarter than that. How can I trust you to handle the truck if you give away our profit?"

All that month he'd been talking like I'd agreed to take over. I said, "We've already been through this. Maybe next summer I can work the truck by myself, but not this year."

"Look," Wrendon said, "when I turned thirteen I started buying my own shoes and all my own clothes. I delivered papers and worked all sorts of odd jobs. For nowhere near what you're getting."

He downed his mug of beer and poured another from his pitcher. "Tell me what I have to do to make you care," he said. "To not keep coming in here every Sunday, saying you've got shrimp left. Crossing your arms like you could give a shit."

Aggravated, I leaned back from the table, and as I did, he grabbed my elbow hard enough to pull me forward. "Stop pouting like I'm some bully," he said. "Sit up and tell me what it'll take. Name your price."

"I can't help it if people aren't interested," I said. "Maybe we should sell less. You've said yourself that times are tight."

"I can go out there," he pointed to the door, "work that truck by myself, and be home by four o'clock on Sunday. What do you make of that?"

I glared at his glass, knowing the truth. That if he did sell out by four he wouldn't come home. Instead he'd come here and spend what he'd made. He let go of my arm and stood up with the empty pitcher, bumping into a chair on his way to the bar. I looked at my watch. Seven-thirty. He came back with a full pitcher and a small calculator. "Remind me how much money I'm paying you."

"Fifteen dollars a day," I said. As if he didn't know.

"Now tell me how much was that guitar that you drew in here a month ago, and what kind of difference it would make if I gave you a quarter for each pound you sold."

I said, "It's not about the money."

He poured another beer and started figuring on the calculator. "It's always about the money," he said. "No wonder you're so bad." He multiplied the pounds of shrimp I'd sold by twenty-five, scribbled something on the paper, and poked in a decimal. "Look at that," he said. "Look at that and realize you're breaking me."

It read, *$38.50*. What my pay would be for just one day. I tried not to react but felt my eyes widen.

"That's after you gave away fourteen pounds," he said, "and closed with another sixteen. Let's say we work something out. I'll have you work the truck every other weekend and get someone else to work it the weekends you're off. That way you've got some extra money and I'm not bringing in so much help."

He was serious, and I was interested. But I was nervous to let on. He was like Buddy and would say what he needed to close the deal, just to have the satisfaction. I'd learned the feeling. I said, "I'll think about it."

"No more thinking," he said. "How much thinking do you figure Buddy does before he's willing to help me? You realize I could just make you do it, right? You've already hustled me into giving you more money. You've suggested I meet you halfway, and here I am. Let's try it out a couple of months with you running the van yourself. And if it's not what you want, then we'll talk about me going ahead and hiring someone else for good. How does that sound?"

"You just said I could switch out with somebody."

"Or whatever," he said. "What I need right now is yes."

The sun came out as fast as the rain, making the dark road shine. The mud and green grass brightened. Cars started slowing down to check us out, but no one stopped until finally a brown Volkswagen bus pulled onto the shoulder, splashing through puddles and passing us by. I heard it back up, and it appeared in the side doors. Gray smoke poured out the tailpipe, and the engine sounded like a lawn mower. Faces appeared behind the windows—a man in the driver's seat and a woman in the passenger's side—sitting and staring at us, deciding. I thought, *Come on*. It rumbled and shook, and I wondered if they'd leave. Until finally the engine cut out and the van settled down. Buddy looked at me and said, "My ass is asleep from sitting here. Take these folks and at least get rid of the little ones. Show me you can do this and we'll go."

The whole family poured out. Stepping over puddles and tiptoeing through the mud. Five total. The little girl's stringy cutoffs and stretched out, faded T-shirt were probably handed down from her brother. The mother held the hem of her dress with her right hand, and the grandmother was wearing a white straw hat with a wilted dandelion in the band. I thought, *Hippies*, and had no idea why they'd stopped. Only the father was wearing shoes. Brown sandals.

The grandmother arrived first. Smiling, she talked like she was trying to hold her dentures in her mouth. "Heyya, sweetheart," she said.

"Afternoon," I said. "That sure is a pretty flower."

"This old thing?" She touched her hat. "It's probably dead, hon. This one gave it to me at a truck stop in Texarkana." She hip-checked the boy, and he stumbled to the side. She reached for his hand before he fell. The little girl covered her mouth, and I waited for the man to finally step up. He wore glasses with earth-toned frames, and his hair hung shaggy, swept to the side. They all seemed to have missed out on Woodstock and were still in search of it. I expected him to say *Heeeyy, maaan,* so I said it. Just like that.

He gave me a confused glance and said, "How's it going? I just stopped to see what you were selling."

I ran through the shrimp like Buddy had.

The guy said, "I don't know. Maybe if you could do the big ones for five bucks, we could talk. Once you weigh in all of the ice and the water, I'm paying double what I'd pay at the grocer. Besides you don't have enough of the little ones to reach five pounds."

"Tell you what," I said. "I'll weigh in all I've got of the $4.99s, and if it doesn't come to five, I'll make up the difference with the mediums."

He stayed tense. "I don't know. I'm mainly interested in the big ones."

No way he could afford those. But I knew not to push too hard just yet.

He opened the farthest left cooler again and picked up one of the jumbos. "Can you take off the head and weigh it out? So I can compare?" He held it up to me with the tips of his fingers. The kids kept trying to climb in the van, and I was about to tell him no when he went ahead and tore the head off the shrimp and tossed the body up on the scale. Flinging the head on the ground, he smeared the yellow and blue liquid of its insides across the cooler. "Compare that to one of these others," he said, picking another jumbo from the cooler. Again he flung it on the scale. The boy picked the head up from the ground and started chasing his sister.

"You see?" he said. "It's half the weight. You either head them or sell them cheaper. Otherwise you're cheating people."

I thought, *Forget it,* if only because he was being a dick. But another part of me wanted to see if I could do it. "I'll sell you the mediums for $4.99," I said. "But I'm not coming down on the big ones."

"That's a rip-off."

I looked at Buddy. He waved his hand low and with stiff fingers, telling me these folks weren't worth the trouble. I thought of what he sometimes said after dealing with people who drove cars that barely ran, who tried to get the shrimp too cheap and had scrawny kids like these. Buddy didn't push anything. He'd only show the shrimp quickly and let them leave empty-handed. Returning to his seat, he'd shake his head as if pulling himself out of a game he could have won. But I wasn't going to do that.

The guy's wife said, "Let's just go."

I didn't care if the whole family starved, if they spent their last twenty bucks so long as I got one over on this guy and got myself out of there. I wasn't considering the guitar, the school clothes, or what my father might say if I sold out. Since that night of the raise, I knew there was no way I'd get out of this, and I'd be dealing with this sort of situation for years to come. I waited until the guy was so frustrated he almost turned, ready to wave me off.

I said, "All right, man, you've got me," and checked my watch. "I'll weigh these jumbo ones, see what we get, and make up the difference with the small shrimp. Five pounds for twenty dollars. That's a better deal than you're going to get at the grocery store. That way you're leaving with what you stopped for." I leaned over the boxes, whispering to the man as if to prevent Buddy from hearing. The guy bent forward. "This is my grandfather's business, and he'll run me into the ground if I give you those jumbos for less than what he paid. I could care less, but they're not mine to give away like that. You get it, right?"

He eyed Buddy and relaxed.

"You'll see. Just let me weigh them."

The rest of the jumbos came to two and a half pounds—enough to fill two adults, maybe—and enough small ones to fill two more. Either way, they would all go to bed hungry. I took the guy's ten and two wrinkled fives. Watched as they walked back to their van, the mother slapping the shrimp's head from the boy's hand. Sitting down, I said, "That kid will have about another pound of those things to run around with once they're finished pinching them off."

Buddy said, "Twenty bucks could have fed those kids for a week. Bread and peanut butter. Some decent food maybe." He shook his head and looked up at me. The sun shone on his face and he squinted. I couldn't tell if he was smiling.

I said, "It's not my job to make pals," and wrote the sale in the notebook. Now I only had a few small ones left, and we could leave. As I started to climb in back to take down the scales, a car pulled up alongside us. A beige Mercedes with gold trim. The driver got out, overweight with a suit that matched his car's paint. I felt the guilt start to rise. He stepped in the middle of a puddle, wearing ostrich skin boots, while he walked over. He laid his hands on top of the coolers with his wallet already out, a pinky ring buried in the folds of his skin. "Hope you got a lot left," he said, "because I'm going to need all of it."

"We don't have much," I said, lifting the lid on the medium-sized shrimp. "Some family just bought us out on all the big ones."

He searched the inside of the box and said, "You're kidding me," and turned to his left, as if considering going after these people who bought his shrimp. Then he shot a look at me, as if to say I should have saved them.

SALT WATER

On the October morning after Buddy passed away, I woke up on a beach in Panama City beside a seawall. An old man was kneeling in front of me, a metal detector slung over his shoulder. Headphones were wrapped around his neck, and I could hear the machine beeping. The white beach was behind him, and he said, "Are you all right?"

I sat up quickly and leaned back.

"I'm not going to hurt you," he said. "How did you get here?"

I swallowed hard and looked out over the water, at the bright line of sun still coming up. My mouth was dry. I said, "My dad. I need to find him."

"Of course you do," the man said, seeming relieved. "Where is he at?"

I looked left, down the beach, and slowly remembered the night before. How I'd gotten here. I remembered the empty hallway with white walls and white floors, in the hospital where Buddy was staying. My father and I had been in Florida for a week, staying at the river house. We came to see him every day, taking the elevator up. Whenever we got to his floor, Wrendon said to wait in the hall for a second while he went in first. So I sat in a plastic chair. Minutes passed, and eventually he'd come out, waving me in. But this time the wait went longer. A nurse came running and went inside.

I'd never noticed the sounds of the machines until they were gone. Now there were voices. Wrendon came out, and the nurse followed. She wiped her eyes with her collar, and they hugged. I stood from the chair as he walked toward me, felt his hand on the back of my neck, gently pushing as we started down the hallway toward the elevator. I realized we were leaving and turned around to try and run back to the room. Wrendon grabbed hold of my collar.

We drove around a while, up the two-lane roads with swaying palm trees and tall streetlights, stopping once to buy a Cherry Coke and a bottle of Wild Turkey. It was something he never drank except on his birthday, and I knew to steer clear of him when he did. It made him mean, asking my mother why she looked like she did. What had happened. Why the place was such a mess. Why I didn't have more friends or play sports. What the fuck I hoped to do with all those records. It made his jaw flutter and his teeth grind.

Wrendon kept the bottle tucked between his legs. We drove around through the night, both of us drinking from our bottles, until the air smelled like salt water. I finally said, "Where are we going?"

He pulled into an empty parking lot and said, "Here."

I looked out at the water, the white lines rolling in.

Wrendon opened his door and said, "Get out."

On the beach, Wrendon stopped, so I stopped. I had never seen him cry, and I tried to keep my face straight. It seemed like one of us should.

"Buddy couldn't say much," Wrendon said. "But he wanted to make sure I told you good-bye. I meant to call you in the room, but I didn't. I wasn't sure if you could handle it. Now he's gone, and I'm sorry. You should have been there."

Buddy had asked for me every day. Sat up straighter when I walked into the room, and he smiled bigger. It didn't make sense. I'd stayed with him while he got sober, and we had worked the truck together. While Wrendon was gone. I said, "Why would you do that?"

He tried to reach for me, but I backed up.

I said, "You should have."

He said, "Just wait. Uncross your arms and let me explain."

I stepped away, turned, and ran down the beach. I pressed harder, and his voice fell away. I knew, with his boots on, he couldn't catch up, and I kept running until my lungs burned and there was nothing around but the sand and sound of water pushing in. Until I was tired and finally stopped and sat by the seawall to cry by myself.

The old man held out his hand, but I ignored it, squinting against the morning's sun. I nodded in the direction I'd come from. I said, "He's back there somewhere," and started moving.

II

STAGES

Just after Buddy died, a Safeway opened around the corner from Wrendon's shop. His business started thinning, and after New Year's he sat down with my mom to say he wanted to sell the store while he still could and use Buddy's inheritance to buy Greener Acres. To start all over. The owner was retiring, and the price was unbelievable. It came established and with a steady clientele. "A lifelong dream," Wrendon said, something I'd never heard before. As he talked, my mother glanced down at his glass of Coke and whiskey, what he drank now instead of beer. She said it'd only make more trouble. She wanted to use the inheritance to buy a car, to replace the one she had that broke down so often she was afraid to drive it very far. She wanted us to get a house, to get ahead and have something of our own.

He said the bar would only put us that much closer. We could have everything.

But she said no.

Throughout that month, they fought differently. With his business slipping away and the owner of Greener Acres getting offers, Wrendon would come home most nights, nice at first but with a calm and settled anger in his eyes. When he eventually brought up the bar and she said no, their fights moved faster. He'd finally ask her why they married in the first place, if she had so little faith in him. When she fought back, he threatened to leave but said he couldn't, because how in the world would she pay all the bills? How long could she handle being alone? She didn't date before they met and sure as shit couldn't find someone now. Once the fights reached this point, she stopped yelling and kept her lips pressed together, staying this way until he got frustrated and left, slamming the screen door closed.

But one night in late February he came home holding a set of rolled papers and a thick, green bottle. He called us into the dining room and said, "Sit down." Uncorking the champagne, he said he'd gone ahead with the purchase. As the foam bubbled onto the floor, he explained that the owner had gotten a reasonable offer from someone else. He filled three plastic glasses and set them in front of us. "I had no option," Wrendon said. "I decided it's my money and my choice, and you should trust me."

My mother stared at her glass, and as he lifted his to make a toast, she took a deep breath and threw back the champagne like it was medicine. Setting it down, she kept her eyes set with the same glare she used to end their fights. He said, "Christopher, drink up," and she watched to see what I'd do.

I drank like she had. At first it tasted sweet, but then it burned my throat.

After he left to celebrate with friends, she asked what I thought.

I knew she wanted me on her side, but I was hopeful. "Maybe it will work," I said.

"Maybe it will," she said.

Over the next few months he did relax, and he was easier to get along with. Every so often he would call my mom and ask us to come out. By that spring, I was fourteen and wouldn't consider sitting at the bar with them while they drank. Instead I sat at an empty table in the dark off to the side, watching through the crowd of dancers as the house band played their set. Over those months I became friends with one of the two guitarists, a thin man named Charlie who had a beard and a deep voice. Some nights we sat in the bar's back office and he gave me lessons, playing and singing. I felt proud, carrying in my SG and walking through the bar to the back. I gave him tapes of music I liked—George Strait, AC/DC, the Replacements—and he taught me their songs. He said it was all pretty much the same, theoretically.

When I wasn't in back practicing or up front watching the band, I shoved quarters in the jukebox and pinball machine. One Friday night, with the band between sets and the jukebox running, the music stopped. Playing pinball, I felt someone grab my collar and start hauling me through the bar. At first I thought it was a cop, freaking out that I was there. Or some drunk woman wanting to dance. But I couldn't turn to see and kept moving backward across the sand-covered dance floor toward the stage.

Standing beneath the bright lights, I looked down at the riser's red carpet, its cigarette burns. Charlie stood in front of me, a cigarette dangling from his lips, holding his blonde Telecaster. I was already sweating and looking for Wrendon to come stop this, but the lights were too strong to see past the stage. As Charlie set the guitar over my shoulder, other band members walked to their instruments, and I felt their steps on the stage. Heard the drums and cymbals moving. The other guitarist turned up the volume on his amp and started tuning. I looked at Charlie and said, "Don't do this."

"Just play a few you know real well," he said, fitting the strap. "Don't do that fast shit. Mind the crowd. Do some Strait and Patsy Cline. It'll be odd, singing a woman. But you're kind of an odd kid." He ruffled my hair and patted the strap on my chest as he stood. "Close with something slow," he said. "For some reason people like that. Think of this as your house, and they're your guests."

A crowd was already gathered, and more people were coming up. Men in cowboy hats and women wearing dresses stared up at me, smiling. I tried to smile back but knew I was only making a face that said I had no clue what I was doing.

Charlie stepped up to the microphone and tapped it. The bar started to settle until he said, "Hey y'all." His voice came loud through the speakers all around, and then no one spoke. "This here's Chris Saxton. He used to be a shrimp man, but now he's gonna play some music."

I felt the rush of their applause, wondering how I was going to get the hell off this stage with all these people down in front and no space to get between them.

He loosened the microphone and brought it down to my face. Covering it with his hand, he said, "Sing from your chest, to the back of the crowd. Belt it when you know you should. Don't look at people up front and don't start conversations. Even if they talk to you. I'm serious. You got it? Don't talk. Except to say thank you after the songs. Do it right. Sing loud, and don't stop if you screw up. Because nobody here," he nodded toward the band, "is going to stop for you."

He stepped into the crowd and out of the light.

Now I was alone, the whole room watching, and I felt the heat of the lights. I looked at the bass player, Red. He yelled over, "Where we going?"

I cleared my throat and said, "Dwight Yoakam?"

"Are you asking me?"

I said, "Dwight Yoakam."

From behind me, the drummer said, "Which one do you want?"

I turned around and looked at him through the cymbals. "Little Ways."

"You need a count off?" he said.

I didn't understand the question, but I didn't want to make him repeat himself so I stepped up to the microphone and closed my eyes. Feeling the metal against my lips, I eased back. I knew that people were in front of me and the band was all around, but in that space I felt apart from them. Feeling my shoulders tighten up, I wrapped my hand around the neck of the guitar, found the strings and the first chord, and took a deep breath.

The drummer said, "I guess he don't."

I heard myself before I knew I was singing. Felt the kick drum behind me and my voice caught up in it, my right hand finding the rhythm. My voice was everywhere, all around. It sounded weird, but it was mine, from my chest. "All you have to do is stay in key," Charlie had said. "Even if you think you sound like shit, don't try to sound like no one else." I kept my eyes closed for a while but finally opened them, knowing it wouldn't make a difference. I thought people would still be standing there, staring up. But they were dancing. A woman passing by locked eyes with mine and winked, and I had to stare at the ceiling not to laugh. Looking down, I saw my parents moving around with the crowd, two-stepping in a circle across the floor, shuffling and spinning from the dark into the light, back to the dark. Their cheeks were pressed together, and they looked calm. For a while, I tried to follow them as they danced but knew I couldn't. To keep it up would wreck the song. So I decided to let them go and concentrate on keeping time.

HANDS

During the last year of my parent's marriage, Wrendon got in the habit of taking in strays. Not vagrants really, but people down on their luck who frequented Greener Acres. My mother had been right. As spring and summer passed, rather than seeing him more often, we saw him less. He used the bar to justify the late nights and the nights of not coming home. He put a green cot in the back office and slept there. But sometimes, when he came home, he would bring someone with him, and every so often I'd wake up on Sunday mornings or get home from Garfield Middle where I'd just started eighth grade to find a new person sitting on the couch with the remote in their outstretched hand, flipping through court television. To cover their keep, my father assigned some job around the house. Painting the walls, replacing or fixing something, and I was told to help out.

In September, there was Sarah, a brown-haired woman desperate to leave the situation with her husband. She would stare out the window that looked on the porch and the driveway, her chin propped on her hand like she was waiting for someone to pull up. She took her husband's calls and, like Theresa, stayed in the bathroom. One night I heard her say, "Honey, you can't shoot their dog." She stopped a second and said, "'Cause they ain't got one." Two weeks later the husband's truck pulled in the driveway, and Sarah was smiling as she walked out the front door, down the steps, and rode away.

Just before Thanksgiving, there was Robby. He had a thick mustache, always wore a red tank top, and claimed to lay carpet. A woman had filed sexual harassment complaints at the place where he worked. He said he'd only asked her out, but I could tell by the way he overhanded his fork and talked with his mouth full of food that he was lying. He was supposed to replace our carpet but did nothing unless I was home. Eventually my mom found a porno stuck inside the VCR, still running. All she'd wanted to do, she said, was watch the goddamn evening news. That's when we realized how Robby spent his days and why nothing was getting done. Wrendon happened home that night and, seeing the new carpet frayed and bubbled, told Robby to hit the road. When he refused, Wrendon dragged him into the yard, punched his face, and flung his suitcase out after him.

More people came and went. Usually they stayed two weeks, or until they got thrown out. Each of them had their own annoying quirks. Some refused to pick up their clothes, and some wouldn't clean the knives they used to constantly make sandwiches. Others brought hard liquor or drugs or sex into the house. Early on I asked my mom why we did this, and she brought up a time when she and Wrendon first came to Texas. Without jobs or money, they had to live out of their station wagon, eating bologna sandwiches. "No one would help us out," she said. "No one would take us in."

And while these people lived with us, no matter my cold stares, they always envisioned a permanent place in the family. I flinched when they ruffled my hair and asked how my day went. Didn't answer when they said "Good morning" or "Good night." I thought it was bad enough with Wrendon gone all the time, but now we had some thirty-year-old replacement wanting in. I heard the same story. The rules did not apply. No one understood. I met many a desperado. How many times I was misquoted Robert Frost, I do not know. After a while, I tuned them out. I came to the notion that everybody moves their own hands. Somewhere along the line they had created their situation. But most people preferred not to deal with the consequences. Yes, you took the road less followed. And look where it brought you. Here with us.

* * *

Daniel was a Sunday person. I found him asleep on our couch one morning in March before anyone else was up. I walked softly through the living room, checking him out. He was wrapped in a green blanket, his stubbled face pale and worn, and he had the stale beer morning-after smell of the bar. Near his feet, beside the couch, were his boots and a nylon duffel bag. Here we go again, I thought.

Usually these people were closer to my dad, but I knew my mother and Daniel were friends. I remembered him from those Friday nights when she and I went to the bar. For a while after that first night with Charlie's band, Wrendon let me play sets, singing covers early on in the night. Starting out, I was nervous. But Charlie said nervous was part of it. You just yell out all the antsiness and trust yourself, he said. Eventually those first few moments got to be my favorite part. After that nothing else in the world mattered. As I played, the dark room was usually half-filled with people, two-stepping or sitting at the small wooden tables that filled the room. My father shot pool and drank with his regulars while my mother sat alone at the corner of the bar, reading one of her novels and sipping a diet cola. When I finished, she usually slipped the book in her purse and we left.

But sometimes Daniel bartended and we stayed later into the night. Whenever this happened, she kept her book closed on the bar and drank beer after beer, leaning forward so they could talk over all the people and music. He was lanky with thick blonde hair combed off to the side. Lots of women smiled and chased him with their eyes, but he always went back to my mother, resting his chin in his palm beside her. They would laugh and carry on. I thought he talked weird. His vowels were drawn out, and he had a flippant airiness to his voice. On those nights, once my set was done, I played video games or watched Charlie's band, eyeing my mother and Daniel from a distance. Wrendon ignored them entirely, something he didn't do when other guys came near.

Because of the way Daniel acted and spoke, people jokingly referred to him as the bar's token fairy. No one seemed sure or wanted to know whether or not he was actually gay. There were rumors that his grandmother raised him, as if this explained everything. Of course he never brought a guy into the bar, and he claimed to keep a little lady at home. When people suggested he bring her up, Daniel fanned his face with his fingers and said, "The smoke gets in her eyes." People teased him constantly. A voice-mock here or limp wrist there. I didn't get it, but they liked him well enough and would defend him if the jokes went too far. My father knew he could trust Daniel to tend the bar and not get drunk. He worked only for tips. Wrendon never gave him a dime.

I hadn't seen Daniel in a while. We hadn't been there since November, almost five months. My mom was tired of going, and I was tired of playing country covers and dealing with Wrendon's mood swings. These days he drank more than ever, going from kind to mean in a minute. I had started up a band with a few friends from school who'd also never gotten into sports. Brian from chemistry who played drums, whose favorite bands were the Grateful Dead and The Who. His best friend Jerry who played the bass and liked Motown and punk. My friend Casey who also played guitar and had a garage where we could practice. His dad was an old hippie, had a record store in Fort Worth, and was cool with it. I sang and played guitar, and at our first practices we stuck to covers. Every Wednesday night after practice, each person wrote the title of a song on a slip of paper and tossed it into a ball cap. Whatever song Jerry pulled from the cap, we had to learn over the week. Brian always suggested songs that were impossible, by people like Jimi Hendrix or Led Zeppelin. Casey and I could never get them down between practices, and the mistakes we made resulted in new songs of our own.

We called ourselves The Earliest Ending, and I used poets like Wallace Stevens and William Carlos Williams, people I read in my English class, to make up lyrics. Casey's dad said we sounded like a cross between the Rolling Stones in their early stages and the Beatles in their middle stages, only with better drums. I thought we didn't sound like anyone. Because of practice, Wednesdays were my favorite day of the week. I liked playing with the other guys, arranging the sounds, and the feeling when everything came together. Friends and girls would come over and stand in the corner of the garage, watching us play. I thought about songs all day. When I woke up, throughout classes in school, and when I lay in bed at night. I kept my guitar propped on its side on the floor beside my mattress and fell asleep with my right hand slung over, running my fingers through the strings.

Making breakfast that Sunday morning, I wondered what Daniel had done to find himself crashed on my couch. Probably some issue with the sensitive-eyed mystery girl. I wondered if she busted him with some guy in their bed, the two men naked. White and sweaty. But the picture came too vivid and gross, and I let it go. *Fag* was a word I'd heard more than once from kids at school when I was younger. I had a nasally voice myself and walked with a bounce when I didn't think about it. And gay people were almost always on the news these days. Wearing tight shorts and screaming in parades. Shriveled in their hospital beds, talking in lispy voices. It was all weird and scary, and I couldn't imagine having one of those freaks in my house.

I hadn't seen my parents together for a week but guessed by his Timex on top of the TV and his boots by the door that Wrendon had spent last night at home. These days I got nervous whenever he came around. The current argument involved some woman named Loren. I overheard my mother talking about her, saying she'd recently moved to town from Florida and sometimes waitressed at Greener Acres. Most of his staff was made up of people working under the table.

That my father slept around was no secret. As I got older, I'd learned his pattern. He was the type of cheater who kept girls on the side. He and my mother went rounds: he kept a girlfriend until my mother found out; she would confront him and cry and, still, the relationship went on until he decided to end it. He would tell my mother he'd realized what he lost if he lost her. His drinking eased up and he stayed home more often, and they'd make plans for a better future. Life got better for a while. Then he'd start going out more nights of the week, and stay out later. Eventually staying gone a full night or two. Lately he'd gotten unbearable, floating in and out of the house, the whiskey making him pick at everyone and start arguments. Finally he'd walk out, saying, "Fuck this."

These days when he threatened to pack up, he asked my mom if that's what she wanted. I wondered, given his new girlfriend and the bar, if this is what he'd meant when he mentioned starting over.

Still my mom put up with it. Even with her steady job she couldn't make ends meet on her own. Earlier that winter, after a particularly vicious fight, I asked her if we should go. She could find somebody else, someone better who deserved her, and I could get some sort of job, maybe sacking groceries. But she said, "You're fourteen, Chris, and you've got a lot to learn. You don't leave a bad thing figuring on a better one. You don't get rewarded just for leaving."

I placed three plates on the dining room table, with folded paper towels and silverware beside them. I hoped we could eat, just the three of us, in peace. I opened the kitchen curtains, and sunlight sparkled through the table, casting a shadow across the linoleum floor. I set down the plates of hash browns, toast, and scrambled eggs. Walked to my parent's room and tapped on the door.

My mother said, "Just a second."

"I made breakfast," I said.

She came out after a couple minutes, smiling and tapping her cigarette into her palm. Wearing a nightgown, her long brunette hair was held back with a comb. She looked at the dining room, said "Wow," and went to the kitchen to grab a plate for Daniel. I almost asked her to let him sleep.

Wrendon walked in, slow and slightly hunched over. These days he was thinner, with his cheekbones standing out and his face always red. He took a chair at the opposite end of the table and laughed at all the food. "You've been watching Julia Child again, haven't you?" he said. "I thought I told you to steer clear of that show."

I thought he looked kind of pathetic. "I just figured it'd be nice," I said, "to eat like a family."

"Like a family," he repeated, more to himself than me.

Daniel followed my mother. "Just make yourself at home," she said, pulling out a chair for him.

"You sleep all right?" Wrendon asked him.

"Sure did," Daniel said. He sat down and fidgeted, getting situated. "You cook all this, Chris?"

My mother said, "You know Daniel."

Yes, I nodded. Greener Acres's token fairy, come to freeload off of us for a while.

"Daniel's going to be staying with us," she said.

"He's going to fix up the roof," Wrendon said. "With your help, of course."

I imagined us up there, with no one else at home, and him pulling something fruity. My mother picked up the plate of eggs, forked some out for everyone except me, and went for the toast. I said, "I have homework after school, and band practice on Wednesdays."

"When did you stop eating?" Wrendon asked, scooting the eggs toward me with his fork.

My mother said, "He's stopped eating meat." She lifted the hash browns and shoveled some onto my plate, then everyone else's. "Something he learned in health."

"I hear it's the healthy way to go," Daniel said.

"It's a way to grow a nice set of tits," Wrendon said. "Besides, egg's not a meat."

"It's no big deal," I said. "I'll just eat toast and hash browns."

My mother looked at me, getting anxious. "Maybe a little?" she said.

I thought of a joke I'd heard in school and said, "The yolk is liquid chicken."

Everyone cringed. Wrendon scratched his jaw. "You hardly open your mouth," he said. "But when you do, this stupid shit comes out."

My mom said, "Wrendon."

"What?" he said. "You know it's stupid. Don't you?" He looked at me.

"Why are you making an issue out of this?" I said.

He stood and circled the table, holding his plate of food. Standing beside me he dumped it all on top of mine, tapping his plate so it emptied. He sat down, balled his napkin, and nodded at the mound of yellow and brown in front of me. "Eat," he said.

I stared at the food, knowing I wasn't going to touch it. I kept my hands on my lap. Even Daniel was staring at me, wondering how I'd react. I knew it was best to stay quiet. Knew from years of watching how people looked, acted, and talked. From those days in the truck when people came up, just wanting to hassle me, and how my mom handled Wrendon when he got like this. The best choice was silence. But I didn't care about what I'd learned. "You can't just walk in here and do this," I said.

Wrendon glared at my mom. "You make him do it."

She said, "Stop."

He pushed away from the table and stood. "You wonder why I don't come home. It's shit like this."

My mother turned to me. "Eat your breakfast, go to your room, and don't come out until I say." She followed Wrendon to their bedroom, and I could hear her apologizing.

All the food sat on the table, hardly touched. Their chairs were empty. Just Daniel and me. He picked up his plate and scooped the rest of his eggs on mine. At first I was confused, but he switched our dishes and said, "Now hurry up and eat."

I understood what he was doing, and I knew he meant well. So I got up and took my food to the trashcan, threw the plate and everything in, and left him sitting alone at the table, knowing exactly where we stood.

I stayed in my room until early that afternoon, replaying the morning. Wondering if I should have given a little, at least for her. Maybe he wouldn't have taken off. Even with the constant fighting, I wanted him home. When someone knocked on my door, I knew it was my mom. We had a rule in the house—between her and myself, anyway—that no one entered without the other's permission.

I said, "It's open."

She had been in the flower bed all morning, cooling down. She sat in the chair beside my desk and pulled off her gardening gloves. "About this morning," she said. "About all of it. I wish I could explain your dad sometimes. He gets these phases. And lately he's got a lot on his mind. Times are tight, and the regulars aren't coming out like they used to. He's doing all he can to keep the bar from folding, and I've had to pull from my savings to cover the cost of the roof."

"I don't get it," I said. "He can't stick around himself, but he brings these people to stay with us. If he's going to stay gone, just stay gone. But don't stick us with these losers."

"You know Daniel is my friend," she said, "right?"

I said, "I'm sorry."

"It's good he's here," she said. "That he can fix the roof. Last spring's storms did a number, and we won't make it another year. With him getting materials wholesale it cuts us a break on this month's rent. It's a windfall, really."

"How long did he say it would take?"

"If he was only doing our roof, five days," she said. "But since he's got his own work it will be longer. I'm not going to hound him to rush the job. I'd say two weeks."

I thought of all the extra time it would take. I was already doing badly in some classes and this could cut in on the band.

She picked up her gloves and went to the door. "He's probably not going to need your help often, but I want you up there in case he does."

"Even on Wednesdays?"

"Unless he says so," she said. "And be nice about it."

Soon enough I saw that Daniel was different from the others. He wasn't at ease with the situation. He left for work before I got up, didn't leave his blankets or pillows strewn on the couch, and kept his clothes folded in his bag. He worked quickly, leaving his own job at three and beating me home from school by an hour. By the time I walked up the driveway that Monday, he was already pulling shingles off the roof. I changed out of my school clothes and scaled the shaky aluminum ladder, growing more hesitant the higher I went. I moved slowly up each rung, sure the whole thing would fall back any second. When I reached the top, I practically crawled onto the roof. Standing up, I tried to find my balance by holding my hands out to the sides, keeping level. Not looking anywhere but the gray shingles at my feet, I dug in the soles of my Converse to get a better grip. Once certain, I straightened up and looked around, seeing the train tracks behind the house, the black rooftops of the stores along the highway, and the sun setting beyond them.

Daniel didn't waste a moment. He stopped working and pointed with his axe-hammer to a pile of ripped up shingles at a corner of the roof. "Go ahead and toss those in the bed of my truck," he said. His beige Toyota pickup was backed into the yard. "And do your best not to send them through the rear window." He waited for me to laugh at his joke, but I didn't. As I started to move, he said, "Chris."

I said, "What?"

He waved his hand along the center of his body from neck to waist. "Center your gravity," he said, "and keep loose." He bent at his knees a few times.

I did the same, saw what he meant, and went to the corner. As Daniel nailed down the loose or curling shingles around the house, I sent the old ones spinning to the bed of his truck. I decided to make a game of it, counting how many I got in. Within half an hour I'd cleared them all.

Standing on the edge and peering over, I didn't hear when he walked up behind me. But the instant he put his hand on my shoulder I started to slip. I tried to regain my balance and find my footing but couldn't do it until he grabbed my elbow and held me steady. I pulled away. He looked me over, put his hands on his hips and nodded toward the pickup. "When I was your age, my uncle started me out by taking me with him on summer and weekend jobs. He gave me a nickel for every one I got in. What are you up to?"

I stared at the ground, knowing I'd made fifty-five. Eight lay on the ground. "Is this all you need? Because I've got homework."

"I guess that's it," he said, starting back toward the spot near the top where he'd been before.

I climbed down the ladder, got to the ground and threw the eight missed shingles into his truck.

He called my name again, and I looked up. Standing at the edge of the roof, above me, he said, "Your mom also left a to-do list on the refrigerator. Dishes and things. So there's that before she gets home."

I almost walked away but stopped and said, "Hey, Daniel."

He stayed where he was.

"I was just wondering. Do you think that's the first time she's left me a list of chores on the fridge?"

He didn't respond.

I almost added that he was the last person on earth who should tell me what to do. But I knew it would only get something started and I went in.

All of Tuesday I wondered how to approach him about the possibility of not working the next night. In three months none of the guys in the band had missed practice. By the time I got home that afternoon, Daniel had two-by-four scaffolds placed like shelves along the sloping sides. The new shingles had arrived, and they were stacked on the rooftop in a line of brown paper rectangles. When I got up there, he started to explain the work ahead. He held a large white sketch pad, and all the tools were laid out on the roof side-by-side.

"First thing we'll cover," he said, "are the materials and gear. I'm not trying to make a roofer of you or anything, but when I ask you to get me something, I want you to get it. This," he held up a shiny, pebbled shingle, "is a three-tab asphalt. These," he pointed, "are nail holes. These are the cutouts, and this shiny black stuff is self-sealing adhesive."

I realized he hadn't yet removed all the shingles. "Don't you need to pull up the rest of them?" I said, suspiciously.

"Not with asphalt or fiberglass shingles, though that's a good question. Up north it's too much weight if you kept adding on, what with snow and all. So, yes, up there you'd pull up all the old roofing. Or replace it section by section as things rot. But that, keep in mind, is a Yankee thing to do."

Another joke. I kind of smiled.

"Now these are the numbers I've figured," he said, pointing at the sketch pad where he had drawn our roof in pencil. "You and your folks have a 1500 square foot roof here. Each of those bundles contains twenty-seven three-tabs. Three bundles make what we call a square. Each square covers a hundred feet. In order to figure out exactly what we'd need, we have to calculate the square footage of the roof and divide by one hundred."

I tried to keep up, but he started carrying numbers and might as well have been writing Russian, considering my attention span and weakness in math. He stopped and said, "Should I talk slower?"

I thought he was making fun of me. "It's not rocket science."

"Yeah, but it's not basic math either. I'm just saying. It's better if you tell me to slow down. Otherwise, I'm none the wiser. You've got to speak up."

I said, "Okay. Slow down."

"Well, there you go."

Speaking slowly, nodding at me and making eye contact, he continued, and I got it. From measurements, Daniel moved on to explain the other supplies and tools he used. Galvanized ring shank nails, builder's felt, ridge shingles, and drip edges. We covered the names of materials as we worked. Daniel spoke loudly and clearly, making sure I understood what he meant. By that evening I was moving around the roof freely, knowing where things were, where they went and what they were called.

As evening approached I knew I needed to ask him about band practice. He stood, looking everything over.

"Look," I said, nervous, "about tomorrow night."

He waved his hand. "You've got your thing," he said. "That's fine," and continued checking the roof.

Nothing came this easy. I said, "Are you sure?"

"Why wouldn't I be?" he said.

He didn't even look up.

Over the rest of the week, I caught Wrendon coming and going when he made random visits to check the roof or grab clean clothes. I walked behind him around the house, to their room or to the kitchen, where he fixed himself a drink. He asked short questions like "How's school?" without stopping what he was doing, and I drew out the answers, going on about a Spanish quiz or theorems on a geometry test. He nodded and climbed in his van, hardly responding. Watching him leave, I got the sense of having played a one-sided game of catch. I kept tossing him balls that he put into his pocket.

Those nights, after dinner, Daniel sat with my mother at the dining room table. He told her about the people he worked with and the apprehensive customers who took time off their jobs to spend the day in lawn chairs, watching him repair their roofs and making sure they weren't getting ripped off. They would ask, "Who's that?" if a new employee showed up or "What's that for?" when a fresh stack of shingles arrived.

Before, whenever my mother tried to talk about her job, about the other women showing up late and taking long lunch breaks, the long hours, and how she sometimes had to bring home paperwork, Wrendon ignored her. But Daniel listened. I realized I'd never known much about what she did, if she had worries, or how she liked it. But they spoke until the sunlight was gone from the windows and all they could do was sigh and lean back in their chairs. She looked rested and smiled often.

She told Daniel about my problems with geometry. I was failing all my quizzes and on the verge of failing the class. On Wednesday night, when I got home, I let him check over my homework. He sat behind me on the couch, using the same flat eraserless pencil he used with the sketch pad. As we worked through problems and he explained his corrections, I forgot about the way his voice rose and fell, stopped squirming thinking any second my dad might come through the door and see this guy leaning over me. Over the week the math got easy. The angles and theorems came together.

We talked more as we worked, and I got to know him better. As we moved further along, adding shingles toward the edges of the roof, he told me about growing up with his grandmother after both of his parents died in a car wreck. He graduated high school, enlisted in the army, and started roofing right afterward. He liked to bartend for extra money, and he liked being around people. I realized I had been wrong about him being gay. He was nothing like those people on TV. His voice was just lispy, and you forgot it after a while. He was a man who spent his days at a steady job, who made time to talk with my mother. He was willing to help me out with homework and talk about school without questioning my social life. So when he leaned over me at the couch while we did the math—smelling like sunburn, his hands thick and coarse—I felt okay with it. The only thing I feared now was Wrendon coming home and wrecking the easiness that Daniel brought into the house.

At times I considered asking Daniel what had happened. What had been so bad that he agreed to do all of this work on our house in exchange for so little. But I knew better than to pry into other people's lives, and I didn't want to risk embarrassing him.

The second Friday he was with us, I got an A on my math quiz, and he congratulated me by handing over one of his old suede tool belts. Sitting on the roof, we laughed about it, knowing once he was gone, the belt would probably collect dust. By that time we were almost done. We had flashed the new shingles along the bend of the house and were working our way to the ridges and edges. Daniel would stand by while I measured out the three-tabs before cutting them down. He let me make mistakes without any harsh corrections, instead throwing me another shingle and saying to start over. When Wrendon stopped by that day, I waved from the roof.

He went in for a second and reappeared. Standing beneath us on the ground, looking up, he seemed smaller. "Hey, Chris," he said. "Why don't you come down here a second?"

I looked at Daniel. "We're pretty much done for today," he said.

I went down the ladder, skipping rungs toward the bottom, and jumped to the lawn.

"What's up?" I thumped the porch light while walking through the door.

"In here," he called from the bedroom.

"Did you see the new roof?" I said. "It looks good, doesn't it?"

"Better than I'd expect on a rental house," he said. He tossed his old shirts and jeans on the bed. I wasn't surprised. I put my hands in the pockets of my new tool belt and rolled the nails around in my fingers. "How's school?" he said.

"Pretty good," I said. "I got an A on my geometry quiz."

"And your mom?"

I felt my mouth turn, wondering why he would ask me this. "Why don't you ask her yourself?"

"Because I'm asking you," he said.

"We're fine," I said. "We're good. Daniel's been helping me with my math, talking a lot with Mom." I hoped he could take a hint.

"What do you mean? Talking a lot with Mom?"

"I don't know," I said. "After dinner. They hang out. It's been cool. I never knew him so much before, but he's been great."

My father stopped moving and straightened up, as if struck by a thought. "So they just sit around and talk?"

I said, "Yeah."

His eyebrows raised, and his head cocked back, surprised. He searched the room like he was trying to find something. Suddenly his face changed and his jaw set. He gazed up at the white ceiling and fixed his eyes there.

Later that night, he called from Greener Acres to talk to my mother. Rather than sit at the table with Daniel, she went to her bedroom and spoke to Wrendon on the phone, the long clear line stretching from the hallway, through the living room, and into her room. She would come out, go to the kitchen, grab a beer, and shut her door. At one point I realized she was drinking them less quickly and had to trace her fingers along the walls to keep straight. Daniel and I sat on the couch watching TV, but I could still faintly hear her. As the night went on, she got louder, cussed every so often, and fought back loosely.

"I'm not coming up there tonight," she said. "I've told you a hundred times why not. Yes, I am happy. Chris was right to tell you that. He pays attention to me, Wrendon. And he respects me all the time, not just when he wants something."

Daniel grew tense, stared at the floor, and sometimes cringed at what she said. I knew she was talking about him, but I didn't think he should hear all this. I had my reasons for listening to them argue. It helped me gauge what might happen later that night. If she forgave him and the fight ended softly, that meant Wrendon wouldn't come home. I'd sit up late with her, watching TV as she drank more beers, until she fell asleep on the couch. But if she hung up the phone so hard that it clattered and didn't ring again for a few minutes, that meant to head straight for my room and turn out the lights, that his van would pull up in about ten minutes.

He'd shove the door open, and they would start in. Looking at Daniel, I wondered if he had some sense of what might happen and what he would do if Wrendon showed.

She was still on the phone when I went to bed. In the dark, with the murmur of her voice across the house, I considered the possibilities. Everyone had the same thing on their minds. Months had passed since my parents had gotten along. In a way, I wished my father could be more like Daniel. That he would actually come home and stick around. Over the years there had been good times, off and on. But lately he was so far gone. I knew we might be better if he packed everything in his bags and moved out. For the first time I let myself imagine Daniel staying with us, as it seemed things were heading. I thought back to when I saw him at the bar, the way my mother acted around him, brightening up. And I knew he liked her too. I decided if they wanted to be together, that would be okay. I imagined letting Wrendon go so he could start up on his own, as he wanted, and a sudden ease spread over me. I was happy and fell asleep that way.

Muffled voices woke me up. I saw it was one o'clock and realized Wrendon had come home. I tiptoed through the dark, went to the door, and cracked it open. I could barely hear her talking. My mother said, "I've seen her up there. I'm not stupid. I know it's serious. We've been through this, and I'm sick of it."

I expected Wrendon to tell her she was drunk, but she kept talking.

"I don't know what to do," she said. "I guess I keep hoping things will change. But we keep moving in these circles. Coming back to the same place. The only difference is I'm older."

I was glad to hear her say how she felt. She sounded sure of herself, confident. She started speaking more softly, so I opened the door and walked on the edges of my feet through the hallway.

"Right now all I want is for us to leave," she said. "Cut the losses and go. It seems this bar was the final straw."

I came to the doorway leading to the living room. Pressing my shoulders to the wall, I turned slightly to see inside. The living room was empty, but she and Daniel were at the dining room table, sitting across from each other. Their arms lay outstretched, her hands on top of his. "Haven't you been happy these past two weeks?" she said. "Can't we try it for a while?"

Daniel shrugged softly and pulled his hands away. "I think you've had a lot to deal with tonight."

She placed her hand on her chest. "But this is how I feel," she said, starting to cry. "You always said I could tell you anything."

"Emily, you know how much you mean to me. You *and* Chris. But I can't give you what you're asking. What would I tell him someday?"

I tightened my fists, not wanting him to say it.

"When would Chris be old enough for me to sit him down and say I'm gay?"

I didn't want any more of this. Didn't want to be a part of the words they were using.

Daniel said, "If you want to leave Wrendon, then you should leave him. You can make it."

"I can't," she said, crying harder. "I can't afford it with the two of us."

I felt sad for her, and angry. I had thought Daniel was different from all the people who came before, but he was worse. We'd never let anyone else in. I walked back down the hallway, grabbed the phone, and shut my door. I turned on the desk lamp and dialed Greener Acres.

Music was loud in the background. A woman smacking gum said, "Is this Emily?"

I caught my reflection in the mirror on my dresser. A tear hung off the corner of my nose. I didn't even know what I wanted to say to him. I wiped it off, tried to deepen my voice and said, "No."

"Oh," she kind of laughed. "Well, I ain't seen him except once tonight. Earlier when he took off with Loren. Probably headed up the road."

"Do you know where I can reach him?"

"I ain't the faintest fucking clue, sugar. You might try her apartment, if you got that number. Or just accept he's found someone new."

She thought I was some woman, an old girlfriend. The music

got louder, and I could barely hear her. In the distance, she said, "I don't know, and I don't give a shit." The receiver clicked, and I sat there, staring in the mirror.

The next morning, I woke up angry to the sound of rain on the roof and a tarp being dragged across it. I walked to the kitchen and found my mother nursing a cup of coffee, her face puffy and hair tied back. She said, "Morning."

I ignored her. She couldn't even bother making breakfast.

"Are you okay?" she said.

"I'm fine." I opened the refrigerator and realized I wasn't hungry. "Did Wrendon call?"

"No," she said, looking up from her cup. "Why would he?"

"He just lives here," I said and walked past her to my room.

As the rain kept up throughout the weekend, I barely spoke to them unless they spoke to me. I knew the truth now, and I wanted Daniel gone.

By Monday the warm spring sun had returned. I came home to find him working at the top of the roof, nailing in the final row of shingles. He wore a sweat-splotched T-shirt and dark green ball cap. He kept at it, not seeing me walk by.

In the living room I heard the shuffle of his footsteps above. I flipped on the TV while heading to my room to grab new clothes, and I went the bathroom to change. The screen door slammed, and I thought it might be Wrendon on one of his visits. He usually came home on Mondays. I heard tap water running and footsteps getting louder as he approached the bathroom. The knob turned while I was standing with my shirt wrapped inside out around my elbows, over my head.

"Oops, sorry," Daniel said, and shut the door.

I yanked the shirt down over my chest, hurried to finish, and went to the living room. He was standing at the television, drinking water.

"In this house," I said, "people knock before walking into the bathroom."

"Sorry about that," he said.

I recognized the dark green cap he wore as my father's.

"We should finish up the roof pretty quickly today," he said. "After that there's your to-do list on the fridge."

"First off," I said, "about these lists my mom leaves." I walked to the kitchen and pulled it from the fridge. "You might think I'm an idiot at math, but Ms. Ludwig taught me how to read in first grade, and I haven't had a fucking problem with it since. And secondly," I said, "why don't you toss me my dad's cap before you go and fuck it up with all of your queer-assed sweat."

"What's wrong with you?" he said.

I held out my hand. "Give it to me."

He pointed. "This old thing?"

"Yeah, that old *thang*," I said.

It landed in my palms. Sweat soaked all over.

"Check the name on the inside tag," he said, "before you get all huffed up."

"Huffed up," I said, underneath my breath. I pulled the white square from the inside band. In smeared and faded purple ink, it read *Daniel Lansing*. I tossed it back at his chest. "Is that your handwriting or your boyfriend's?"

"My grandma's, I think." He put the cap back on. "Whatever's possessed you, I want nothing to do with it. I'll finish the roof by myself. Just get the list done before your mom gets home, and start your math. I'll check it over after dinner."

As he started for the door, I reached and tried to shove him out. He quickly turned around and grabbed the bones in my wrists. I tried to pull, but he held tight. I said, "Let go," and kept trying to push him out. He spun me around, wrapped his arms over my arms, and held them tight to my sides. He hoisted me off my feet, and I couldn't move, though I struggled. I tried to kick him and said, "Stop it. Let go of me, you faggot." But he wouldn't. I said, "Stop," twisting harder, and he held tighter. I tried to shake my shoulders loose and throw my head back to catch his nose but couldn't do either. I felt warm tears on my face and wanted to reach to wipe my cheeks, but my arms stayed tight. I kicked his knees with the bottoms of my heels and did connect. But instead of letting me go, he squeezed harder and held me there, struggling to get loose. Until I was exhausted and breathing hard. "I saw you at the table on Friday night," I said. "I know everything. All about you. You should have never set foot in this house."

His arms loosened and my feet came to the floor, but he still gripped me.

With my back to him, I said, "Are we so terrible, Daniel? That no one wants to be with us? Am I so stupid and weird? Is she so bad that he can't come back? That you won't even try?"

He let me go and stayed quiet. I felt ashamed and started walking toward my room but felt a tug on the back of my shirt, pulling me back. His hand on my shoulder, he turned me around. I looked down, avoiding his eyes.

"You need to look at me," he said. He held my shoulders and said, "Look up at me."

He was calm and even-toned. "I love your mom very much. And if I could, I would stay. But I can't." He paused a second so this could settle. "We are friends, Chris, and you know that. That I care for you. If I could, I'd do anything to help you. But you guys have *got* to take care of yourselves."

I realized something. "You're leaving soon, aren't you? Once the roof is done."

"You were right," he said. "I shouldn't have come here in the first place."

"I didn't mean that."

"You did," he said, and put his hand on my shoulder. "And that's fine. You should say how you feel. Right out with it. No bullshit. Though of course," he added, "there are better ways to do it."

I wiped my cheeks and held my chin up.

"I've got to go ahead and finish up tonight," he said, looking outside at the roof. "We're just about done. Are you willing to help me out? Because I need it."

I said, "Yes."

"Good," he said. "Now wash your face and meet me up there."

We worked into early evening, putting down the final shingles. Just as the last nails were in, my mother pulled into the driveway.

She had a trunk full of groceries, and we went down the ladder. In the kitchen, as we were unpacking the bags, the front door slammed. We looked at each other as if we'd been caught doing something wrong.

Wrendon traipsed in through the archway separating the kitchen from the dining room. He held a glass, smelled like the bar, and was grinding his teeth.

"You home for dinner?" my mother asked, her voice tense. She stood by the counter, putting cereal boxes up in a cabinet.

He walked to her and wrapped an arm around her waist and pressed his cheek to her lips. She pecked him quickly but kept her head back, looking at him curiously.

"I'm only here for a second," he said, "to grab Daniel."

She said, "What?"

Daniel was filling the refrigerator, and he turned toward Wrendon, surprised.

"We've got a big tournament on the pool tables tonight," Wrendon said. "I stopped off to see if you could come and help out."

My mother said, "On a Monday night?"

"Should be a pretty big crowd," Wrendon said. "I could really use a hand. And you could probably use the tips. Now with you moving to your new place."

My mother looked at Daniel. "You didn't mention you'd found a place."

Daniel tilted his head to the side, like he had a question he wasn't sure how to ask.

"The leasing agent called the bar," Wrendon said. "I guess you gave him that number. I think his name was Shane something. Is that right? Shane called Greener Acres asking around for you today. Says you can even move in tonight, if you like. Things checked out okay."

My mother said, "Well, that won't be necessary. I mean, Daniel, you're more than welcome—"

"Shane?" Daniel said.

Wrendon spoke slowly, measuring his words. His face settled into the same pushing glare as the night he dragged Robby out of the house. "Shane Chapman called today, and he's been trying to get a hold of you. Everything checked out okay."

I could tell Wrendon was up to something. That he and Daniel were talking through us.

My mother said, "What's going on?"

Wrendon nodded. "Go ahead and grab your clothes and we'll head out. I'll explain as we go. Plus we need to talk a few things over. Payment for all you've done here."

Daniel said, "I'm going to change first."

Wrendon nodded. "Sure thing."

Once Daniel left the room, my mother said, "What's going on?"

Wrendon stepped away from her and leaned against the kitchen counter. He said, "That son of a bitch has AIDS."

I almost called him a liar, but my mom beat me to it. She stepped back and shook her head. Smiled, confused. "No, he doesn't."

"You think I'm making this up?"

"I want you to stop it," she said.

"That's the real reason he's here," Wrendon said. "He got tossed out because his boyfriend got scared." He looked at her. "Shane's not a leasing agent. It's the man Daniel was living with. And he didn't call the bar, he actually *came* into the bar. Late this morning, when it was empty. I thought he was lost and needed directions, until he started asking me questions about our houseguest. If I had seen him. I could tell the guy was drunk. A total wreck, almost crying. That's when he told me everything."

She said, "Everything."

"I guess Daniel got tested a few weeks ago," Wrendon said. "Found out that he was sick and told Shane. And Shane of course put his ass to the curb. He was living out of his car and in motels up until a couple weeks ago. I thought something was wrong, and he told me his girlfriend threw him out for messing around. That's when I offered to let him stay here in exchange for patching the roof. Biggest fuckup I've made in a while. Anyhow, Shane got tested, and it turns out he's clean. Now he wants Daniel back, if you can believe that."

"What'd you do?" she said. "When Shane told you this?"

"I told him to get the fuck out of my bar before I whipped his

ass. Which is what I'm about to do with Daniel, once we leave."
He finished his drink. "I'd do it here, but I'm sure you'd get
involved."

"You're unbelievable," she said. "You're going to beat Daniel
up when he's sick?"

"Don't you get it?" Wrendon said. "You don't just bring some
disease into people's homes. Even he knows it. And just because
you have some crush on him doesn't warrant my not knocking his
head in."

I couldn't believe how easily he threw all of this around.

"What are you talking about?" she said.

"You think I don't know?" He looked at me. "I figured it out
last week. Talking to Chris."

I said, "I never said anything like that."

"If you thought something was happening between me and
Daniel," she said, "why would you wait until now? If you were
sure on Friday night? Why didn't you kick him out then?"

Wrendon took a long drink, finished his glass, and dumped the
ice in the sink. "I figured out, when we were talking, that nothing
was happening," he said. "You don't have the spine for it." He
rinsed the glass and shook out the water. "Besides, who else was
supposed to finish the roof?" He set the glass on the kitchen counter
and crossed his arms, leaning back. "And now there's this, all I've
learned. For all we know the whole damn house is infected."

"It doesn't work that way," I said.

"You learn that in health, too?"

"Everyone knows it," I said.

"You think I don't see when you're trying to make a jab at me?"
he said. "Leave it to you to stick up for him. Keep that up and
you'll end up just like him someday."

I swallowed hard. I knew what he meant but couldn't believe
he'd actually say it. "You're serious?"

"You think I don't see it? The way you act?" He started counting
on his fingers. "With the cooking and the cleaning. You don't play
sports. You never talk about girls. The way you walk and the way
you talk. It's why you don't have any friends. Just that goofy little
band. The last thing you need is to think that's okay. Otherwise

you'll end up like him. Dead because of what you brought on yourself, with no one but strangers to take care of you."

"And what about you?" I said. I waited and looked at my mom. She didn't know the truth about Loren. Not like I did. There was the chance this woman would go off to the wayside like others before. That he'd clean up. But I was beyond pissed off, wanting him gone, and now for good. I thought of what Daniel told me, to get it out. I said, "I called Greener Acres at one o'clock on Friday night. I wanted to talk about what I'd said that afternoon. To apologize. But as it turns out, I don't have the number to Loren's apartment. Or the number to wherever you two went. Is that what I'm supposed to be? A liar who never comes home?"

"Compare our situations," Wrendon said. "Daniel's and mine. Tell me whose shoes you'd rather be in."

My mother turned her head sharply. "What were you doing up at one?"

I didn't want to say it out loud. But as she stood there, I could see her face turn down once she realized I had heard them at the table. "Either way, the roof is done," I said. "Isn't that what you two wanted? Why you brought him here in the first place? Just let him go. He hasn't done anything wrong."

Daniel walked into the room. His face was clean-shaven, his hair combed to the side, and his duffel bag slung over his shoulder.

"You ready to leave?" Wrendon said.

Daniel glanced at my mother. "I'm probably not coming back tonight," he said, "so you can lock up when I go." He turned to face Wrendon. "Unless you're coming back."

Wrendon dangled his keys. "I'm all set."

Daniel looked at me. "I guess this is good-bye," he said.

As we shook hands, I said, "Take care of yourself."

"I will," he said.

"Come on," Wrendon said.

Daniel nodded and shifted the duffel bag on his shoulder. I realized he was taller than Wrendon. Healthier and sober. In better shape. He wasn't scared, not even slightly.

As they walked out, my mother stared at the front door. The van pulled out of the driveway, leaving the kitchen with a quiet hum. Grocery bags still on the counters, half-unpacked. We stayed where we'd been, and I had no idea what to say. As I turned toward her, she stepped forward and slapped my face. "You had no right," she said, her finger in my face. "Do you get that? No right." She walked away, leaving me there by myself with my cheek stinging.

For two days, we didn't speak. I wouldn't look at her. She came home, went to her bedroom and went to sleep. On Wednesday night, after I got home from practice, she was waiting for me at the dining room table with a paper sack at her elbow. It was strange to see her alone there with the light on. She said, "Sit down." After apologizing for hitting me, she said she'd spoken with Daniel on the phone the day before. Wrendon hadn't tried to beat him up after all, only dropped him off at a bus stop and said to stay away.

"I'm not ashamed of him," she said. "Not who he is. Not our friendship. I know he's sick, and I know why. But I don't care for him any less. He turned to us because he had nowhere to go, and I believe we're luckier for it. Don't you agree?"

I said, "Yes."

"And in this time, here with Daniel, I've had a lot to consider. Your father's got no right to act this way. To say these things to you or me. And I'm fed up with it. Like you are, or so you've said." She unrolled the bag, reached inside and said, "So I got these." Two brass doorknobs, still in their plastic cases. "I was never too mechanically inclined, but thought maybe with your handy work around here you could manage. That is, if you're okay with this."

I weighed one in my hand. It was solid and shiny and would look strange on the old door. I said, "I am."

"Do you have the tools you'll need?"

"Daniel left a Phillips-head screwdriver in the belt."

"And that's enough?"

I said, "I think so."

And it was.

The next night I woke to Wrendon banging the door from outside, yelling for us to let him in. He explained he'd been right. That he had saved us. He swore he'd change for good. Just let him in.

I stayed in my room, expecting my mother to turn on the porch light and open the door. But she didn't. I watched from the space between the curtains in my room as all the lights in the house went out, one by one. The dining room, the living room, and their bedroom. Wrendon pounded on the door, paced the driveway, and yelled a while longer, shaking the hurt out of his hands. He got angrier and used them to punch the walls and cup his mouth when he yelled. I thought he might break a window, but he didn't. Instead he walked to his van and drove away.

I got out of bed and went to the hall to take the phone off its cradle, only to find she'd already done it.

He kept calling all that month. We were used to him being gone, but now we couldn't let him come back. He moved in with Loren but still called from the bar. Some nights I got stuck talking to him. I heard the alcohol in his voice. He would ask if I missed him and if I'd ask my mom to try. I said I couldn't. This was her choice. Sometimes he asked if I would come see him at the bar, or if I wanted to have dinner at Loren's. I said I was busy. Two weeks passed and he said, "Am I supposed to just accept that you won't see me?"

I wouldn't reply.

He said, "Be honest. Tell me how you feel about this. No more bullshit. Say it outright."

I was frustrated and started crying, but didn't want to show it. I said, "I told her to throw you out, before Daniel even came here."

I waited for him to say something. Instead the phone clicked and went dead. I went to my room and fell asleep. After that night he didn't call again. April passed and so did most of May. My fifteenth birthday came and went without a word.

After my birthday, my mother said we needed to talk. I expected this to be about Wrendon, that she was considering taking him back. Instead she said that Daniel was sick with pneumonia and would likely not make it long, and I should see him if I wanted to.

I said, "Of course."

We went that day, driving deep into Fort Worth to a ragged-looking, redbrick hospital. We walked through the incontinent-smelling halls and found his small room crowded with people I knew from the bar, others I didn't. Rain tapped against the tinted window. He lay on the bed underneath the bright lights, wrapped in a white blanket. His face sunken and blue eyes wide. I had forgotten how blue his eyes were until that moment. Suddenly he saw us and sat upright, waving us in past all the people. I bit my cheek as he scooted over on his bed, patted the space he'd made, and said, "Come here, you two, and sit down beside me."

GHOSTS

I t was June when I saw Wrendon again. Casey was driving me home from band practice when we pulled in the driveway. The van was parked beside my mother's car, and I thought, *Dammit.*

Casey said, "Is that your dad?"

I said, "Yep," opened the door and grabbed my guitar case from the backseat. Walking slowly up the driveway I took my time moving between the two cars, eyeing the living room window. Inside the house a million things could be happening. A big fight. Them making up. I didn't want either. Walking up the porch steps I listened for yelling, but there was only a soft murmur, and I pushed the door open. They were sitting apart and talking in the living room. Him on the recliner and her on the couch. He looked up, and I saw he was different. His face tan and eyes clear. A can of Schlitz in his hand instead of the glass of Coke and whiskey. She had her own beer on the coffee table, and they were relaxed. I could sense they'd arrived at something. I looked at her. "What's going on?"

They glanced at each other, unsure how to say it, or who should speak first.

"We've been talking," she said.

"And I was hoping," Wrendon said, "that you'd consider coming over to mine and Loren's tonight for dinner. What's it been now? Two months?"

I didn't want to. There were days I still missed him, and I was struggling to stay pissed. I was afraid of us sitting alone in the van, having to explain myself face-to-face. Or deal with him trying to win me back. I didn't want to meet this woman, and I hoped my mother would give me permission to say no.

"You'll be back in a few hours," she said.

He nodded.

I wouldn't talk unless I had to, and if he started in on anything, I would put it back in his lap. "Let me put my guitar away."

We drove quietly in the van until he turned the radio down. He cleared his throat, and I prepared myself.

"I know you're upset," he said. "And you've got every right to be. I'm sorry. Sorry for all of it. Something clicked when Buddy died. Something I can't explain. I've been terrible before, but never that bad. The whiskey's done though. Loren and I are getting a house out in Burleson. And I'm selling the bar. The papers go through later this month. I'm not getting back all the money I paid, but I'm getting enough to give me some time and get us this place. A modular home, so I can build on it."

I'd never once heard him apologize. I was jealous he was getting this house, something my mother had wanted all along. But we'd wanted him gone, and that was more important. "Time for what?" I said. "Are you going to get a job?"

"Me? Hell, no." He patted the dash. "I'm going to sell shrimp, like you and Buddy did, out of the van on the side of the road. I still have the signs and coolers. I'll make as much as I did with the shop, only without all the overhead." He even sounded different. Not just hopeful, but with a plan.

He wanted to keep talking, but we pulled into the parking lot of an apartment complex. It looked like a motel, with rain-filled potholes and rusted cars parked throughout. I followed him to a light blue door, and he went in, calling "We're home," as if to warn her. The television was turned up loud, and Loren stood from the couch, stubbing her cigarette in an ashtray. Blonde and extremely skinny, wearing jeans. She looked nothing like my mother. The apartment smelled like cheap perfume and Lysol, and she forced a smile as she stretched out her hand.

Within an hour I understood my father better. Why my mother never stood a chance. Not just against Loren, but anyone like her. She was confident and loud, drank beer after beer without losing herself. She didn't care what people thought. I wondered why my father had put my mother through all those years of their bad marriage.

Even though Wrendon was living there with Loren, he seemed like a guest. Everything in the apartment was hers. All the photographs on the walls and all the furniture. They planned on having steaks for dinner, but I reminded him I didn't eat meat. Loren looked annoyed. Not at me, but the situation. "You're sure you're fine just eating potatoes?" She must have asked a dozen times throughout the meal.

Later that night, after many more beers, she spoke more. About growing up in Florida, along the coast, and having only recently moved to Texas. Her boyfriend had started cheating within a month. "And I don't take that shit off anyone," Loren said. "I don't need any man's support. I dumped his sorry ass that very night, and the next day I walked into your dad's place, asking if he needed help. Someone to bartend or cocktail. The plan was to save enough for a bus ticket." She reached for his hand. Stared in his eyes. "But I guess that wasn't in the cards."

Wrendon didn't say a word. I knew she was trying to help me understand that fate had brought them together. Of course I didn't say anything about him calling the house that first month.

Back in the van, driving home, he asked my take.

I didn't know what I was supposed to say. "She seems nice," I said.

"She is nice," he said. "A little more open than I'd like, but I guess that's who she is." He picked back up where he'd left off earlier, about the business. "Here's the deal," he said. "What I wanted to talk about. Sometimes I'll have to drive down to the coast on Thursdays to get a haul of shrimp, five hundred pounds or so, and work Friday through Sunday. I know things haven't been great between us. But I was hoping you could make the trip once in a while during the summer. Just to keep me company. You got your learner's permit in April, didn't you? I'll let you drive the van, if you want, and we could stop off at the beach."

I wondered if this was how he talked to my mother all those times she took him back. I'd get to drive, and I'd get to go to the beach. I didn't answer right away, but he waited. I said, "Sure."

Hesitant, he said, "I was also hoping, once we get the house, you might stay over some weekends, working the truck now and again. I can't offer much for child support, but this will help out. I'll put you at what you were earning before the bar."

The money would be good. I needed a new amplifier. Something louder. "As long as it doesn't mess with the band," I said. "Casey and Brian have their licenses, so we've started playing shows. Mostly parties."

"You're really doing that?" he said.

"It's what you're supposed to do," I said.

By the start of July, he'd gotten the business going and moved into the house in Burleson. I stayed with him every other weekend, working the truck. Sometimes he worked with me, but more often he dropped me off and went to the bar. On Thursdays we made the trip to the coast. He let me drive, and we stopped at the beach for an hour before heading to the warehouses that sat on the docks, where the shrimp boats unloaded. Driving through the night with the coolers of shrimp stacked in the back, he sat in the passenger's seat, drinking beers and telling stories I'd never known. Those first years in Florida, just him and his mother. The hard times that followed when Buddy came home from prison, and when he left them without saying good-bye. Wrendon talked about the women he'd dated growing up, and meeting my mother. The best woman he'd ever known, he said, and the worst thing he'd lost. He always seemed surprised when telling me these stories, as if he thought I already knew them.

But one trip in late August, Wrendon hardly talked for most of the drive. Down to the coast and at the beach, he stayed reserved and to himself. I wondered if something was wrong with Loren. If they were splitting up. As we drove back that night, I asked what was going on. Still he wouldn't say. Instead, every so often, he fidgeted with the glove box, tapping the button to make it open and pushing it closed.

At nine o'clock, as we were passing through Huntsville, a town with nothing but a prison and no steetlights, he finally leaned over, turned down the radio and rolled up his window. I glanced at him but concentrated on the road, lining the hood ornament with the reflective white lines on the sides of the highway, my trick to keep the van steady. He put his cigarette out and lit another. "You see this hill," he said, "coming up?"

I looked ahead and said, "Yes." It went up steep, so hard you couldn't see past.

"One night, making this trip by myself, I was right about here when I saw your granddad's ghost sitting beside me, in this chair where I'm sitting now."

I thought he was joking and said, "Yeah, right," but he wasn't grinning, just watching the road ahead. I said, "You saw Buddy?"

"As real as me," Wrendon said. He shook his empty beer can, rolled down the window, and tossed it out. Reaching behind his seat, he grabbed another and flicked ice off the top. "I was going around eighty or ninety miles an hour when I hear this voice come from beside me. Clear as day. 'Wrendon, you slow this son of a bitch down.' I looked over, and there he was. Do you remember those short sleeve button-downs he wore? How he kept his hair combed back?"

I remembered his white face and wrinkles. I rolled up my window. "So what did you do?"

"I slowed down," Wrendon said, "to about sixty or seventy, when he says the same thing. 'You slow this son of a bitch down.'"

I watched the road, imagining Buddy's deep voice. I didn't mean to let off the gas, but the dashes of yellow lines on the road got clearer. I wanted to tell Wrendon to stop.

"So I did," Wrendon said. "I slowed down. By the time we reached the top, I was doing about twenty. And as I came up over this hill, the engine died completely." He took a long drink from his beer. "I looked to my right, and Buddy was gone. I coasted over, and do you know what was on the other side? Have I told you this before?"

I tried to see up over the hill and said, "No."

"A semi was jackknifed in the road. A big red Peterbilt with the trailer turned over. Spread out across the highway. Like a wall."

I saw it. The red truck with its face turned toward us, the large rectangular trailer lying over the road. Our van was nearly at a standstill, there in the dark. I could have counted out the black tar lines in the road, like little cracks.

"What are you doing?" Wrendon said. "Speed it up." He waved his hand in a shooing motion.

I pressed the gas, my right foot aching from being stiff all day.

"I wouldn't be here tonight," Wrendon said, "if your granddad hadn't appeared. I would have driven straight into that semi. It would have killed me. But it didn't. And do you know why?"

The road got smooth again with the lines flowing beneath us. I sat back, feeling sweat on my hands.

"Because my dad was still with me, keeping an eye out."

I checked the rearview mirror. The road was empty. The night before us hung in the sky, the large pine trees lined the road. I had stopped looking at the hood ornament and knew I wouldn't need to do that anymore. My arms stayed tight, and I realized Wrendon wasn't finished.

"You don't know it," he said, "but you and I come from a long line of ghosts. Buddy saw his dad sometimes, after he died playing cards. I want to tell you this because, whatever happens, I will always be around. I still talk to Buddy sometimes. Not just at his gravesite, but in my prayers. You should do that too, someday, after I'm gone. Don't feel foolish. I ask him questions, and I get answers. Sometimes I do it because I miss him, and I know he'll be listening. I do it so he knows I remember him and somewhere he's still alive."

"Why are you telling me this?" I said.

He didn't answer right away.

"There's the chance," he said, "coming up, I'll need to lean on you a while. I need to make sure you can handle it. That you understand where I'm coming from, when I tell you. So I can depend on you, and you know you can always depend on me."

Wrendon said he wasn't sure how to put it. As I picked up speed, he finally opened the glove box and reached inside. He took out three pamphlets and said he'd gotten them from his doctor the day before. I glanced over and saw what he'd been holding back all day. On the pamphlets were cartoon drawings. Empty bodies in black and white. The only colors were red tumors, like little balloons, inside the throat. And for the next hour, as I stared down the road, he read aloud. With words like *benign*, *malignant*, and *larynx* taking shape inside our lives.

HOME

In the months between my father and stepfather, my mother only brought one man home. During the spring and summer after they split up, while Wrendon bought his new place and was starting up his business, she spent most evenings at the house, getting used to being alone. She'd never gone out much, but in the fall that I was fifteen, as Wrendon went through radiation and I spent every weekend working for him, she started going to bars with friends. First only Fridays and Saturdays, then every night of the week. I'd always been a light sleeper, and during this time, I woke from something as simple as a light switch turning on across the house. When she got back I listened as she sat up by herself. Watching TV, drinking beers, and stumbling around. Slurring cuss words at no one.

On that one Friday night she must have thought I was asleep. I heard him first, saying, "Let's hit the bedroom," and she said, "No, here on the couch." They were drunk, laughing and clumsy. Their voices were hushed, and then they weren't. As they got louder, I stared at old glow stars tacked to my ceiling, now faded white. I turned on my side and stared out the back window, wanting to leave. After a while the noises settled, and I fell asleep. Sometime later I woke again and went down the hall to the living room. The yellow light from a lamp was on. Aside from that, the house was silent. She was sleeping on the couch on her stomach. Snoring, naked and alone. I reached to turn the lamp off but pulled my hand back, deciding instead to leave it on. Hoping that when she woke up later, this would hit her like it hit me.

After that she never brought another man home, and she wouldn't sleep in her room. I heard her tell a friend that if she tried to sleep in the bed, she just laid there, feeling like a failure. She stopped going out to bars unless I stayed with Wrendon. After his treatment, the cancer went into remission and he started working more often. We switched off every other weekend so my band could play shows.

For a while he didn't drink, but soon his old habits returned. When he picked me up on Fridays, I could smell smoke in the van. If I asked, he shook his head and said, "Nothing like before." I couldn't understand why he would take such a risk, but I knew it was useless to ask him to stop.

On the weekends when I stayed at our house, my mother drank at home, and by October she was drinking every night of the week. Sometimes I woke in the early mornings and found her passed out on the couch in her nightgown with the TV still going. The coffee table covered with beer cans and overfilled ashtrays. I cleaned it up, went to her cold bedroom, grabbed her a quilt, and went back to bed. Later I'd find her at the kitchen table putting on makeup and getting ready for work. I'd grab cereal, sit down, and she would ask how I slept. I said, "Fine. How about you?"

She held her compact to her eyes. "Fell asleep watching TV, and after that I went to bed."

I usually left it at that, not wanting to make her feel worse. I finished breakfast and took off. But one Friday in November, I finally said, "I see you there at six sometimes, right before you wake up for work."

She didn't respond.

"You don't have to sleep on the couch," I said. "It's your bedroom, too. It's not like you did something wrong."

Still looking into her compact, she said, "What time is Wrendon picking you up tonight?"

"Around seven," I said, stirring my cereal. "But you know how that goes."

She kind of smiled. "How's he doing?"

"All right. But he keeps bugging me about staying more weekends. Maybe all summer."

She swung the mirror aside. "Are you considering it?"

"No way."

She relaxed, checked the clock on the wall, and dropped her compact in her purse. "You're going to miss your school bus."

I hauled my dishes to the sink and grabbed my backpack. "See you Sunday," I said and went out the front door.

Heading into the gray morning, I felt her relief follow me up the driveway. Now the house was hers, and she could wake up how she wanted, without the coffee table clean or the ashtrays put away. Without the guilt or me to consider. Standing by the side of the road, I glanced back. I didn't know what she wanted, but I had hoped for more than this. The better life that she had coming. That was the reason we'd locked him out. To move on.

When I got home from work that Sunday, the house felt different. She was smiling and trying to hide it. Finally at dinner on Thursday, I asked.

She balled her napkin. "I met someone last weekend," she said. "His name is Davis."

I said, "At the bar?"

"I was just sitting there with the girls," she said, "when he walked over, very shy. He introduced himself and asked if I'd like to dance." She got more wound up as she spoke. "So I said yes, and we walked to the dance floor. During that first song, he said he'd been wanting for weeks to ask, but he could never build up the nerve. Can you imagine? All that time and I'm just sitting there." She went on to explain that he was forty-three, divorced, and didn't have any kids. He worked the line at GM, liked to fish and rebuild pickups. He had a knack for broken things. That night as they danced, she practically fell asleep on his shoulder. He said he liked the way she smiled, that she was pretty, and he hoped they'd do this again.

"He sounds nice," I said.

"He is," she said. "We have a date set for tomorrow."

The next night she was a wreck, running between her bedroom and the bathroom with her hair up in rollers. With each pass she was dressed differently. I sat on the chair in the living room, watching her and the TV, with my SG across my stomach. Eventually she stopped, blocking the screen. Her hair was brushed out, and she smoothed down her pants. "What do you think?" she said. "Be honest. I got this blouse this afternoon. Do you think it makes me look silly?"

"Why would a blue denim shirt make you look silly?"

She rolled her eyes and held her hands out to her sides. "Like I'm trying to look young?"

"You look fine," I said.

A car pulled in the driveway. She breathed deep and looked at me as she reached for the door. "It's going to be okay," I said, and she nodded. She waited for the knock, and when it came, she opened the door.

His "Hello" lasted two seconds, and she said "Hi" the same way. I tried to see. She stepped aside and waved her hand. "Come on in."

His dark hair was combed to the side. He wore a brown plaid shirt and brown slacks, carried a bouquet of red roses wrapped in clear plastic. "You look nice," he said, and stretched the flowers out to her. She took them and turned to me. "Aren't they pretty, Chris?" she said.

Davis stayed in the same spot, smiling with his hands in his pockets, barely looking at me. I could tell he was nervous.

"I'm going to put these on the table," she said. "Where we can see them when we first walk through the door." She winked at me and tilted her head as she went to the dining room.

He watched her walk away. Kept on looking even when I knew she was out of sight. "You sure do keep a pretty house," he said, nodding around. His eyes fell on me. "You doing homework?"

I hadn't noticed my biology book on the table. I said, "Yes."

"On a Friday night?" he said. "Shoo-*whee*. When I was your age, I'd have been out partying." He did a little dance resembling the twist. "I ain't surprised though. Your mamma mentioned how smart you are."

I said, "She did?"

He looked at the TV. "*Love Boat*, huh?"

I shrugged and said, "It was on," as if I would never actually watch this.

She came back with her purse slung over her shoulder. Staring at me, she shook her head. "Bed by ten," she said. "Okay?"

I had no curfew, but I got it. "Yes, ma'am."

I said good-bye as they left and, once they walked off the porch, I threw my guitar off and ran to the window. His truck was old but looked brand new. When they reached it, he opened her door. Something that Wrendon had never done, and I thought, *Good.* When they were gone I went to the roses, set in a porcelain white vase on the table. Exactly how she'd said, first thing you saw when you came in.

Each week throughout the next two months, fresh flowers filled the vase. Yellow roses. Red roses. White daisies. Pink carnations. Every Friday she rushed home, changed clothes, redid her makeup and grabbed an overnight bag. Davis pulled up at six. On the weekends that I worked, Wrendon showed up just after they left. On the weekends that I didn't work, I practiced guitar at home alone and went to Casey's on Saturday mornings. Those nights the band usually played parties, though more often we were playing coffeehouses and dinky college bars. Because we were fifteen and sixteen, we had to slip in through the back.

Sundays at dinner, my mother and I would regroup. I would tell her about the shows. The friends' living rooms and garages, the clubs that couldn't afford real bands. She told me about them going to restaurants, the chain steakhouses and buffets, catching up on their weeks, and going to bars. I learned that Davis had moved from El Paso to Fort Worth with his wife ten years before. He woke one morning to find her gone and later discovered her affair had lasted a year. He blamed his "stubborn hardheadedness," and my mother didn't press. She only knew he'd been hurt how she was hurt, and she hoped this was enough, that he'd be faithful.

One Sunday night while we were talking, she said that Davis had mentioned all of us hanging out. Taking a trip or something, to fish.

"I'm around fish all the time," I said. "Working in the van." I imagined us on the shore of some lake, all of us holding fishing rods and him saying, "Shoo-*whee,* ain't this a party."

"You need to get to know him," she said. "Y'all never talk. He says whenever he comes over, you're messing around with your guitar."

"I'm *always* messing with my guitar. Every day since I was little."

"I told him that," she said, smiling and looking down, remembering their conversation. "The other night I told him how you used to follow me around singing, when you were this big." She held her hand out over the floor. "You used to say how you would buy me a new car and house someday."

"You actually told him that?" I said.

"You want to know what he said? 'As much as that kid practices, he can do whatever he wants.'" She reached across the table and took my hand. "You should really give him a shot. Get to know him. He's got a lot to offer."

Davis started to come over for dinner throughout the weekdays. Flowers in hand, with heavy cologne, wearing one of his three button-downs. He sat quietly at the end of the table, listening to everyone speak in turns. More often on those Friday nights that I didn't stay with Wrendon, I went to dinner with them, sitting on the edges of booths at buffets and family restaurants. He spoke more, but not much, and I wondered if he was nervous to be around me, if he actually believed I was smart and would make something of my life.

On Valentine's Day we went to a nicer steakhouse. My mother's favorite, though she hadn't mentioned the wooden pews or dusty pictures. I was surprised they'd brought me along, given the holiday. When the waitress came he stared at the thin plastic menu and said, "Y'all get whatever you want." He ordered a sirloin for himself and the smaller version for her. He was more antsy than usual. As the waitress walked away, Davis cleared his throat and said, "Emily, how long have we been dating?"

"Almost four months," she said. "You know that."

"Four months," he said, as if it were four years. "And in that time you've always talked about believing in people."

I thought, *Shit*.

"Davis, what's going on?" she said.

"Well," he said, his voice slipping. "I've got a proposition for both of you." He was tentative and stuttering. Hands shaking. "You always dreamed of owning a home. And I know four months don't seem like long." Again he eyed me, hoping to get out what he wanted, straining his neck as if trying to force the words. "Well, hell," he said, shaking his head. He stuck two fingers in his shirt pocket. "How about I just show you?" He set a Polaroid on the table, facedown, and managed the last words of whatever speech he had intended: "Don't turn that over unless you trust me."

She reached out and turned the picture over. It was a house. Dark green and L-shaped with a red wooden porch. A chain-link fence wrapped around the yard. Her jaw dropped and eyes went wide, while I pushed back in my seat. She wanted a house like I wanted to play music. Looking it over, she said, "Oh, wow."

"It's almost new, out in Mansfield," Davis said. "My cousin owns it. Last week he got transferred to Houston and needs to sell the place quick. It'd put you closer to your job and me closer to mine. Would only cost us sixty thousand for that half acre."

My mother brought the picture to her face. Leaning toward me, she pointed to a small corner of the yard. "Look," she said, "it's already got a small flower bed and a garden."

I could barely make out either. "Mansfield is thirty miles south. I'd have to change schools, and there's the band. I know we're not some big name, but still."

"All the details can get worked out," Davis said, waving his hand over the table. "What's important to you, I promise, matters to me. But we need to think big picture. And let's face it. Y'all can't keep living in that old rental. Not on the highway. With that big crack in the foundation."

I said, "What crack in the foundation?"

"On the porch," he said. "Surely you've seen it."

I wondered if he had some plan working here.

"I can't believe you haven't noticed," he said. "But I guess if you don't know how to look, you wouldn't." He nodded at me.

"See?" he said. "I'm good for something." The food arrived. "Let's finish supper, and I'll go show you."

The sky was dark when we pulled up, and Davis turned on the porch light. "Right there," he pointed. An inch wide and jagged.

"That's been there," I said.

"Not that big," Davis said, "and it gets wider every few weeks. I noticed it the first time I came here in November. Now watch this." He followed the line with his finger. "Open the door." He traced the crack across the threshold and made an invisible line through the living room, under the brown shag carpet. "These old frame houses ain't nothing but sheet rock held up by two-by-fours on concrete. When the weather dries in summer, the foundation shifts. This crack is headed for the bathroom or the kitchen. It ain't like the place is going to collapse, but one night y'all could be sleeping when a gas line disjoints. Who knows when? Maybe a month. Could be days."

"Can you guess?" I said.

He put his thumbs in his front pockets. "This place ain't safe for all sorts of reasons," he said. "Sitting here on this road, you're lucky no one's broken in. I lay up nights worrying about it. I know you're struggling with bills. Wrendon says that Chris working the van is child support. But that don't pay electric, and it sure as hell ain't groceries. I'm thinking about the long haul here. Don't you want something to keep?"

"How long do we have to decide?" I said.

Davis said, "I know you'll want to discuss this by yourselves. You two ain't had an easy row. I get that. But Chris, you need to give her situation some thought. She might not say all she's thinking because she loves you so much, and she don't want to hurt your feelings. But I promise she wants this. And you should let her have something for once in her life. You'll be headed off before long. And where does that leave her? I understand you hardly know me, but I don't think I'm that bad. Hell, you might even come to like me."

"Of course I like you," I said. And in a way I felt sorry for him having to say this. I turned toward her, standing at the edge of the porch light. She was looking at me, and I realized she had been the whole time.

* * *

Early Sunday evening she came to my room and sat down at my desk. I saw the picture in her hands. She'd kept it nearby all weekend. "It's pretty. Don't you think?"

"What does he mean, 'Let you have something for once'?"

"He doesn't mean it like you think," she said. "Like you've been denying me of anything. But you have to admit." She looked around. "What have I got? I work sixty hours a week, and I've got this. A house about to fall down around me. He just said it the wrong way. He gets worried you don't like him. That you assume he's kind of dim or not good enough. But you need to understand, I really care about him."

I felt hesitant, about to say this. "Are you sure he's what you want? Aren't you curious what else is out there?"

She looked confused. "Are you kidding? Do you know what it's been like this past year? All those nights? And you think I should spend more time sitting at bars? Waiting for someone to walk up who's half as good? I don't think I can handle going back to how we were, all that emptiness in those months. What exactly were you expecting?"

I knew what I wanted for her. A doctor or a lawyer, or something like that. Sitting here I realized the likelihood of either, and I remembered the one night. Finding her on the couch. All the nights she spent drinking alone. Since she'd met Davis, those days were gone.

"All I want is someone kind," she said. "Someone who can be steady. Who isn't asking me to be something I can't. I feel lucky, and I wish you did too. But he was right the other night. You'll be gone, off to college or whatever, before too long." She looked at the photograph again, like something real had once been inside it, and now she saw it for what it was. Some flimsy picture. "Because the reality is this. If I call him and say no, that's probably it. I don't think he'll stick around."

It felt strange to have this decision in my hands. All I had to say was yes, and she got everything she wanted. If I said no, she was alone again. "I'm just asking if you're sure," I said. "I trust you, if you're positive this will work." She looked up to see how serious I was. I said, "Have you seen it yet?"

"I wanted to wait for you," she said. "It's not just my decision."

"Promise me this," I said. "If we move, we'll make arrangements where I can get to school and back. Where I can make every practice. Nobody misses. Plus we're getting all these shows. I know he said what he said, but I need to hear it from you."

She said, "No one will get in the way of that."

"When do you want to check it out?" I said. "Tomorrow?"

"We can go right now, if you want." She turned and looked out the window. "There's still some daylight, and he's waiting by his phone for me to call."

After Davis picked us up, I sat by the passenger's side window of his truck and watched as we passed the pawnshops and convenience stores, took I-20 to Mansfield and CR-157. Everything spread out. A Winn-Dixie, a family video store. Braum's, a run-down Texaco. We drove up two-lane backroads before turning down a single gravel lane. Chain link fences wrapped around trailers in yards. Lit-up front porches. Dogs ran beside the fences. I saw families through some of the front windows, eating dinner in their dining rooms.

Davis eased into the driveway at the end of the lane. The house was larger than I expected. The siding looked brand new, and the roof was in perfect shape. The grass had just been cut. In the front window, a man and woman stood from their chairs. The porch light turned on, and they came out. "How y'all doing?" the man said. He looked like Davis, with his squint. "Glad you made it. Suze and I were getting worried."

Davis led, and my mother walked beside me, her right arm loose over my shoulder. She said, "Do you like it?"

I said, "Yes."

She squeezed my shoulder, let go, and started walking ahead. We formed a line up the pathway, over the porch, to the front door. Davis opened it and stepped aside at the threshold, letting us through.

We moved in quickly, in early March. Davis sold his trailer for the down payment and gave away most of his furniture. My mom sold off her romance novels, taking them in several trips to used bookstores. With the extra money they bought a new bedroom set and a glass-topped dining room table. We decided I could stay at my school since I would get my driver's license at the end of May, when I turned sixteen. They bought my mom a used Taurus and agreed to give me her old Bonneville after Davis tuned it up. He said it just needed a new radiator. Give him an afternoon, and he could fix it. That simple.

Our routines hardly changed, only now they included him. I came home, studied at the coffee table in the living room while watching TV, and Davis got home afterward. He changed into a white T-shirt and jeans, went outside and worked on the rusted, light blue pickup he was fixing, parked in the side yard under an A-frame.

During dinners my mother and I ran through our days as we had for years. Davis sometimes stumbled into the conversation, interjecting or cutting us off. But we stayed patient. A month passed before he started talking more about his job at GM, how all the "bigwigs" were asking employees to put in overtime without compensation. When he and my mom talked about money at the table, the air tightened. Property taxes were more than his cousin let on. There was propane and the garbage bills. Repairs to make. One night, a few weeks after we moved in, he brought up possible layoffs and cutbacks in hours. My mother said, "If that's the case, we'd better put off that clutch for your project truck. Especially if we're going to fix up the Bonneville for Chris." She gathered the plates from the table and went to the kitchen.

Davis looked as if he'd been cut off midsentence. "Ain't nothing happened yet."

The dishes hit the sink, but she didn't respond. She was trying to keep from talking, where an argument might start.

The next Wednesday, when I got home from school, he was already home from work, in the yard underneath the jacked-up truck. Inside the house I grabbed my guitar and went to the kitchen for a glass of water. Casey was coming any second to pick me up for practice. The front door slammed. "Chris, you in here?" Davis said.

I stayed at the counter, holding the glass, wondering what he wanted. I said, "Yeah?" He walked in, wiping his fingers on an old red oil rag. "Did you take a half-day off?" I said.

"Can you help me with the truck?"

I looked at the clock on the microwave. "Casey will be here in five minutes."

"Won't take nothing but half a minute," he said, putting the rag in his back pocket. He started toward the front door and said, "I won't get your pretty hands dirty. Come on."

He'd never said anything like this before. I followed him out, wondering if he'd been kidding. He messed around sometimes and told jokes he'd heard at work. He even made fun of his own thickheadedness. Still, I was apprehensive. Once we got outside, he pointed and said, "Just hop up in the cab and press the far left pedal when I say." Lying on a plywood board on the ground beneath the truck, he slid under the engine.

I climbed in the cab. The seats were threadbare and smelled like oil. The steering wheel was hard plastic, stained with grease. Metal tools banged at my feet, underneath the floorboard. I checked my watch and kept turning toward the driveway. Davis said, "All right," and I pushed the pedal beside the brake. "Now quit," he said, and I did. Looking down at the dusty mats, I saw a white plastic bag and a receipt folded in half. I leaned over and picked it up.

Ford 1965 F100 clutch..............*$125.96.*

Davis said, "What are you doing?" from under the truck. "Stop pressing the goddamn pedal."

My foot had pushed it when I leaned over, and I let up. By that point he was already on his feet, black fluid on his cheek, glaring through the windshield. I was still holding the receipt when Casey pulled up.

"Sorry about that," I said. "I was checking around for him."

"You were off in fucking la-la land," he said. "Like always."

It caught me off guard. "Are you mad at me for something?"

He waved me off. "I'm only kidding. But next time I ask you to do something, don't talk back to me. Now go on."

I ran inside, got my guitar, and walked out to Casey's car. As he put it in reverse, he said, "What's wrong? You look pissed."

Davis stood beside the truck with his hands on his hips, staring vacantly at the fender. I said, "It's nothing. Let's just go."

The next afternoon he was home before me again, and I knew now for sure his hours had been cut. Again we worked on the truck. The sun beat down through the windshield and the smell of oil gave me a headache, but I didn't complain. He was nicer, and this time I paid better attention, even when I had to lay on the sheet of plywood beneath the engine and help him out. At the bathroom sink I couldn't clean the grease from underneath my fingernails, and he'd been right. I was irritated at them being dirty, at the thought of having to eat and go to school like this. While we ate roast beef that night, my mother noticed my hands. Grinning and surprised, she said, "Were you helping?"

I lifted my shoulders. "I just sat there pushing the clutch." Anger flickered across her face, and worry spread through his. For the millionth time in my life—and the first time with Davis—I wished I had been smarter with what I said and kept my mouth shut.

"You got a clutch?" she said.

"I got it at some old junkyard," he said, trying to sound indifferent. He looked at me as if I could confirm this.

"Every bit makes a difference," she said. "Especially with you doing half days."

"I told you that's only temporary," he said. "And besides, how else is Chris going to learn about cars? He starts driving pretty soon, and I bet he can't even change oil."

I shook my head. "You don't want me messing around with your truck," I said. "I ruin almost every mechanical thing I touch. Vacuums, bikes. You'll be lucky it doesn't explode."

My mom said, "He's not kidding. He wrecked three vacuums at our old house."

"That excuse probably frees you from all kinds of work," he said. "But you ain't too good for it. No one is."

"We get the oil changed at a shop," I said. "It's just as cheap."

He looked offended. "You probably think you'll get everything done for you," he said. "But I've been thinking, watching you this past month. And it's high time you did more. All you do is play guitar."

I looked at my mom. "I work," I said. "There's school."

"And there's the shrimp truck," she said. "He works more than I did when I was his age. Plus his dad's been sick—"

"Let him talk," Davis said. "So you have school and the shrimp truck. What's that do for us around here?" He swallowed his food and pointed his fork at me. "That's right. Not a thing. You might think I'm kind of thick, but there's a lot that I can teach you. And you'll be glad once you know."

I knew it was best to let this go. He was waiting for me to react so he could add to what he'd said. He seemed different now, enjoying this argument. Not the guy who asked if I was doing my biology homework. Who did the little dance, and pointed out the line in the front porch. No one spoke throughout the rest of dinner, and I suddenly sensed that something was missing from the table— the flowers, always there, loud and bright, at the old house.

With the truck now off limits, Davis made me his project. Every day I came home and he met me on the pathway with one of his worn-out tools. He had a sentimental streak for dated lawn equipment. A weed trimmer, tree pruner, hedge clipper. Tools with wooden handles and rusted blades. He demonstrated their use, handed them over and stepped aside. I always got it wrong. He shook his head, snatched it back, showed me again, and we'd repeat this several times. Finally with his face red he said, "Here, dummy. Do it right." Practically shaking.

Now furious, I magically got it.

When he left me alone to work, the tools always fell apart. The spool sprung from the weed trimmer. The hinge on the clipper came unscrewed. Whenever something broke, Davis had me stand aside while he fixed it. "You'll need to know this," he kept saying. But I learned nothing. He worked too fast, saying what to get from his red toolbox. Standing in the hot sun, I stared at the house and knew I needed to practice or do my homework or I'd be up late. He snapped his fingers in front of my eyes.

More often at dinners he was the only person talking. He'd learned not to mention his job, so instead he went on about me. Getting louder and more pointed, as if I wasn't at the table. I'd get up, put my plate in the sink, and go to my room, but I could still hear him across the house, saying I couldn't follow the most straightforward instructions. That I didn't pay attention. Asking my mother how in the world she let me slide so long. Finally she'd come to my room. She seemed more tired in my doorway than when she'd come home from work. "You need to look at him when he talks to you," she said. Or, "Try harder to get it right the first time."

I did get better and steadily gathered a growing list of lawn and housework. But nothing could help his tools. I came home one day, and he was waiting with his rusted lawn mower. It took fifty pulls to start. I spent three days mowing our half acre because the mower broke in every way. I flooded the engine. The dusty pull cord snapped. The spark plugs lost fire. On Friday the blade fell off entirely. At dinner that night, he said, "I swear to God, he's got some gift. Like that King Midas. Except everything he touches turns to shit." He thought this was funny, and I could tell he'd been working on it all afternoon. My mother's shoulders were falling more with each sentence. He finally said, "I honestly wonder if he *means* to break my tools."

I set my fork on my plate and said, "Maybe your tools are shit."

She said, "Chris, don't."

"Why would I break them? So you can hassle me about it? Do you think she even cares? As if she doesn't have enough to think about?"

"Go to your room," she said. "Right now. And don't come out until I say."

Lying on my bed, I listened as he yelled. He went about this much differently than Wrendon. My father rarely raised his voice, and he gave guilt trips, working us inside out, individually. Davis was the opposite. He never talked about her, only me to her, and in that way, he broke her down.

Her footsteps came faster than usual. "Go out there and apologize."

I chewed my lip and stared at the ceiling. "So I can get him off your back? Forget it."

"Get out there," she said, "or you're grounded and you won't have practice at all."

"You think that will work? Having me spend more time with him?"

"Maybe you'll finally learn some patience."

"Maybe you should learn less."

"Two weeks," she said and slammed the door.

I thought I'd be okay, but the two weeks lasted forever. Small arguments erupted, and I knew I could get grounded longer. I only felt safe in my own room. I considered going ahead and moving in with Wrendon, but that meant living with two strangers, and I didn't want to leave my mother. All I needed was to wait this out until my sixteenth birthday, when I would get my license. I could practice more and get out with friends, away from Davis. So I paid closer attention. Not just to what he showed me, but how he acted. His temper was short; he had to be right; and anything less than total agreement meant you were challenging him entirely. Like her, I apologized if I did something wrong, and he would make a big deal of forgiving me, saying all he wanted was to make me a better person. Because he had to get the last word in, the trick was not in not talking back, but in not speaking at all. If I kept quiet, he had nothing to build on. Slowly we learned to get along. But to her that only meant the grounding worked.

In April, when his hours got cut again, his temper got shorter. He was upset because of the bills and because he didn't have money like before. He complained about the groceries, saying we needed to cut out cereals and ice cream, foods we all didn't eat. He picked constantly. My hair was too long. My clothes too baggy. I played my guitar too loud, even when the amp wasn't on. I stayed in my room or at my friends' houses too much. His comments were often questions put to her after the fact.

"Does he have to shut the door so hard?"

"Did he ask if we needed chores done before he left?"

"Are you going to say something, or should I?"

I wondered if he was upset because of the new bills and having me in his space. Sometimes he threatened to move out. I knew the instant Davis said my name she might look up across the table or come to my room and say, "One more week." I rarely knew when it was coming, only when it was done. Every so often, I cut in and berated myself, saying I was an idiot, trying to make it a joke, and that sometimes worked. But more often he simply agreed, and I still got grounded. There were a few times, right after she gave me another week, when Davis actually said, "You don't always have to ground him." She'd throw her hands up like she could do nothing right. "Fine," she said. "You're not grounded." But most of the time, Davis shrugged as if the punishment was inevitable.

As my sixteenth birthday approached, I managed to stay out of trouble. The house had never been calmer. That night, while we were sitting at the table, I asked my mother what day of the upcoming week she could take me to do my driver's license exam. As the candles burned on the cake, Davis suggested I should wait until summer. There was no sense in getting a license if I didn't have a car. I looked at his face and knew from the way he talked, he had no intention of fixing the Bonneville, either because he couldn't pay for parts on his own truck or because he didn't want to do it. My mother looked caught off guard but tried to act like this was planned. Davis asked what was the rush, and where in the world did I need to go anyway?

I got grounded more often, and the band came apart. Practices were sporadic. Our shows, when we had them, were terrible. False starts and bad timing. After the sets I told the guys that I was sorry. They all said it was okay, but their irritation was obvious.

We had a show scheduled one Friday in June, but that afternoon Davis decided to fix a clog in the kitchen sink, and he refused to use a drain cleaner. He lay inside the cabinets, every so often sticking his hand out and calling for a tool. Plastic pipes were spread all over the floor, and I knew we'd never finish in time. I stared at the clock on the microwave and kept wishing he'd let me go. The more my mind drifted, the louder he got. At one point I realized he'd been shaking his hand a while. "Give me the goddamn wrench," he said.

"Which wrench?" I said, looking down in the box.

"The pipe wrench," he said. "What do you think?"

I pushed the tools around. "Can you describe it?"

"Are you that damn stupid?"

This was the part where I was supposed to apologize, let him forgive me, get my gear, and head out. But after he asked if I was stupid, I heard my mom say from another room, "What's wrong?" Davis settled back, and I knew this was it. He was about to yell something and she'd come running into the kitchen.

Before he could, I turned on the faucet and felt the cabinet shake. He said, "What did you do?"

I heard the water come up and saw it rush into the sink.

I ran past her, to my room.

Davis chased me, with his face and shirt wet, and I tried to shut my door. But he lodged himself between it and the jamb, and I let go. As I backed toward my bed, I said, "I'm sorry, Davis. That was really stupid," and I meant it. But he was too focused to hear. He said, "You think you're so much better than me? That you can act however you want?" He grabbed my arm and raised his hand, flat and open.

My mom grabbed his wrist and said, "Don't."

Catching himself he stopped quickly and settled down. He threw her hand off, looked us over, and shook his head. "You two can have each other."

She watched him walk out of the room, and I could tell she wanted to go after him. "How could you do that?" she said. "All he wants is to show you how to fix things, that way if you have similar problems in the future, you can take care of them."

"You don't actually buy that shit, do you?"

"One month," she said. "After school you come straight home and go to your bedroom. You come out for dinner only after we're done, and even then you keep your mouth shut. On the weekends that you don't stay with Wrendon, you stay in here unless we have chores, which you will do without question. Otherwise meals are the same as throughout the week. No stereo, no television, no phone, no guitar. No more Wednesdays and no more weekends."

I shook my head. "Why are you doing this?"

"So you'll learn to keep your mouth shut."

"Like you did with Wrendon?"

"Two months," she said.

"You can't just do that," I said. "Throwing out these random numbers because you're afraid he won't stick around. I can't help if I'm not like him. If he doesn't like me. Didn't you know this before? That he's impatient? I hardly knew him, but you said we'd be fine. Now I'm working on cars and fixing sinks? Getting yelled at because I don't already know what to do?"

"And no show tonight," she said.

"I can't cancel," I said. "They're counting on me. If I keep doing this, it's all over."

"Call Casey," she said, "and tell him."

I followed her down the hallway. As I picked up the phone in the kitchen, she went outside. Davis was leaning against his truck, smoking a cigarette with his thumbs in his pockets. As I dialed the number and let the phone ring, she apologized and told him I had been grounded. But Davis wouldn't look at her.

Casey picked up, and I told him what happened.

He said, "Should I just come get you?"

"I can't leave like that and expect to come home."

Davis finally lifted his eyebrows and nodded, agreeing she'd done the right thing. She relaxed, and they walked around to the front of his truck where he lifted the hood.

"Do you think we can even make this work?" Casey said. "You know as well as I do, the shows sound like shit. Everyone's getting frustrated."

I could tell he hated to say it, and now I knew they'd been talking. I didn't have an answer except to tell him I understood. But I didn't. Hanging up the phone I looked out in the yard at the two of them together. Davis pointing out something in the engine he needed to fix. She'd let him get whatever he needed.

I stood and watched them through the kitchen window. Sixteen years old, but I felt eight. I practically ran my father's business, paid his bills, and took care of him while he went through cancer. I didn't complain and got great grades. I had a good band playing shows. The only thing I'd ever wanted, and I had built it up myself. Now everything was falling apart because it rested on these two people.

I stayed in my room the rest of that night, thinking about what would have happened at the party. Arriving with all our gear, setting up in front of people as they waited. The jittery moments before the set and hanging out with the other guys. Standing in front of the microphones, turning everything on. The certain quiet of being wrapped in all that noise. Feeling like something.

I paced the floor. As the sky grew darker I looked around, wishing I'd said yes to Casey. But that was done. At nine-thirty the TV in the living room turned off and their bedroom door shut. For another hour, I left my bedroom lights off and stared at the clear night sky, wanting to go, to be anywhere but here. Over the months, the house seemed to have gotten smaller, and now my room felt tiny. *Certainly*, I thought, *the world is bigger than this*.

Sitting at my desk and looking out the window, I thought of a small college bar we sometimes played on Friday nights. The Freedom Club in north Fort Worth, next to TCU. A place where underage kids got pitchers for three dollars. Bare lightbulbs hung from the ceiling, and red candle jars sat on the tables. There was a small stage in the corner. The owner was a Rastafarian guy with long dreads, but he let bands play almost anything.

In the dark I stood up, went to my closet, and put on a fresh T-shirt and my shoes and thought, *Don't*. I knew the Bonneville wouldn't make it because of the radiator. I might get there, but not back. That left only my mom's new car. I made myself sit on my bed and really consider what might happen. Getting pulled over. Going to jail. But these seemed like empty words. To see how it felt, I stood up and crossed the room and picked up my old acoustic. Held the neck in my hand. The more I moved the less I thought. It seemed like steps adding up, and I'd eventually turn back. Outside my room I could hear Davis snoring, so I walked carefully down the hall, across the living room carpet, to the dining room table, and there I stood still a moment, searching for my mother's keys. But they were nowhere. For a second I realized what was happening, thinking I should quit. Until I spotted Davis's keys and picked them up. I went to the door, turned the knob, and shouldered through. Standing on the front porch, I pulled the knob and felt it click. I stared out over the yard, the cars in the driveway, and the gravel lane. The open sky. I was outside now, with my guitar in my right hand and the keys in the other. If I drove safely, played a few songs, and came back before one o'clock, I'd be fine. Going back inside now, I ran as much risk getting caught. So I continued up the cement walkway, lifted the gate latch, and reached the door of his truck, blood warm in my ears.

I drove up the gravel lane with the headlights out and stopped at the paved street. I could turn back now, but I was already at the road. Reminding myself to fill the tank, I pushed the gas, flipped on the lights, and started moving. I turned one corner, and then another, gaining speed as I got farther away.

The next morning, I sat up in bed to knocking on my bedroom door. Morning light spread across the carpet and walls, and I remembered. Driving out to the small club. The white paint on the cinder block walls outside, the parking lot light shining down on all the cars, and the mural of Africa in red, green, and yellow. Asking the owner if I could play. He said, "Sure. You know the deal. Just come in back when I come get you." At eleven he came outside to the truck, said I was on, and I walked in. Up on the small stage I took a stool by the microphone and played an REM song. I didn't look up until people started clapping. A cute girl up front yelled, "Another!" and I kept going. Mostly requests and covers. Hank Williams, Cyndi Lauper, Lionel Richie. Also some of the band's songs, though it didn't feel right to play without them. Before I left the owner said to come back whenever I wanted. I was excited but drove carefully. Remembered to stop and fill the tank and got home at one forty-five.

My mother pushed through the bedroom door, looking worried. She held the phone out and said, "It's Wrendon."

As I took it, she sat on the edge of my bed, already trying to read my face. I held the phone up to my ear and said, "What's going on?"

He cleared his throat. "I need a favor, if you can do it. I've got a doctor's appointment at one, and I can't afford to let the shrimp sit around. I was wondering if you could work the van for me. I know it's supposed to be your weekend off."

I said, "What's wrong?" But I already knew.

"I'll explain when I come get you."

I looked at my mother and she could see what I was thinking. The cigarettes he wouldn't stop smoking. The bars the doctors said stay out of.

"I'll pick you up in half an hour," he said.

That Sunday night, after getting home from work, I showered and sat at the table for dinner. Steak and potatoes. I hadn't eaten since noon, and it was almost eight o'clock. Davis cleared his throat, sat up in his chair, and said, "We need to talk."

"This can wait," my mother said. I could tell she had asked him not to say anything just yet.

I placed my hands in my lap and braced myself. I'd forgotten about Friday night. After Wrendon picked me up Saturday morning, he said his cancer was back, worse than before. That following week he would start aggressive chemotherapy, and there was recovery. Sure to last into the summer. He said he needed me to work more weekends, agreeing to let me close up early on Saturdays that I had shows. Now, after working through the weekend, I was exhausted.

But Davis had no intention of waiting. "You know," he said, "every Saturday that you're not working, it's your job to cut the grass. I realize this weekend was different, but you have to understand. It's your responsibility and you could have done it before you left."

"You're kidding me," I said, relieved and disheartened all at once. "You want me to mow the lawn right now? After the weekend I just had?"

"We understand that," he said. "So your mom and I figured you could do it tomorrow morning."

"I have to get ready for school in the morning," I said. "Why couldn't you just do it this weekend?" I looked at my mother and waited before continuing. Thought, *Fuck it*, and kept my voice steady. "Or what about tomorrow? You've got the extra time now, don't you?"

The calmness zipped out of the room, just like that.

"So you'd rather do it tonight?" Davis said.

"I'd rather you did it when you had the fucking chance," I said. "I'd rather you weren't such a dick, and such an idiot about everything."

My mother said, "Get outside right now." There was fear in her face, and I realized she was scared for me.

I said, "Fuck this," and stood up.

Davis did the same, put his hand on my chest and said "Sit down," pushing me back. "Your mom made dinner."

I grabbed the arm of the chair and stayed on my feet. "You don't touch me," I said.

"Davis," my mom said. "Stop it."

"Stop it?" he said. "Shit. I can stop it." He walked in the kitchen and came out with a grocery bag, shaking it open as he walked toward their bedroom. "This son of a bitch thinks he's too good to live under my roof with me. Too good to do anything. You want me out, I can go."

"All of this makes sense," I said.

My mother pointed and said, "Get out there now."

"This is bullshit," I said, "and you know it."

I mowed the grass with only the porch lights in the front and the back, casting a tilted shadow of the house across the lawn. It took two hours, but I needed to get it right. Otherwise, I'd have to mow again in the morning. I wondered the whole time what they were talking about inside, if he was serious about leaving. As I finished and turned off the mower, I saw my mother standing outside by the front porch, with her arms crossed and waiting.

"Is he leaving?" I said.

She shook her head and prepared herself for what she was going to tell me. "From now on," she said, "when Davis tells you to jump, you ask 'How high?' You say, 'Yes, sir' and 'No, sir.' Think before you talk. Also, I'm going to start setting aside your earnings, and we're going to ask you to stop playing guitar in the house. That you only go to practices and shows when we have nothing for you to do around here."

"Can I breathe?" I said. "Did he give you permission for that?"

"You get along fine when you're grounded, and I can't keep doing this."

"Do you *want* me to live with Wrendon?"

She paused a moment and said, "No."

"I've considered it, but I don't want to," I said. "I think of all those years, when he was gone. All the shit you and I went through when it was just us."

"But now it's not just us," she said. "And I'm tired of taking sides."

"You take sides?"

"Don't you get it? If he leaves I'm *worse* than before. Stuck with a house I can't afford and a son who will move on. You're already gone most weekends. Can't you try to make this work?"

"Can't you see that I'm trying? Do you realize this is the first time we've really talked, just you and me, since we moved here? And we're outside in the dark?"

She looked around and accepted this. "It's how things need to go," she said. "I promise it will get better." She started to turn and waved me in. "Come inside and finish your dinner."

I pushed the mower to the side of the house and followed her up the porch steps.

She stopped a moment before opening the door, turning around and wanting to say something else before we went back inside, where Davis would hear. "Maybe I expected too much from you," she said. "You've always been so grown up. You hardly ever played with toys or anything like that. Maybe it was Wrendon, learning to live with him. Or maybe I pressed you too hard. But I'm surprised."

I said, "At what?"

"At you taking Davis's truck the other night," she said. "Didn't you even stop to think what could happen if he found out?"

I reached for the doorknob, but she had it and I couldn't get around. She wanted an explanation. I said, "No."

I took a shower, staying in half an hour. After a while I sat in the tub, letting the steaming water run over my neck and spine. I fell asleep with my head against my knees but woke to what I thought was Davis pounding the door and saying I'd been in there too long. By now the water was running cold. I turned it off, got out, and dressed. Walking into the hall I saw the house was dark and they had been in bed a while.

Keeping my light on, I took my backpack out of my closet and set it on my bed. I packed a week's worth of clothes and laid my

SG in its case. When that was done, I sat at my desk and looked around. My records, acoustic, posters, all of it. With the case in my hand and my backpack slung over my shoulders, I got up and turned out the light and shut the door. I walked down the hall and went to the dining room table, pulled out my key ring, and took the house key off. I didn't try to be quiet. I set it down beside my mother's on the table. Davis's set was on a white notepad where he left it every night, that way he wouldn't forget and lock himself out. An old habit from his old place, when he had no one to call. I had forgotten to put them back on the notepad when I got home on Friday night, and I realized she must have found them on Saturday morning before he woke. I picked them up and worked the Bonneville's keys off of his set, hoping the car would make the drive.

When I got to the door, I pulled it open and turned the switch inside the knob so the house would stay locked once I was gone. Pulling it shut on the front porch, I felt the humid air and started down the front steps, up the walkway, to the gate, wondering if she'd heard me leave and if she'd get up if she had. I closed the gate, turned around, and glanced back at the house. Here in the dark, it seemed gray and the windows were all black. Except a moment when a small light came on in my room, cast from the hall. And, for a second, I wanted to go inside and talk to her, like we used to. But there was nothing left to say, and I'd have to knock to get back in.

III

HUSTLE

I could see my breath in the cold Sunday morning with the sunrise layered beneath the pale sky. February, now almost a year since I moved in, and the grass in Wrendon's backyard was frosted from last night's rain. I pulled a large cooler from the shed to the van, gripping its handle and walking backward with my knees bent. Eight o'clock and I'd just shown up, supposed to have had the weekend off. But Wrendon called Casey's an hour before to say he needed me home. He couldn't work. I didn't need to see his face, only hear his voice to know he hadn't slept the night before. That he was nervous about seeing his doctor on Monday morning and had sat up waiting for the right time to call. I packed my gear inside the Bonneville, wrote a note, and left.

The smell of grease poured from the back door of the house. From frying eggs and bacon and the hamburger he was cooking for my lunch, and my stomach grumbled. It crossed my mind, how I'd gotten by not eating meat before I moved here. How Wrendon and Loren didn't want to work around it, and it hadn't seemed worth the fight. Now I couldn't remember what that had been like, or why it would have ever mattered. As I considered this, the cooler hit a rut and I pulled too hard, causing the box to topple over. The lid fell open and fifty pounds of shrimp and ice rolled out. The small pink bodies lay on the ground, now speckled with grass and mud. I put my hands on my hips, stepped back and said, "Shit."

Wrendon was suddenly in the back doorway of the house, looking out. He wore faded Wranglers, a polo shirt, and his old Saxton's Seafood cap, too big for his head. Months after chemotherapy, and he was still thin. When I first arrived this morning he was tense and apologetic. But now he seemed relaxed. He pressed his shoulder against the screen door to keep it open, holding a large skillet. Steam rose and evaporated. There was a time he would have freaked at seeing me do this, but the cancer had softened him up. He pressed a tight smile and said, "Are you okay?" I waved him away, and he went inside, letting the screen door close.

After the shrimp were picked back up and set into a different cooler, hosed down, drained, and set in clean with the others, I grabbed the two sides, bent, and lifted. Setting it in the van between the two other coolers, a jab of pain hit my spine and I remembered to lift with my legs. But these days the pain didn't matter so much—my back ached constantly. I climbed in and went through the sinks and cabinets. All these new things we'd installed over the fall after having been shut down twice for failure to meet new health code regulations. Linoleum floors, hot water, and a water pump that stopped working last week. I turned the faucet knob to see if he had fixed it, and he hadn't. I lifted the metal hanging scales out of the sink and saw the glass face was newly cracked. I thought, *Jesus Christ*, and looked up at the house. Last week the van had started running like it was missing and needed a tune-up. Now that I had my license, I drove it myself and always worried it would break down between here and Trader's Village. I checked underneath the cabinets to see if we had the shellers and crab boil. Plastic bags and paper sacks.

I wiped my hands on the inside knees of my jeans and crossed the yard to the house, opened the door that went in the kitchen. Wrendon was standing at the stove. He pointed with a fork to a plate of scrambled eggs, bacon, and grits. In his dry and burnt-out voice, he said, "That's yours."

I ran my hands beneath the faucet, picked up my plate, and sat at the table. I could barely taste anything but butter because the shrimp smell was thick on my hands. Through a window I looked at the van in the backyard. Its doors still open and the three coolers sitting side-by-side. It smelled like pine cleaner and soap but would later reek of shrimp and old water, even with this cold.

I thought of the Monday morning last June when I showed up after having left my mother's. He and I sat on the porch and drank coffee, staring out at my car, with its hood still popped to let it cool from the night before. I asked if I could move in, and he said to call my mother. While he went through chemotherapy and recovered, I worked every weekend that summer. Though he'd said I could have Saturday nights for the band, it wasn't enough, and The Earliest Ending almost split. There was no time for practice. Instead, I needed to spend Wednesday nights making phone calls, trying to get someone from the bar to drive down to pick up the shrimp on Thursdays and work for us on Fridays. I worked every weekend, and shows were out of the question—there was just this. Eventually Casey called to say he and the guys were going to try something new with someone else. I asked him to wait until the end of summer when Wrendon could hopefully do more.

The cancer went into remission, and by September he was healthy enough to drive to the coast himself and work every other weekend. When we started switching out, I went back to playing with the band that autumn. At first he made the effort and stayed out of bars, fixing up the house and tending his garden. But Loren still went out, and he sometimes went with her, eventually going on his own on those free weekends when I worked, staying in the smoky rooms all day. One night in November I asked if he wanted to get sick again. He said boredom will get you quicker, as if this was funny. But recently something had changed, and he had started acting differently. Coughing often and trying to hold back the coughs, each time with a look like *dammit* spreading over his face.

Now it was winter. I looked outside at the van and considered his appointment, knowing what this meant and how it wouldn't take so much to lose the band this time.

Wrendon set the van's keys in front of me and sat down. I considered his thin elbows, thin arms, and bony hips, and the twenty pounds he was still gaining. Wondering how he would spend the day, now that he had it off. After a few bites my stomach started to settle, and I noticed the sun had risen further over the van, past the shed and the garden. I figured maybe I'd sell out early, get home, and make a day of this. But with the cold weather no one went to Trader's Village. No one stopped, and they wouldn't until spring. Right now we barely paid the mortgage and electric. On the corner of the kitchen table sat a stack of bills, rubber-banded together. Wrendon was letting them go unpaid, planning to make them up once business steadied. I worked for free, and I was fine with that. As long as I had time for practice and shows. I swallowed and took another bite.

Wrendon said, "How's your breakfast?"

I said, "What time is your appointment tomorrow?"

He looked down. "I'm sorry I had to call you home, Chris. But at least you had your Saturday."

"You need to fix some things," I said. "The water pump's still broken, and the face on the scales is cracked. It wasn't like that when I worked last week."

"Happened yesterday," he said. He set his elbows on the table. "Do you have your little space heater? Did you remember to pack up the cord, to plug it into the cigarette lighter?"

I nodded, still staring out the window. My fingers were pink and burning from the ice, but I was used to it and tried not to think. Just let it go and finish my food.

At Trader's Village, the sun left in the late morning and didn't come out again. All that day the temperatures stayed in the thirties. Dark gray. Wind pushed, shaking the van. I kept the space heater on and stayed in front. Hardly anyone pulled over, and those who did said I should give away what I had.

After haggling with one customer for ten minutes, trying to get him settled and gone, he finally agreed to five pounds of the jumbos. He wore mirror sunglasses despite the weather, held one of the doors to block the wind. I could see myself bending and standing in the two lenses. Lifting shrimp from the cooler to the scales, watching myself with my bright cheeks and nose, I accidentally straightened up too fast and tipped the scales with my shoulder. The guy jumped back as cold water, shaved ice, and limp bodies slid down my back and scattered across the coolers and the floor.

He threw up his hands and said, "Ah shit, man. I ain't paying for them."

I shook my head but kept my mouth shut. Turning back to the cooler before he could talk again, I dug my hands into the icy brown water.

He stood on his toes and looked at the scale. "Now I see how much ice you throw in there."

I said, "Are you kidding?"

"Keep giving me attitude and I'll go someplace else."

"I always toss in extra." I tipped the scale, giving him a better view.

He crossed his arms. "I'm fucking cold. Speed this shit up."

Once weighed, I emptied the shrimp into a small white garbage bag, spun it, and wrapped the bag inside itself, twirled it again, and snapped a brown sack open behind me. Slipping the bag in, I rolled the sack end-over-end and put a tab of white masking tape over the edge. I wiped my right hand across the thigh of my jeans and asked the guy if he needed a sheller, picking one up and handing it to him.

He held the wide end in one hand and jabbed the pointed end against the palm of his other. "It's a big plastic shrimp," he said. "What the fuck would I do with this?"

I took it back, headed one of the jumbos and pressed the pointed tip against the center of the shrimp's body. Gripping it loosely, I pushed the tool along the single vein that ran through its middle. When the pointed end poked out, I held the shrimp tighter and twisted the larger end of the sheller. It pried the body apart, removing the legs and central vein, its nervous system. I pinched what was left. "Rips off the skin and tears out the nerves," I said. "Leaving you with nothing but meat and muscle."

"You want to do that with all of them?" He waited for me to smile and waved the sheller off. "How about you cut me a deal on that crab boil?"

"You're going to boil those?" I said. "They're too big. They'll taste like rubber."

"Man, how old are you?"

"Sixteen."

"Look here," he said. "I've been making shrimp that way all my life. So what the hell do you know?"

"It's another five bucks for the crab boil," I said, setting the box beside the bag.

He tossed down a five and picked up his things. "Have fun cleaning up that mess," he said. "Probably take your mind off that stick up your ass."

"Sure thing," I said, taking his money and thinking, *Fuck you*. After he left I wrote the sale in the spiral notebook, opened the register and slid the twenty beneath the cash drawer. I tossed the sheller up to the dashboard and turned around to clean my mess.

The longer I ran the van, the more I took care of business and held my own, better than Wrendon or Buddy ever had. These days we couldn't afford to throw out the leftovers, and that meant sometimes freezing what was left on Sunday nights to add them in with next week's load. During that winter we sold next to nothing and had to freeze dozens of pounds. Sometimes we did this two weeks in a row, turning them so brown we had to splash in a capful of bleach. Throwing them out meant burning good money, not paying the mortgage. Knowing this, I wouldn't hesitate to look people straight in the eye and say, "We drove these up this morning. Straight off the boats." Or, "Sure, you can butterfly these popcorn shrimp. Fry 'em on up. They'll taste better than any jumbo. But I've also got these tiger shrimp I've been hiding for someone special." I'd say, "Listen up. I'm damn near giving these away to you. But only now. This second. You can take it or you can leave it." Most people reached for their wallets.

On Thursdays I sent someone south for the shrimp. Usually a guy from the bar who I could trust. Unless I had that week off school or we didn't have the money to pay someone. Then I went myself. I was doing well enough in classes and could lie to my teachers, saying I had to help my father with treatment. Once I got down to the coast, I did business with a Vietnamese guy named Huong whose pit bulls lived off the fish guts and squid on the docks. Every so often I stopped off at the beach and stayed and watched the sun set into the water, then drove home in the dark.

Now it seemed the cancer was gone for good, and I was hoping Wrendon would take over. I needed more weekends for myself. Not just for shows, but to date and have a life. Normal things my friends did. Casey's father had offered to let me work at his record store, and I could spread out the hours. There was no reason, if Wrendon was healthy, he couldn't work the truck himself or pay someone else what he paid me. I also hoped it would get him out of the bars. "Maybe this summer," he said. "But right now things are too unsteady." I knew if he had his way I'd work the van every weekend, leaving him to do whatever he wanted.

Sitting in the front seat, I held my fingers in front of the space heater and looked across the road at the apartments being built in the once-empty fields. I had homework to finish but knew I wasn't going to school tomorrow. Instead I'd drive with him to the doctor so he wouldn't face it alone. With no insurance for specialists, he went to the dingy hospital in south Fort Worth where Daniel had gone two years before. Homeless people hung out in the doorways, taking in the heat when the doors slid open. Wrendon sometimes saw nurses stuffing morphine in their pockets, and his doctors were always changing. Young and overconfident, brimming with different suggestions, though everyone agreed the laryngectomy would solve it. I had seen people who'd undergone this surgery, with their larynx removed. When they spoke, if they could speak, it was through the sides of their mouths, and they sounded like they were pinching their noses. Wrendon said to forget it. He made his living with his voice.

"Just imagine. One day here, the next it's gone."

"That could be you," I said. "The next day gone."

Wrendon tried to look on the brighter side of radiation and chemotherapy. He said his teeth had never been great, so when he had to have them pulled, he got perfectly straight dentures. And his hair was already falling out before chemo. But when he couldn't eat much, that got to him. The left side of his face swelled baseball-size for a while.

The doctors had told him to stop everything. No more bars, no more beer or cigarettes. But that meant forgetting the life he was used to. Start being conscious all the time. Face up to all the losses and deal with everything head-on. In a way, I understood when the drinking started again. Even the cigarettes. I tried to tell him to cut it out. But who was I to tell him to quit?

Once my fingers thawed, I leaned back in the chair and waited for someone to stop.

Around two o'clock, a woman pulled up in a black LeBaron. Wearing a red blouse, black skirt, and black hose, she barely made it across the gravel in her heels. She was pretty, and I thought she might be on her way home from church. I said hello and gave her the spiel. When I finished she looked around inside the van, up at me, and said, "Where do you go when you need to use the restroom?"

I said, "I'm sorry?"

"That's what I thought," she said, tapping the coolers. "Mr. Saxton, I'm here with the Texas State Health Department. You need to stick tight while I grab my things."

As she walked off, I scanned the van to see if I could fix anything right away. I needed to get the permits out of the glove compartment, and at least one of them was expired. A large stain from the earlier spill was still on the floor and the notebook page where I marked the day's sales was smeared. There were the broken water pump and cracked scales. She was coming back already. I could do nothing but dig out our permits, sit on the roughest-looking cooler, and wait.

She carried a clipboard and a Polaroid camera, saying to open the van's rear doors. As she climbed inside, she pulled on latex gloves and asked for my permits. I handed them over. She laid them out on the counter and took a picture. She picked up the expired one and said, "Toss this." Glancing over the other, she said, "You've got one for Texas but not Grand Prairie. Where's that?"

"Texas means Texas, all inclusive."

"You know better."

She waited for me to try again, but there was nothing I could say. The lack of permits was enough to shut us down, but she kept going. With her checklist on the clipboard and camera ready, she slid a metal pen from her pocket, clicked it, and walked to the front of the van. Looking over my pre-cal homework on the passenger's seat, I thought she might start making corrections. On her checklist she made note of the paper bag that had held my hamburger and started picking through the van. Used the tip of her metal pen to move things around. The Ziploc bags, the paper sacks, the crab boil and shellers. After measuring the scales and making note of the cracked face, she stuck large thermometers inside the coolers. She sat on one of the cooler lids holding a handful of shrimp, yanking their heads and peeling back their skins. With a look on her face like she was picking through garbage, she said, "Some of these appear to have been dropped on the ground. And all of them are at least three days old." She dropped a few in a plastic bag. As she moved along she kept snapping Polaroids, laying the pictures on top of a cooler. Each one developed from green to dark colors, caught in bright flashes inside thin white frames.

The longer she stayed, the dirtier the van seemed. With the coolers open, the rotten smell filled the air. Stringy whiskers of dried shrimp hung from the scales. The thirty-gallon coolers were faded burnt-orange, and most of their drain plugs were corked with baggies. The makeshift brown cabinets of plywood and screws were splintered and warped beneath the weight of the sinks. All these things I'd never noticed. She asked how often I mopped the floors. Where I kept the drained water. Again, where did I go when I needed to use the restroom?

I knew I needed to hustle her but couldn't get a word out.

She opened the door of the wooden cabinet, took out a small flashlight, and leaned inside. With her back turned, I felt an urge to scrub the floors. I considered dumping water all over the photos. As she poked around underneath the sink, I finally started talking. "The water pump broke an hour ago," I said, "and I've used towelettes to clean my hands since then. I change the ice regularly. Two or three times this morning."

She said, "Uh-huh," and pushed further inside.

"I drain the old water into large plastic jugs that we give to a neighbor with a squash and tomato garden. You could call her yourself, if I had the number. I close up shop when I need to take restroom breaks and walk to a convenience store up the street."

She came out slowly, her right hand closed in a loose fist. Staring forward and looking stunned, she half-listened. "On a normal day," I said, "my dad would be here to tell you this himself, but he's got a doctor's appointment tomorrow. We just found out that his cancer that was in remission has come back. That's why I'm out here alone today. And I'm positive he's got the permits."

As I finished she held her palm out with something small and black in the center. Two tiny pellets, the sort I'd seen in Wrendon's shed or behind the fridge in the old house.

"Shut the doors," she said.

I recognized what she was holding and wanted her out of the van that instant. I said, "I don't know what those are."

"You have rodent problems," she said. "Not to mention your van is a mess and you don't have the permits to set up in this county. Therefore I'm shutting you down right now." She took another bag, dropped in the pellets, and started gathering her things, looking disgusted.

"Just let me sell what we've got left," I said, finally speaking from my chest. "I wasn't kidding about the cancer. What I said just now."

"According to my records this is your third offence this year. I'm going to see to it personally that you never set up here again. I realize your predicament, but you have to understand the implications. Time and again, you have failed to comply with our minimal regulations. So go ahead and get your things together. I'll stay until you're done."

She stacked the pictures on top of the clipboard, walked out the back doors and waited outside.

While I packed the signs, she paced beside the van. At one point a brand new red Mustang pulled up. A man and his son of about ten sat up front in matching blue shirts and sunglasses. The gold wire frames made the kid's face seem small. When the man reached over and rolled down his son's window, the health inspector walked over. "This truck has been condemned due to health code violations," she said. "There's a grocery store down the street, if you'd like to get seafood."

I moved faster. The kid looked up at me, crinkling his nose so the glasses wouldn't slip. He waved, and I ignored him and the Mustang took off.

Before the woman left, she said, "So we're clear, the next time you guys park here or any other place in this county, I'll confiscate your shrimp and have your truck towed." She gave me a copy of the checklist with the citations checked off. "Show this to your father. Each offense is worth a ticket. He needs to call tomorrow morning to find out what he owes."

Looking it over I thought of Wrendon having to call before going to the doctor. "There's no way we can afford this."

"Most of the citations will be revoked once your dad agrees to shut down. But if he opens back up, he'll have to pay these fines and more."

"This is our business," I said. "It's all he's got."

"You'll figure something out," she said. "People do." As she walked away, she said, "Take care of yourself, Chris."

I wondered how she knew my name and figured she saw it on my homework.

After she left, I closed the van's doors and sat on the cabinet, setting my feet on top of a cooler. There was the sound of passing cars. Light came through the windows, but the van was almost dark. I stared at the linoleum and remembered the day at the hardware store when Wrendon and I picked out the pattern. Beige with yellow diamonds, it was supposed to hide stains but didn't. Beneath the flooring laid a sheet of plywood. We had measured and cut it to go around the cabinets. Beneath that wood was the corrugated metal floor where I had followed Buddy and learned to talk like he could. Where he said a million times to speak up and pick my words wisely. Don't give people time to think. Know what they want to hear and believe in what you're saying. Look in their eyes and they will trust you.

All I'd failed to do with this one woman, and now I needed to call Wrendon.

I walked to the convenience store and tried the house, but no one answered. When I finally reached him at a bar, he said to set everything back up.

I said, "Do you understand what could happen if she comes back?"

He said he wanted to see how the van looked when she saw it, but I just walked back and left it the same.

Half an hour later he stepped out of Loren's Escort and told her to go. He was angry and for a while wouldn't look at me. Gripping the back of my neck, he steered me toward the passenger's side. As I sat down, he circled around and climbed in. Instead of starting the van, he gripped the wheel. "I'm not mad at you," he said. "You should know that. But you've got to tell me exactly what happened."

Handing him the checklist, I described her going through the van and all she'd seen. As he glanced it over, I said, "She took pictures and found mice stuff under the sink, and that's when she shut us down."

He looked up. "She found rat turds in your truck?"

I didn't answer right away. It was that word and how he said it, making me feel the grime and stench of the van all over my skin.

"Didn't you notice it when you cleaned this morning?" he said.

"We clean the van when we get home," I said. "That way this sort of shit doesn't happen. You worked yesterday when I was at Casey's. That's not all she found. There were all kinds of things." I pointed to the slip, but he tossed it on the dash.

"I'm still trying to understand how you let this happen."

"You're the one who can afford to go to bars instead of fixing up the van," I said. "There were the permits, the scale, the pump."

Wrendon shook his head as if he hadn't heard. "All of it," he said. "Down the tubes. Do you have any idea how bad this is? I put everything I had in you, and this is how you take care of business?"

So much, I thought. *One can only be leaned on so much.* "You've put everything on me," I said, "and there's a difference. I couldn't change what that woman saw."

"You could have if you wanted to," he said, starting the van. "Instead it was old Chris. Afraid to speak up when he needs to, always saying the wrong things."

We drove half an hour to some bar. The small, square building was painted brown, on a highway between a junkyard and a liquor store. The neon sign above the door read in orange cursive letters, *Orange Blossom Special.*

"What are we doing here?" I said.

"I can't just throw away what's left."

"So I'm going to sit in there all night while you ask people if they want shrimp?"

He pulled the keys from the ignition. "Stop talking to me like this. I told you why we're here. Now get out."

For the next five hours I sat at a corner table in the back beside four pool tables. I went through my homework and read ahead for the week, wishing it was anything but math. Layers of cigarette smoke hung around the ceiling. Women playing cards argued with men at the bar over the volume of the television. Wrendon was among these men watching TV. Every so often a cocktail waitress came over with orders to fill in the van, and I went back outside. Hung up my scales.

At one point I came back to the table and found a paper plate of chips and a brisket sandwich. While I ate, a bleached-blonde woman shooting pool with a guy in a cowboy hat kept winking her caked-blue eye at me. I tried not to pay attention, but eventually she walked by and said, "You're gonna be so handsome someday."

Her boyfriend smiled. "That's old Fishhead's boy," he said, nodding at Wrendon.

They made a quiet joke and laughed. She didn't look at me again.

I started to eat, and after a while I noticed the bread on my sandwich smelled like shrimp from my fingers. I spit the food into a napkin, got up and walked to the men's restroom. It smelled like old piss, but no one was inside. I washed my hands and tried to get soap from a nearly empty dispenser. I thought, *This fucking sucks.*

A pay phone hung by a condom machine, and I walked over.

In the background Davis said, "Tell him to call from his dad's at a decent hour."

My mother whispered, "Hold on a second and let me get up. I need to put the dog out." Since I'd moved in with Wrendon, Davis had bought her a German shepherd to keep her company. She'd told me his name, but I kept forgetting. Her voice was soft and hurried. I pictured her cupping the receiver, her eyes as scattered as her voice, getting up out of bed and lighting a cigarette. I heard the screen door slam and the dog's barking grow distant. She picked up the phone in their dining room.

I asked how work was going. She whispered, "Fine. Real quick. How are you?"

Real quick. I wanted to tell her how my back ached all day. About being stuck in this bar, missing school, and this stupid woman with her idiot boyfriend. I explained the van and that afternoon with the health inspector. "Does he expect me to take care of everything?"

"I'm sure he'll find a way to have the van set up next weekend," she said.

I shook my head. "Not this time."

"Can you set up someplace new?"

"We tried a different flea market a while back, but nothing sold."

Her screen door opened and closed again. I could hear the dog running around on their linoleum. She said, "I know things were tight here with Davis, but we've been talking and he's agreed to ease up if you come back. Plus if you're working for Casey's dad at his record store that will get you out of the house."

This felt good to hear, but it was impossible. I couldn't leave him. "Wrendon's been coughing again. Worse than before. He has an appointment in the morning."

She was quiet. Knowing, like I did, what this meant.

The phone in the bedroom picked up. Davis said, "Chris, this business of collect calls after eight o'clock is bullshit. We've got to be up early for work. Emily, it's time to get off the phone. Tell Chris you'll talk later. Tell him to call on his dad's dime."

She said, "I miss you, Hon'."

"Sure thing," I said.

Davis hung up his line.

She said good night and hung up hers.

I turned around to leave, but Wrendon was leaning against the door. I wondered how long he'd been there. "Who were you talking to?" he said.

"Time and temperature," I said.

He took me by the elbow and guided me through the bar. I felt a whirl of caked eyelids, yelling, and smoke all around. We walked through the parking lot and stood by the back doors of the van. Cars sailed by on the highway behind him, pushing cold air on us. My hair blew in my face. Still gripping my arm, he looked in my eyes. "I've raised you to be the type of person who can talk straight with people. The type of person who handles his problems. Now you're your own boss. I can't make you do anything, including help out. But you came to me. Remember?"

I said, "I know."

"And I've always said you could go back to her whenever you wanted. So if you want to go, give me the word and I'll take you right now. But decide. Because I need to know whether or not I can depend on you."

I searched the pavement at my feet, wanting to tell him yes, I wanted go. Knowing I couldn't.

He let go of my arm. "You think I don't know what you're going through these days? I went through the same thing with Buddy. And the one thing I learned is how we have to stick together."

Something in his voice made me look up. How it got softer. And something in his eyes surprised me. A look I knew. Whatever I said now didn't matter. Wrendon was waiting with a reply. He was set with how he'd work this. How he'd hustle me to stay. He was willing to make me feel guilty, though I'd done nothing wrong. And he wanted to seem confident. But in that same look I saw something else, in the corner of his eyes. A glint of fear. What would it mean if I left him right now, with him sick and broke? Not just to the shrimping business, but everything in his life. All the cheating and drinking and cigarettes, not sticking around. All the truths about his life that he pushed to the side and tried to ignore, now growing clearer. I looked him over, his face and body. His narrowed chest inside his shirt. His ankles ill fit at the bend in his white tennis shoes. I felt sorry for him and wanted him not to be afraid.

"Wrendon," I said, "this sucks. There's no other way to put it. But the situation with the van is nothing we haven't dealt with before. We'll get it fixed and be back out there in no time, and this sort of problem won't happen again." As I spoke, I stayed intent on his eyes, just as he and Buddy taught me. With the same steadiness I could have had with the woman that afternoon but did not because I needed to cut loose from this, I spoke from my chest and not from my mouth. Before I finished, before letting Wrendon say anything, I said, "It's nothing but a bump in the road, and we'll be fine. I have a feeling. We'll be better for it." I did not let my eyes waver. I believed what I said.

Wrendon nodded, reassured.

"It's already getting late," I said. "I still need to drain the coolers and hose the van down. There are only a couple pounds left. Can't we just call it a day?"

He seemed relaxed again. I'd said what he needed. He eyed the bar and said, "I need to settle up, and we'll go home."

I nodded, and we walked opposite ways around the van. I climbed in the passenger's side and sat down to wait.

Watching him walk back in, I knew he'd stand at the bar and finish his beer in several drinks, bum a cigarette from someone as he waited for his tab, and pay with money I'd earned. I cracked the window to let the night air in. The sound of traffic on the highway. I sat there planning the next few weeks. I knew he'd go into the doctor and they would say the laryngectomy was necessary. After the surgery he wouldn't be able to talk. He would want to get the van going again, and I'd have to convince him the cost of putting it back in working order outweighed our profits. He could collect disability, and I would say this was probably best. Once he agreed,

I would wait another week to tell him I was moving back in with my mother to focus on the band and my upcoming senior year. There was no money set aside for college. It was music or nothing. No plan B. He would be upset, but it was time. There was the chance that he would live, and maybe he wouldn't, but I needed to go.

I looked up at the door, with its glowing orange sign, thinking it had come open. That he had come back out, faster than I'd figured. But it stayed closed. I reached for the notebook on top of the dash so I could figure out my sales. But instead of the notebook, my hand fell on the sheller, where I'd tossed it earlier, and I sat back. Staring at the little plastic tool, I thought of what I'd said to that customer. No skin or nerves, just meat and muscle. As if holding a shrimp, I closed my left hand and slid the sheller's pointed end into my fist. Trying to keep my grip, I turned the tool, but felt it tearing at my skin. And when it hurt too much, I let my fist come open, and saw, in the light, the little red creases cut in my hand from where I'd tried to keep it closed.

LIKE SNOW

After moving back in with my mother that winter, I started at the record store that Casey's father owned. A converted warehouse with cement floors and rows of plywood tables, CDs sectioned and alphabetized in narrow cardboard boxes. LPs shelved along the walls, facing out. Above the LPs, along the ceiling, hung posters of college rock bands. Worn-out, black-and-white posters of jazz musicians, and blurry posters of seventies rock groups. Music played constantly, picked according to the weather. On rainy days, slow jazz, maybe Cole Porter. On colder days, Van Morrison. Warmer, the Beastie Boys or Green Day, and in the summer, Stevie Wonder.

I hadn't seen her before that autumn, and then it seemed she was everywhere. High cheekbones and gray eyes. Brown hair she tied back or kept tucked behind her small, pointed-out ears. Throughout the start of my senior year, when I was seventeen, I'd see her around either at parties or the record store, walking along the aisles alone. Wearing broom skirts, T-shirts, jeans, and sweaters. Faded black All-Star low-tops with no socks. Chewing her lip, she ran her fingertips across CDs, buying several at a time. Music ranging from Tina Turner to Frank Zappa, the Descendents and Iggy Pop. When she checked out, she settled her eyes on me, lingering at the counter while she gathered her things. I wasn't typically nervous around girls. I'd dated over that year, having more weekends freed up. But she was different. Whenever I saw her, I tried to play it cool, to not look at her too long. But it never worked as planned.

One Friday night just before close, I was standing behind the counter, filling out the next week's order sheet. No one came in this late. But when I glanced up, she was there. Wet hair and white T-shirt. "So you called me," she said.

"Excuse me?" I said.

She pointed over my shoulder, and I turned around to the black case of shelves for special orders. "You left a message," she said. "About a Nick Cave import I special ordered. You said it was here."

"That must have been Casey." I looked over the CDs, with names written on slips of paper, taped to the sides of the cases. I found it. "Josie Pride?"

She was digging through her purse, a Dooney and Bourke. Nodding, she pushed a gold card across the counter. "That's me." Her name was punched in black letters across the bottom. As if answering a question, she said, "It's a goofy name, I know. The sort of name you'd give to a hooker." Her receipt printed out, and I handed it over. As she signed, she said, "And you're Chris Saxton."

I said, "How did you know that?"

"It's a good name," she said, and held up her fist. "It's solid."

"Yeah, but how did you know?"

She pushed the receipt across the counter. "I like to keep a close tab on boys who stare me down across record stores and parties. Just to make sure I know what I'm dealing with."

I said, "Yikes."

"I'm kidding," she said. "I asked around. I was waiting for you to talk, but you didn't." She took the slip of paper off the CD and shook the pen. "Now to make an awkward moment even stranger, I'm going to write down my number. That way, if you want, you can call me."

I said, "Thanks," and felt excited as she walked to her car. It sat under one of the lights in front of the store. A dark blue BMW. I wondered how old it was, if her parents had handed it down, or if they'd bought it for her brand new. If she was that kind of person. Casey was walking through the parking lot with two white paper bags, our dinner from Mercardo, with grease stains on the bottoms.

He stopped to talk to her, came inside, and set one of the bags in front of me. I said, "You know her?" trying to sound calm.

"That girl you've been checking out for weeks but won't talk to because you're scared?" he said. "Josie." He took a burrito out of his bag and laid it on the counter, unwrapping the foil. "She dated this guy I know, a year ago. Goes to a private school out in Dallas. Her mom's an urban development planner, and they live in this massive house on Lake Arlington, on a street her mom named after her. Pretty much designed their whole neighborhood. She dances with the Fort Worth Ballet." He took a bite. "Kind of a monster."

I said, "Monster?"

"Don't let that innocent face fool you," he said. "She was born with it. That guy I know, they dated for three months when all of a sudden she stopped calling, and she wouldn't return his calls. Just dropped him completely."

"Maybe your friend deserved it."

Casey shook his head. "He found out she was seeing someone else while they were dating, and that she pulls this all the time. After that he started hearing these stories about other people she'd seen before. Older frat guys. Some coke dealer. Even a girl. All by the age of seventeen."

"So you don't think I should call her."

Casey shrugged. "If you were looking to get laid, I'd say sure. If it was simple. But it won't be like that."

"How do you know?"

"You two would have talked before now," he said. He looked at the slip of paper and shook his head. "I'm not surprised she gave you her number, but I am surprised she waited. She's the type to just go after things. Then the next thing. And the next."

"Maybe she's different now."

"Why would she change?" he said. "People like her, with looks and that much money, don't have to." He wiped his hands on a napkin. "But who knows? Maybe she has. Either way, with all that's happening, you should steer clear of that. If you want a distraction, go for something that won't fuck you over."

I looked at the note, her number in her handwriting. *Call me* underlined. "There's the risk of that in anything."

"Not anything," he said, and thought for a second. "Model airplanes."

"All that glue," I said. "Missing pieces."

He threw out Legos and sand castles. And we went on like this until close.

Through that week, I carried her number in my pocket, and many nights I held the phone to my ear and almost dialed. But I had no idea what we'd talk about. The band? Or my father? I considered what Casey had said. I didn't date girls who were dating other people. With my time split so heavily, I couldn't waste it hanging out with anyone unless I really liked her, and I didn't want to wonder if the girl I was seeing was thinking about someone else. Still I thought about her constantly. While driving to work or school in my Bonneville, sitting on its ripped bench seat, I stared at the faded beige dash and the chip in my windshield, and I thought about her car. I pictured her house when I drove down my gravel road and parked in front of my mom and Davis's, with its yellow lawn and gray chain-link fence. I imagined what her days must be like. The school, ballet. Things I never could have afforded. At dinner I watched and listened as my mother and Davis rattled on about paying bills. Knowing she probably never heard her parents worry about money.

I thought about her every night in my room in the dark when I didn't want to think about Wrendon. Since I had moved, I saw him less and felt guilty about it. After the surgery that past summer, he'd changed entirely. His neck was sunken in and half his jaw was gone. The surgeons had removed part of his left pectoral muscle to rebuild his throat. He couldn't eat solids, only drink Ensure. The chemotherapy thinned him down to loose skin and jutting bones. He was different inside and out. The cigarettes stopped, and he quit drinking. He couldn't talk above a very painful whisper. To build up his strength, he walked an hour every morning. As much as he could, he was healing and getting by, and this time he seemed determined. I only hoped it wasn't too late. Our visits were rare, but he said he understood. There was my job at the record store, the band, and school. Sometimes I had to cancel our planned visits when shows came up, and this got to him worse than anything. But I thought, if he was getting better, none of this should matter.

Lying in bed at night, I thought about Josie's face. I considered this reputation of going from one guy to the next, and it was part of why I wouldn't dial her number. I thought of how she had asked me to call, and I wondered if she was waiting.

The next Friday night we played a set in the corner of some guy's garage. These days our shows were split between house parties and opening for larger bands at clubs in Dallas, paying gigs. We had recorded a demo and were selling them at shows and the store. Tonight the room was crowded, completely dark except two floodlights on the floor beside our feet, angled up. Cigarette smoke clouded the room, with people in front of us at face level. It didn't matter, to be so close.

After the set, I sat in the den beside the fireplace, Casey beside me. The room was hot, all bodies and sweat. My ears hummed and throat hurt. I had seen Josie earlier that night but not since, so I figured she'd taken off, until I saw her shouldering toward me through the crowd, holding two red cups. She finally made her way up and looked at Casey. Thumb over her shoulder, she said, "Beat it."

He patted my thigh, hopped up, and raised his eyebrows, telling me to be careful. I nodded back to say I would be fine.

We watched him disappear into the crowd. She sat to my right and handed over one of the beers. "So, you decided not to call."

"Who are you here with?" I said.

"Nobody."

I said, "No one?"

"If you mean my boyfriend," she said, "he's out in the car. I just thought I'd duck in here, see your band, and grab you this beer while he waited. People try to say he's whipped, but I think I'm lucky to have someone so patient." She leaned into my shoulder, taking a drink. "I came alone."

"So, what did you think?"

"Pretty much sucked," she said, smiling.

We talked through two more beers, mostly about music. I said, "You have the widest range of any person I've ever met. I mean, Lyle Lovett?"

"When I was little," she said, "I used to watch anything with music and dancing. *Solid Gold*, the *Mandrell Sisters*. You name it."

"What about *Hee-Haw?*"

She grinned and peered down at her feet. "Actually, I used to. With my dad, every Saturday night that he wasn't gone on business. He used to play this old guitar. A beat-up Silvertone acoustic. I have it in my room right now, on a stand. He's the one who got me so into music. He listened to almost everything."

"Sounds like a good guy," I said.

"He was," she said, pressing her lips together and nodding. "Past tense. In some ways more than others." She glanced at her watch. "Looks like I'd better get shaking."

I said, "Sorry about that."

"It's nothing," she said. "Don't worry about it." She put her hand on my arm. "He took off when I was eight and died two years later. Plane crash. Small engine. My mom's a freak about curfews, which is why I need to split. But you can walk me to my car."

We stood up, got through the crowd, and headed a couple blocks down the suburban street, streetlamps shining on both sides. "This is me," she said, pointing to her BMW. I remembered then, the money and the boys. Felt myself easing back.

Opening the driver's side door, she said, "It used to be my mom's." Reaching in back, she grabbed a duffel bag full of tights, dancing slippers, and towels. At the bottom were several black and white programs for the *Nutcracker*. She pulled one out and laid it on the trunk, took out a pen and shook it. "I'm going to write down my number by my name." She pointed:

Snow Princess..Josie Pride.

"Do you haul these around with this in mind?" I said.

"Nope," she said. "Do you ever go to the ballet?"

I said, "No."

"Would you be interested in going? I have next Friday off."

I almost said yes but remembered I'd promised Wrendon a visit. I hadn't seen him in two weeks. "I told my dad I'd hang out."

"All right," she said, thinking through some options and coming up with nothing. "Fuck. Couldn't you stay with him next week?"

"We have a show that night," I said. "In Dallas. You could come, if you wanted."

"Not exactly a date," she said. "Are you sure you can't get out of this thing with your dad? Just this once? Make it up during the week."

"I'll talk to him," I said, knowing I couldn't make it up soon.

"Then we're set," she said, opening the door. She tapped the bill. "Do call me. Call on Sunday so I know we're still on."

Back in the garage, now lit up and empty, I was packing my SG and amplifier when Casey came in. "What's with the goofy smile?" he said.

"Guess."

He laid his guitar in its case and snapped the lid. "Just don't say I never warned you."

"She's not so bad," I said. Putting the program in my case, I grabbed the handle and my amplifier. "What do you wear to the ballet?"

"What you wouldn't in real life," he said. "I have some clothes, if you want. That way you're not buying things you'll never use again."

"Cut it out," I said. "Did you get our money for playing?"

He reached in his pocket and took out my fifty dollars. Enough for a tie and pair of slacks, if I stretched it.

Her house was huge, inside a neighborhood of large redbrick homes, on a street named "Josie." Two-stories and wide, with colonial columns in front. Enormous windows all lit up. The lawn was green and sloped down along the driveway. Her car and a black Mercedes sat at the bottom. Driving up, I almost parked on the street beside the mailbox instead of the drive. It seemed the neighborhood, with its big houses and windows, had its eye on me. But I pulled in behind her car, killed my engine, got out, and smoothed the wrinkles from my stiff clothes. After crossing the lawn, I pressed the doorbell and watched through the window as she came downstairs, called over her shoulder, "Good-bye," and swung the door open. Her hair was pulled back. She wore a gold necklace and black cocktail dress. The prettiest girl I'd ever dated, on top of everything else.

Further inside the house, her mom walked out of a room. She had curly hair and a silk shirt, putting on gold earrings. Both looked me over, though entirely differently. Josie quickly straightened my tie and said, "Sharp." Her mom came to the door and nudged her aside. "I'm Carolyn Pride." She held her hand out.

"Chris Saxton."

She peered over my shoulder, at my car, and looked at Josie. "Do you want to take the Mercedes?"

"Night, Mom," she said, and pulled the door closed.

Alone, we walked across the lawn.

I said, "Do you want to take your car?"

"Not unless you want to." She looked at my Bonneville and stopped.

I said, "If you want to make the windows go up or down, you have to connect two loose wires in the console. I'll show you how, once we get in."

She said, "Check."

Walking into Will Rogers Coliseum, the marble-floored hall was filled with people and echoed with noise. Men in slacks and jackets next to women in sparkling dresses, made up like Josie, in bright diamond earrings. Little boys in khakis and button-downs like mine and girls in crushed velvet ran around screaming. Everything seemed new.

Holding my elbow, Josie took me downstairs and backstage, walked me around, in and out of dressing rooms, introducing me to her friends. Dancers, costume and makeup people. At first they stood at arm's length, looking me over, then she said, "He sings in a band, The Earliest Ending. They play in Dallas sometimes." Their shoulders fell, and they nodded, saying, "Sure." At one point I saw an old man in a blue jumpsuit and flat cap pushing a broom. We made brief eye contact, and he winked at me while smiling, put his head down and kept sweeping.

After a while, we went back upstairs and through the emptied hallways. Lights flickered and violins screeched. She pulled me through an entrance draped in thick red curtains, to the lower balcony. The lights went out and violins started. We took our seats in the front row. The curtain rose, and a gang of kids bolted onstage, circling a twenty-foot Christmas tree. Josie pointed. "The girl in the middle is Clara." She glanced me over to see how I was taking this in. I tried to relax, telling myself to stop being such a dork, thinking about how strange it was to be in this place with this girl, at a ballet I couldn't afford. I inhaled deeply, held my breath, and let it out slowly.

Once the performance was done and we walked out, the night was colder than before. When we got through the parking lot and found my car, I said, "Where to now?"

"Someplace warm," she said.

"You want to find a restaurant?"

"Not in this dress. What about your place?"

I thought about her seeing my house. The gravel driveway, the chain-link fence. The junked-out truck that Davis kept jacked up, and I said, "No."

"Do you have a house?"

"I do."

"Are your parents awake?"

"I don't think so."

"So what's the problem?"

I didn't have an answer.

She said, "Get in."

As we pulled off the main road and onto the gravel lane, her brow creased and she turned toward me. Almost asking a question, she let it go and settled back. Her eyes shifted around as we passed my neighbors' trailers. When we pulled to my fence, I was glad it was dark so she couldn't see the lawn or the faded paint on the house. My mother's dog stood barking with its paws up on the fence. Josie said, "It's a lot of land," as if we were buying it together.

"Half an acre," I said, the car still running. "I think they might still be up."

"You can't fool me," she said. "The windows are dark." She

opened her door and climbed out. To calm the dog, she scratched his chin, and as I walked to the fence, she pulled up the latch.

Inside the house, I kept the lights off and took her hand. We tiptoed through the living room and hallway, to my room. I shut the door and turned on the desk lamp. She took her shoes off and walked around, touching posters on the wall. She poked through CDs and some of my records, shelved with plywood and cinder blocks. When she got to my desk, she picked up a picture of Buddy, Wrendon, and me standing in front of the van. "Saxton's Seafood?" she said, tracing a finger along one of the large signs.

"My dad and I used to sell shrimp outside of flea markets," I said. "Up until a year ago, last January." I took the picture from her and pointed with my thumb. "My grandpa Buddy used to be a con man, out in Florida, but he passed away four years ago. My dad lives in Burleson. He had cancer for a while, but last September he had surgery to remove his larynx. He finished chemo in October."

"How's he doing?"

"Looks all cleared," I said. "So we're hoping that's that." I set the picture where it had been. "Pretty awesome conversation."

"It's good to know," she said, still looking around the room. "It's what you've got going on right now, right?" She went to my bed, took my SG from its stand and sat on the mattress. "Besides, I knew. Casey said something about it."

I said, "Terrific."

She kept her head turned down and strummed the strings. "Teach me something."

I sat beside her. "What do you want to know?"

"Something that fucking rocks."

I wrapped my elbows around hers and pressed her fingers on the fretboard. Note by note, pulling the strings beside the body, we went through a song.

I said, "Do you recognize it?"

"Violent Femmes," she said. "It's 'Blister in the Sun.'" She played it faster, finding the rhythm. "What's so funny?" she said. "You're scared I'm better at this than you?"

"It's just cool, to have you here like this."

She looked down at the guitar. "Now teach me some Metallica. Or something by Slayer. Or old Van Halen."

I leaned over and she turned and we kissed. She set the guitar aside, and I pressed forward. Laying back on the pillow, the light from the lamp caught her face, and I was above her, slowly easing my knee between her legs, working them apart and feeling her dress rise. She wrapped her fingers around the back of my neck and pulled my face down to hers. We kissed a while, and I felt the warmth of her through my slacks. I brought my hand to her knee, opened my eyes, and she was staring up, biting her bottom lip. "Are you cool?" I said, and she nodded, pulling me down again. As my hand pressed further, she kissed me harder, until my thumb was on the inside of her thigh. I thought of Casey saying how this would be simple if all I wanted was to get laid, and something in me wanted to stop. Suddenly she said, "Hold up."

I pushed myself up with my left arm, my right hand staying where it was. With an apologetic smile, she snaked her arm inside mine and pulled it loose, so it landed on the mattress. "Sorry," she said. "It's just, I didn't intend this." She put her hand flat on my chest. "Maybe I should have said something, when I mentioned coming over here."

"What were you supposed to say?"

She shrugged. "I don't know. I guess I wanted to see where you live. Are you upset?"

"Why would I be upset?" I said. In a way, I was relieved.

"I just don't want to fuck this up," she said. "I mean, I'd like to keep seeing you. And I'd eventually want to do this," she nodded to the space between us, "if things work out. It's just, I know what Casey told you about last year. And other things he probably mentioned. I have dated a lot of people. And I can be kind of flighty. But I'm trying to do things differently. To not be that person. And this could get in the way of that. Either us doing this, or your being pissed off that we're not."

I wasn't sure what to say, but she was waiting for a response. An okay. I wondered who this person was she was trying not to be, and looking down she seemed nervous. There seemed so much to her—the money, the schools and ballet, even this past. Olive skin, gray eyes, long throat. She was talking beyond this evening, and I'd only hoped to get through tonight. "You don't need to say all this," I said. "I'm glad you finally said something, there at the store. And thanks for taking me to the ballet. It was interesting, though sometimes I wanted to laugh for no reason. But it was fun."

She smiled and said, "Good."

That night, after driving her home, it finally set in. Driving past the lake and lit-up houses, my car smelled like the girl I'd been freaked out about just hours before. We had lunch scheduled for the next afternoon, when she would come up to the store. I was so happy that I ran two red lights, only realizing afterward, the blur of red.

Two weeks later, just after New Year's, Wrendon had a routine checkup scheduled at his otolaryngologist. I was in a good mood. Josie and I were going to see a play that night. I sat beside him in the office, in two leather chairs by a large cherry desk. Outside, it was sunny, the view from the window overlooking the roof and skyline. Wrendon was nonchalant and staring out the window. The week before he'd done a CT scan to make sure everything was clear. There was some tension, but he was casual about it. Every time before, when the cancer was in him, he said he'd felt some warning. But not anymore.

These days, because he could hardly speak, he wrote almost everything down in a small black notebook. Sitting here, it lay spread out across his knee, and he was tapping it with a pen that he had grabbed off a receptionist's desk on the way in. The door behind us creaked opened, and we turned around. The doctor said, "Hello," walking to his side of the desk, carrying a manila folder. He sat down, cleared his throat, and leaned forward. "I called you in today because I have the results from last week's test."

He opened the folder and pushed it across the desk, films of Wrendon's lungs in bright colors. Blues, greens, and reds, with spots of yellow. The doctor pointed. "These are your lungs as of last week," he said, "and I'm afraid, as you'll see here in the pictures, the cancer was more aggressive than we anticipated. While the surgery did remove most of the tumor from your larynx, some was left, and the chemotherapy failed to keep it from spreading. That remainder has since developed into small-cell cancer in your lungs."

Wrendon looked up quickly.

I said, "Small cell. That's good, right? It's not big cell. We can do something."

"Even with early detection, about two-thirds of the people with this type of cancer already have extensive disease. Extensive meaning it has affected both lungs. As you can see in the diagram from your CT scan," he pointed again, "there is a small layer of fluid already around the lungs. More so on the right one than the left, but it's on both."

Wrendon picked up his notepad and jotted something down. He tore the sheet out and pushed it across the desk.

The doctor read it and folded the note in half. "Some people at this stage have two months, others four. You are in the range of the latter, more or less." He closed the file and brought it back to his side. "The important thing now is to start making plans, doing some things you might have put off."

I shook my head. "Surely there's something else."

Wrendon put his hand on my leg.

"You said you thought it was in remission. And now you're saying he needs to take a fucking vacation?"

"I don't mean that necessarily," the doctor said. "All I'm saying is to use this time to take advantage of doing some things you've wanted to do but maybe put off, and to consider the time that will follow. I know it's difficult to hear, but many people don't get this opportunity."

"Can't we do anything?" I said. "More chemotherapy? Alternative treatments?"

The doctor said, "These routes would simply prolong life, not save it. And it would diminish whatever quality remained."

Wrendon nodded. He stood and shook the doctor's hand.

As we drove down the freeway, rain started to fall. Only my driver's side windshield wiper worked. He reached for the floorboard and pulled up a tube of lipstick. He took out the notepad. *Is this yours?*

I shook my head.

He waited.

"Her name is Josie," I said. "She goes to Nolan, a private school by SMU, and she dances ballet." I told him about her. "She's smart," I said. "Buddy smart. And very pretty." Though the word didn't seem to do her justice. "We're going to see a play tonight."

Your mom mentioned some girl. He nudged me with his elbow. *Getting cultured.*

I handed him the notepad. "We went to the ballet once, and an art opening in Dallas. At first it felt weird to do these things. But I like it. Davis gives me shit about it."

He wrote *Fuck Davis* and took the notepad back. *I hope she's not the only one. You're too young for that.*

I didn't want to tell him we'd already talked about this. But he looked at me and wrote, *Oh brother.*

I watched the road for a while and almost said more about her, but I saw he was staring out his window. In that moment, we had forgotten, but now it all came rushing back. "So what's the plan?"

In a low whisper, he said, "Talk to Loren."

I didn't tell Josie right away, but then I had to start canceling dates. We could only see each other on weekends, and I was playing more shows. Our rule in the band was we didn't turn down gigs, and we were getting more offers. Bigger bands needing opening acts. Benefit shows. One night, sitting in a Whataburger beside a large window, sharing a strawberry shake, I finally told her everything about Wrendon. "Are you fine with this?" I said. "We won't be able to see each other so much, and we hardly do right now, given our schedules." It was late January, a month out of the *Nutcracker,* and she was rehearsing for *Giselle.*

"Of course," she said. "Of course."

On weekend nights we went to Fort Worth or shows in Deep Ellum. Sometimes we told our parents we were going out to movies and drove around until I knew my mother and Davis were asleep, and we snuck back in my house. There were nights when the world disappeared. When we forgot about holding back, and I wanted to get everything off my mind. But she said to hold on, to definitely wait, and we rarely did more than kiss.

Over that time, I got to know her better. I stopped worrying so much about money. I went to see her perform, and she came to my shows. Mostly, I knew her as smiling and happy. But there were nights she hardly spoke, even at my house, when all she wanted to do was read. Or nights when we went out and she hardly said anything. I tried to start conversations, but she stayed distant. I knew she'd told her mother about my father's shrimping business, thinking she'd find it interesting, but it only made her like me less. She told Josie to keep her options open, to see other people. I sometimes considered what Casey had said, and on those nights I wondered if she wanted to be someplace else. As if reading my thoughts, she'd apologize for being so withdrawn, saying "I've just got a lot on my mind."

One night in late February, on her eighteenth birthday, we were walking through downtown Fort Worth, trying to find some theater. She was in one of these moods. That afternoon, a cold front had pushed the temperatures down into the twenties. We'd needed to take her mother's car because mine stalled in the cold, and Josie's was in the shop. She was irritated before we left, from her mother hassling us about being extra careful. She wanted Josie to drive, but when we stopped off for her cigarettes, she handed me the keys. I concentrated on the speed limit and not getting hit. But it only made me drive too slow and come close to several wrecks. All the while, she hardly spoke or looked up, except when I slammed on the brakes and she said, "Dammit." Driving through downtown, it took forever to find parking. I was glad to get away from the car, and I hoped she would be too, but she stayed the same.

Now on the empty sidewalk, the cold wind burned my ears. Her black wool coat was buttoned to her chin, her hands stuffed inside her pockets, and she kept her face buried in the collar. She came up every so often to take a deep breath. At one point I noticed her lips had turned silver, and I kept looking. She said, "What's up?"

"Your lips," I said.

"They do that sometimes," she said, "like when I'm fucking freezing." She pulled her cigarettes and a lighter from her purse and tried to light one. But the wind kept blowing out the flame.

She stepped into a store's entryway, and it finally caught. Keeping her arms tight by her sides, she clenched her jaw. It was warmer here, out of the wind, and I looked around at the glass walls. It was a toy store, with huge stuffed bears sitting inside. I had wanted to get her something, but the tickets were all I could afford. She said, "You never think cold weather is all that bad until it gets here. Then Jesus tits." She shivered and looked up, her lips still that color. "The only good thing is the sky. How it's so clear." She nodded, and I glanced up, out of the entryway, as she filled it with smoke. Once it faded, I could see the stars she meant. "The weather guys keep talking about snow, but it never snows here. Not the real kind that's big and piles up."

"They just say that for the drama," I said. "So people will drain out the grocery stores and give them more news to talk about."

She was still looking up. "It's just so hazy, with all the lights. You can hardly see anything. But someday I want to know what that's all about. Not astronomy or physics. Whatever. Maybe it's physics. But how everything relates. Why people feel the need to look at stars and try to make sense of them. Why it even matters."

I said, "You want to figure out why people need to figure them out?"

She rolled her eyes and shook her head. "Don't make me feel stupid, just for talking." She stamped her cigarette, left the doorway and walked ahead, keeping her head down.

I apologized, but she kept walking. We finally found the small theater, got our tickets, and went inside.

The auditorium was small and warm. The show lasted two hours, about some kid who could witch water during droughts but refused to get wet. She stared ahead the whole time. After we left I considered every way to get her talking, but she had this glare that said shut up before I even spoke.

I said, "You're making a big deal out of nothing."

"It's not just this," she said. "I don't know." She looked away, her hair blowing across her face.

We were standing by her car, about to get in. I said, "What are you saying exactly?"

"Let's just get in the car and go."

Driving out of downtown along the freeway, I only wanted to get her talking. To say something. I said, "Which exit is it? 35 North or South?"

Her elbow was propped up on the windowsill, with her forehead in her hand. Looking out, she said, "You don't need to make small talk. You know the way home."

I considered pulling over right there and handing her the keys. Instead I gunned the engine and slipped between six lanes of traffic, exiting 35 North.

She sat up straight and looked around, clamped her hand on the dash and said, "This isn't the right way." She looked at me. "What are you doing?"

The exit put us over the freeway, back down, and headed toward Denton, past the Fort Worth skyline, surrounding suburbs, and well-lit gas stations. I drove another ten minutes, until there were no streetlights. Fields of grass lay on both sides. Before the Decatur exit, I slowed and steered us onto the bumpy shoulder. Hardly any cars were out, and the ones that were flew by. Once we stopped, I cut the engine and pumped the gas. I pulled out the keys and tossed them in her lap. Opening the door, the interior light blinked on, and I stepped on the pavement. Josie got out and brushed past me, saying, "Get in."

The wind blew harder, with nothing to block it. I stepped away from the car. The night air layered my lungs. She sat in the driver's seat and said, "Are you coming or what?" She turned the key, but the engine wouldn't start. I looked at the road, facing north. I knew no matter how mad she was, she wouldn't leave me here. "If you keep doing that," I said, "you'll drain the battery."

"What the fuck did you do?" She slammed the door. "We're in the middle of nowhere, and my mom is going to kick both of our asses if you don't get her car started now."

"Your mom is forty miles," I pointed, "that way."

She kept looking at me. Her teeth shaking and lips silver again. I walked to the car and grabbed her coat. "It was dumb, what I said. But I didn't mean it to come out like that. And if you want to go right now, we can. But you've got to drive, because I'm sick of being in charge of that car. Now, look up."

She glanced at the sky. No streetlights. No haze. She kept her hands deep in her pockets and tightened her coat. Her shoulders relaxed.

I walked back to the car and sat on the edge of the hood, still warm from the engine, and breathed in my hands. Slowly, she came over, stood in front of me, unbuttoning my coat and slipping it off. "How much time do we have left until it goes back to normal?"

"We can go now if you want," I said. "I just flooded the engine. All you have to do is hold the gas to the floor when you turn the key."

"Good to know." She took her coat off too, laid them both across the hood, and buttoned them together, making a blanket. She sat beside me and spread it over our shoulders. "Lay back."

She pressed against my right side. Facing the sky, she said, "Thanks."

More stars appeared each second, and I said, "Sure."

She laced her fingers in my right hand and held it a while, then she pressed it against her stomach, on top of her dress. I felt the small beads of fabric, and she slowly guided our hands past her waist, down her thigh and to her knee, and she pulled her dress up, over her hips. I wasn't sure what she was doing, until she spread her legs and pushed my hand between them, beneath her panties and inside her. She said, "There." I turned my head and looked at her face. Her tightened jaw and small ears. Taking long, shallow breaths. After a moment, she glanced over, smiled, and swallowed. She motioned upward and said, "Stay focused." I turned my head and saw the sky now filled with light. We stayed there as a semi roared past, shaking the ground and punching wind across my face.

The next week, while I was playing another house party, I saw her rushing, head down, out the front door. That afternoon I'd asked her to come out, but she'd made previous plans. I saw another guy following close and two of her friends right behind him. I glanced at Casey, and he was watching her, too. He nodded at my guitar and the microphone, to say keep playing. But I turned the volume down, pulled the guitar over my shoulder and set it against the amp. Casey leaned to the microphone and sang while I pushed through the crowd.

Stepping out into the night, people in coats and knit hats were stumbling across the lawn. A couple houses down, Josie stood backed against her car. The guy's face was inches from hers, and she was laughing with her head turned. Two girls sat in the front seats, lighting a joint. One nodded toward me and yelled out at Josie.

I made my way over, trying to stay calm. I could hear my band inside. She looked up. I said, "What are you doing?"

She pushed the guy off and threw her hands out to me, smiling. Her face was flushed and sweaty and lit up on something. He was surprised, but she seemed thrilled. She hugged me and nuzzled her face against my shoulder. "We've been going from place to place," she said. "I didn't want to bug you."

I cupped her jaw in my hands and looked at her face. Could smell the alcohol on her breath. "What all are you on?" I said. "Your pupils are massive. Are you rolling?"

She nodded. "I didn't want to tell you earlier, when we talked. I know you don't do this because it's expensive. Plus I knew it would make me want to nail you, and we're holding out. Except last week. Man, we should have just fucked on the car."

Her teeth were grinding, and she could barely put sentences together. I knew to let her be, but I said, "What's going on?" Nodding toward the guy.

She didn't stop smiling. "He's nobody. His name is Jack. He has the drugs."

"So you're fucked up with him?"

She lifted her shoulders. "I guess so."

"Look, I'm almost done with the set," I said. "Why don't you come inside and go home with me?"

"Because that would be a *bad* idea," she said, grinning.

I hesitated before asking. "When I came out here, were you kissing him?"

"You think that?" she said.

The girl in the driver's seat said, "Josie, let's go."

"Why won't you stay?"

"Because I'm out with them," she said. "Besides I've been thinking. And not just tonight. But maybe we need to make some space. I mean you too."

I looked at the guy and back to her. "Are you kidding?"

She stepped back. "I know we haven't discussed it. And I knew it would bug you to see me like this. But there are reasons. There are our schedules. And you've got lots going on with your dad. It just feels tight."

"And this is how you want to talk about it?"

"It's how I'm thinking it through," she said.

The girl started Josie's car. She looked back and said, "Hang on!" She turned to me and said, "I can't just stay here with you, and we do need to talk. But not like this." She looked down and shook her head. "I'm fucking it all up."

I said, "If you want to go, then go. But if you do, don't call me tomorrow."

"God *dammit*," she said. "Stop it." Her friend honked again, and Josie suddenly looked sober, but also lost. I knew it was mean to do this while she was so messed up, but I couldn't imagine her leaving with this guy.

"I've got to go," Josie said, backing away toward the car. "You have to trust me. I'll call tomorrow, and don't not answer."

"You go with him," I said, "and it's done."

"You're being a jerk."

"Me?" I said. "Fuck that. You're the one who thinks you need to do things differently." I started walking back toward the house and heard the car door slam behind me. Now I had a sense of what she meant that first night, what Casey warned me about. I went inside and finished the set, furious. Pushing through faster, not talking between songs. Afterward, while we were loading out our gear, Casey said, "Are you hanging out or going home?"

I said, "Home."

A month passed, and she disappeared. We got further into winter, and the weather turned colder. February skies turning into constant gray. I wasn't friends with anyone who knew Josie well, so I had no way of knowing what was going on. I decided it was for the best. Now I could concentrate on Wrendon. Even still, playing shows, I sometimes thought I saw her in the crowd. Girls with Josie's hair and her ears, standing toward the back of the room, in the dark. I would get hopeful and nervous, until the houselights went up and I saw it wasn't her.

Once I stopped looking, she came back. One Saturday night while I was working at the record store, I glanced up and saw her walking along the aisles. Her hair was shorter, and she was wearing tortoise-shell glasses, a white T-shirt, and jeans. She didn't look at me, and Casey rang her up. They talked a moment, and I went in back to grab some register tape we didn't need. When I came out, there she was, smelling like cigarettes and perfume. "Got a second?"

I was suddenly scared to talk to her. I said, "No," and tried to move, but she blocked me.

"I think you owe me five minutes," she said. "Away from here."

I said, "I'm not the one who showed up on ecstasy, pinned to a car, saying I needed some space."

"There's more to it than that," she said. "And I think you know it."

"Look," I said, "this is done. We finished that night, and now you're dragging it out. I don't need an explanation."

She stood there thinking, chewing the side of her bottom lip, her eyes wet. Unsure of what to do. She looked prettier than ever, and I felt mean for thinking this, and for what I was doing. I didn't mean a word of what I said, but I knew I needed to show her I could drop this as easily as she could. It was the only way I could hang on to her, if I wanted to.

Wiping her cheek with her palm, she turned away, walked alongside the counter and out of the store.

That night, I was studying at my desk when something tapped against the window. It stopped and started up again. I walked over, opened the blinds, and Josie was standing in the yard, looking up. Wearing the same white shirt and jeans, the same glasses. Her right hand was full of pebbles and she was about to throw another. I opened the window and looked around for her car.

"It's at the end of the road," she said. "Can I come in, or are you going to keep acting like you don't want to talk to me?"

I said, "All right," took out the screen, and reached down for her.

Once she was inside she walked around, picking through my

albums. "I've missed this place," she said. "I've wanted to come over so many times."

"How did you get out?"

"Climbed down the lattice," she said, picking out a Janis Joplin album that she kept stashed to the side. "The alarm code is my birthday. I do it sometimes, just to drive around and blow off steam. A lot more when you and I were going out, after I'd come home and fight with my mom about us dating. For a while, I started driving further, just to see how it felt. Even on school nights. Denton and back. College Station and back. I've been to Austin a couple of times. Three hours each way. I've walked up Sixth Street at two a.m., then come back. I grab a couple hours of sleep, wake up and go to school." She opened the album and looked at the inside cover. "Sometimes I wonder what would happen if I kept going. Just grab an exit, east or west, and push the gas. It'd be that easy." She shut the album. "I have friends in New York. Some in LA. All of them dancers. I know I could land something. Maybe start school."

I felt jealous. "Do you want me to put that on?"

She shook her head and put it back.

"You never told me you snuck out," I said. "You could have come over."

"It was my time alone," she said. "But I have missed you. I've wanted to talk to you every day. To let you know I didn't just bail, that I wasn't kissing that guy that night. But you did act like kind of a dick, to assume."

"I know what I saw," I said, sitting at my desk. "I only asked what you were doing."

"That's not true," she said. "Deep down, you were waiting for something like that to happen. You always worried that things were ending. Because you thought you didn't have enough money, and you knew my mom didn't like us dating. And there was what Casey told you, and what I let on. Though I promised I wouldn't fuck around, and I don't lie."

"Is this what you wanted to tell me?"

"No," she said. "There's more." She pulled her cigarettes from her pocket, and I grabbed an ashtray from my desk drawer. "There's what I wanted to tell you that night. About why I needed some space. I haven't been completely honest with you." She lit one up and cracked the window.

"What do you have to tell me, if it's not about some guy?"

"You should know what happened that night of the party, after I left you there," she said, ashing her cigarette. "I was upset after we talked, and I made my friends drive me home. I felt like shit and couldn't stop crying, even when I got home. Part of it was the drugs, and I was starting to come down, but there was also what you said. My mom found me in the bathroom and took me to the hospital, where they realized I was having a nervous breakdown. I was embarrassed about all of it. I still am. I know this sounds so nuts. But for a while, my mom was used to it. I've been hospitalized once, about a year ago, for six weeks. That's when they found out all kinds of shit. High anxiety. Manic depression. The kinds of things that jealous boyfriends and gobs of ecstasy don't help."

I knew she was trying to make a joke, but for some reason, it all made sense. The heavy mood swings, all those nights. As she said this, I could see her in the stark light of a hospital room, sitting on the edge of a bed. Head tilted, in a white gown, with bare feet. Clutching the edge of a blue-sheeted mattress.

"But it's what I wanted to tell you when I said I needed some space. I was getting fucking exhausted, and my mom could see it happening. I was trying to juggle school and rehearsals, and I'd been worrying about you, with your father. One day I would think that I could be this good thing for you as all this shit was happening with your dad, and the next I would think of all the time you were wasting on me, when you should be with him. The thing is," she shrugged, "I wanted to keep seeing you. But in reality, it was wearing me out, trying to balance everything. I stopped sleeping. Stopped eating."

I looked up, and she was waiting for me to respond. "Jesus Christ, Josie," I said. "I didn't know any of this. I mean, I never even knew you wore glasses."

She smiled and reached up, held the edges of the frames, as if remembering they were there. "Another thing," she said, lifting her eyebrows. "I'm dyslexic. Up until I was fourteen, my mom and doctors thought I was mildly retarded. I had to take these remedial classes. Could barely read anything. And math? Fucking forget it." She crossed her arms and looked down. "Up until one afternoon in a ninth-grade typing class, when we had to do these scaffolding exercises, and mine were all perfectly wrong. They sent me to the school nurse, and she knew right away, just by looking at my printout. Ten years. My doctor says, along with my dad taking off, that's to blame for most of my problems. All this pent-up aggression I can't get over. So this is it: Me, laid out. All of the wrinkles that can't be smoothed. But you should know. Only I ask that you don't tell anybody."

I said, "Scout's honor," and held up three fingers. "It's just so strange to hear this now."

She said, "Now you tell me something. Something you've never told anyone."

I looked at the picture on my desk, of me standing in front of the shrimp truck. "I don't know why," I said, "but lately, I've been thinking about these days I used to work the van by myself. There were these women, every so often, who would come up in their Jaguars and Town Cars and spend eighty dollars at once. More than I made all week. They used to flirt with me like crazy, and it pissed me off so much. It made me wish I never wanted money again, and that's when I first started up my band."

"You see?" she said. "I never would have known that if I hadn't come over here tonight." She leaned back against the records. "I think when we were dating, I was trying to be different. I mentioned it that first night, on your bed. But then it got to be for you, and not for me. And it felt wrong." She stared out the window. "I wanted to be better than I have been. Maybe more than I'm capable of being. Does that make sense?"

"I don't want to sound mean," I said, "but I don't know who you are."

"But you do," she said. "Let's face it. More than you think, given our lives, we are really similar. Fuck the money my mom has got. Boil it down."

I thought for a second. She said, "Can I ask you something?"

"Sure," I said.

"Why were you so interested in me?" she said. "I mean, you're cute. You've got your band. You could date all kinds of girls. But you knew, what Casey said, that that night was a possibility. Plus we weren't sleeping together. Why waste your time on me?" She thumped her glasses. "I know it's not these."

"You want a list?"

She turned back to the window. "I could tell you that I like you because of your eyes. But the way I'd say it, you'd know it's not just because I think they're pretty."

"Maybe I don't want to know," I said. "Not even for myself. Maybe I don't want to figure it out, enough to explain."

"How about this?" she said. "Give me one reason you'd want me to stay here tonight. If you'd want me to. What you could learn from me."

"You can walk away from anything," I said. "But then, it's also something I hate."

"You hate it because you can't do it," she said. "But that's the reason I'll never be a great dancer, though I'm a good one." She took a deep breath and nodded. Settled, better. "To be honest, sometimes I wish it wasn't in me. I have to fight hard to stay with anything. You, on the other hand, have to fight to walk away. So, in a way, we're learning the same thing. It makes sense." She put out her cigarette and stood, closed the blinds and stayed in front of the window.

"Be honest," she said. "Did you miss me? Otherwise I'll go right now. But tell the truth."

I said, "I do."

She took off her glasses, placed them on the windowsill, and pulled her shirt up over her head. Now she was only wearing her jeans, and she started to unbutton them.

"Are you sure?" I said.

"It's who I should have been from the beginning," she said. "This feels more clean."

That night in bed beside her, I sat up in the dark. My alarm was set for three. Plenty of time for her to get home, she'd said. I scooted away and turned on my side, the blankets lifting as I moved. I wanted to make this work, and I tried to stay awake. Her brown hair was tucked behind her ears and her eyes moved around like she was dreaming. Breathing softly in and out, sucking her lips as if kissing something. Her small breasts rising and falling. Her thin rib cage and the bones of her hips.

I woke to knocking at my front door. My mother and Davis were at church, and I got out of bed. When I opened it, she was standing on the porch. Clouds and gray sky behind her. Wearing her black wool coat and the clothes from the night before, with her mascara smeared and her bottom lip swollen. I could tell she hadn't slept. Holding her empty duffel bag, she shouldered past me and headed straight for my room. I followed and shut my door. She dropped the bag on the bed and went to my closet. "I need to borrow some clothes," she said.

"What's going on?"

"I've been driving around since four," she said. "I left as soon as she went to sleep. Right after she gave me this fucking lip. Do you have any of my cigarettes?"

I found a pack of her Marlboros in my nightstand. "Your mom did that?"

She shook one out and bent her head to her lighter, her hands shaking. Sitting down on the carpet beside my dresser, she held the cigarette between her fingers and pulled her knees to her chin. "She kept following me around, saying she knew."

"That she knew what?"

"That we fucked," Josie said. "What do you think?" She thought for a moment. "Of course, she didn't know for sure until I told her." She looked back up, shaking her head, eyes welled up. "I can't believe I told her everything. All the times I've snuck out. The night of my birthday. All of it. That's when she hit me, and I left."

I groaned. The look on her face, pinching her lips together and staring across the room. "What are you going to do?"

"I'm staying with this guy named Stephen," she said. "He's my friend Allison's boyfriend, and he's the only person I know with an apartment who my mom won't call."

I said, "How long?"

"I don't know." She sounded frustrated, and I knew to ease up. She was the one with the busted lip, and I'd have done the same thing if someone hit me. But even she seemed to realize this all sounded sketchy. "I'm on your side," I said. "I'm just trying to understand."

She put out the cigarette and stood. "I'm going to need a couple things," she said. "There's the chance my mom will call here, and if she does, I need you to tell her that you haven't heard from me. Except once this morning. I called to break things off. That will at least get her off your back."

This seemed to be the only part of her plan that she was sure of. I thought about last night, lying in bed, and felt this slipping out of reach.

She pulled a pair of jeans and a sweater from the bag, undressed and pulled the clothes on. She wiped her face and cheeks. "Just one more thing," she said. "I need you to wait up for me tonight. I'm going to drop by around twelve."

I said, "I'm spending tonight with my dad."

She sat on the mattress beside me, and I felt it fall in. "Look," she said, thinking aloud. "Things are going to be weird for a while. I'm not sure when I'll get to see you again. Could be days. Could be a week or more. If we don't hang out tonight, I'm not sure when we will."

I said, "I'll see what I can do."

I passed through the metal gate surrounding Wrendon's house. Every time I came over these days, the air got colder and the sky seemed to darken. Throughout that year he'd started planting young oak trees in the front and sides of his yard. They were fastened to wooden stakes with white kite string, and bent in the wind. I parked between the white van and Loren's Escort.

I walked in the house, and the heat pushed against me. Holding the screen door so it wouldn't slam, I saw Wrendon on the couch, watching TV. I already felt guilty for what I was going to do. I heard Loren on the phone in the kitchen, and the house smelled like hamburgers. Wrendon waved me in. I sat down in a chair beside him. A spiral notebook, the kind we used in the shrimp truck, sat on the coffee table, with his handwriting in blue ink.

"What are you writing?" I said, nodding toward the notebook.

He flipped the page over and waved his hand like it was nothing. He wrote something on the fresh sheet. *Are you hungry?*

"I ate before coming over," I said. He knew I didn't like to eat in front of him.

A little for Loren.

I said, "Fine."

Go say hi to her.

As I walked in the kitchen, she hung up the phone and went to the stove, wearing a powder blue blouse, slacks, and heels. Whenever I came over, she went out. These days, now that Wrendon stayed home, she hardly left. Without looking up from the pan, she said, "There's potatoes in the oven. I wasn't sure what you'd want for breakfast, so I got waffles. Is that okay?" Her eyes fell over me. "Or are you not staying the night?"

I realized I was still wearing my coat. I said, "I can."

She wiped her hands on a towel that hung from the refrigerator handle. "You know he'd appreciate it," she said. "He hardly sees you anymore."

"What if I stay until eleven-thirty? He'll be asleep when I go."

"Whatever, Chris. That's fine."

"It's up to you," I said.

The timer on the stove began to ding. Loren said, "Go spend some time with him. He needs to talk to you."

I took off my coat and went back to the living room. Wrendon was watching a western. "Loren said you wanted to talk."

He pushed the notebook forward with a pen on top of it.

I need you to make a list for me. Things you want.

I pushed it back and looked up at the TV, knowing for sure now that I shouldn't leave. "What are you watching?"

The notebook slid back, and I pushed it away again. "I don't want to."

He cleared his throat, swallowed, and held the edge of the table. In a whisper that sounded like his tongue was pressed against the back of his throat, he said, "I need this. I have to let Loren know.

181

Pictures. Rings. That kind of stuff. Don't make it tough on her. Or me. I'd like to think there's something of mine you want."

Loren spoke up from the other room, saying, "Supper's ready."

We ate and watched TV until a car pulled in the driveway and Loren put on her coat. She said, "Good night, you guys. Have fun."

After the car left, Wrendon asked if I wanted to rent a movie. I told him I needed to leave at eleven thirty. "I got scheduled to open the store at nine."

He pushed the notebook forward. *What's there to do that late?* Before I could answer, he took the notebook back and winked at me. *Same girl?*

"Yep."

He reached into his back pocket and pulled out his wallet. He pushed a five across the table.

"What's this?"

For Eckerd's drugstore.

It took me a minute to realize that he meant condoms. I pushed the money back and told him I was set.

He wrote something else and pushed it forward. *Consider the list over the week. It means more than you could know.*

I said, "I'll work on it."

After a couple hours, Wrendon started nodding off in his chair. He tried to stay up, and would a while, until his head dropped down and he started to sleep more heavily, with a wet sound coming from his throat. Eventually I touched his shoulder and said, "Why don't you go to bed. You don't have to stay up for me."

He nodded and put his hands in his pockets, getting up.

"You want some help?"

He raised a hand to say good night.

I said, "I'll see you later this week."

Once he was gone, I sat at the table with the notebook in front of me. I couldn't write anything, and I considered not leaving. He'd be surprised and happy to see me in the morning. But eleven thirty came and went, and I worried I wouldn't get back to the house in time. A car's headlights waved across the living room. I went to the kitchen sink and rinsed my face with cold water. Pulling on my coat, I stepped outside as Loren walked in. "Are you okay?" she said. "Do you want to talk?"

I shook my head. "Nothing to talk about."

I drove like a madman from Wrendon's house to my mother's, gunning the car down the dark backroads. I cranked up the heater and rolled down the windows. Coming up the gravel lane, I saw her car already parked by the fence. She stood beside it and walked to my car as I got out. "I thought you might not show," she said.

"I probably shouldn't have," I said.

She followed me up the walkway, and we moved through the house. I didn't need to guide her, but she grabbed my hand anyway. In my bedroom I turned on the lamp and sat down on my bed. "Why did you want me to come back here?"

She walked across the room. In a careful voice, she said, "I need you to be done with this. I might be taking off, heading east, up to New York. And if I leave, we can't make this last. It sucks, and I know my timing is shitty, but I think it's best to end this here. As much as I don't want to."

I took a deep breath and said, "That's it?"

"No," she said, and sat beside me. "I mean, there's still tonight."

I said, "Get up."

She said, "What?"

"I can't imagine you staying here a second longer." I stood and waved my hand to get her on her feet. "So, up Josie. Now get up. You need to go."

"Why are you doing this?" she said. "You have to believe that when I came over last night—"

"You need to leave," I said. And for some reason, here in the dark, I imagined this with Wrendon, what I would say to him if I could, given all of those years. Him driving himself into the ground and making me feel terrible all the time. Having me write out lists of what I wanted. And for what?

I took her wrist and pulled her up and started walking through the house. We were halfway through the living room when I realized she was trying to pull away from me, whispering, "Wait a fucking second."

"All I've done is wait," I said, not letting go, and I kept moving through the dark.

I opened the front door and pulled her through. It slammed behind us, and we stopped on the porch. Looking out over the yard, snow was coming down heavy, unlike any I'd seen. Thick and swirling. The ground was already covered, on top of the cars and tree branches. We stayed still a moment, looking it over.

Standing behind me, she said, "Maybe I don't have to go. I could just stay here tonight and go home tomorrow morning."

I knew she meant this and wanted to stay, but I wondered if she had just now arrived at this point, if she was shocked because she wasn't getting her way. Maybe the only reason she had come back the night before was for forgiveness, and maybe she had in fact been kissing that guy. Maybe all of it. She did care, and she was being as honest as she could. I only knew for sure that I was tired of other people deciding for me, who stays and who goes. I was exhausted. I took the first steps off the porch, down to the walkway. I waved her along and said, "Let's go." Continuing up the concrete path, she followed with her head down. I went through the gate, to her car, opened the door, and said, "Get in."

She got inside and put her hands on the wheel, staring ahead. She glanced up at me out of the corner of her eyes, blinking hard. I pressed the door closed and began walking toward my house. I thought she might start the car and drive off, but she sat still for a moment. I wondered if she was waiting for me to stop. But I didn't, except the moment she cried out. One full breath, hitting her palm on the wheel, and I quit moving. Feeling her scream, it was so loud. I continued through the gate, up the walkway toward the house. With her head bent, she cried with one hand over her eyes. She started her car and backed up as I climbed the steps. I stood at the door until I heard her at the end of the road, pulling away. When she was gone, I turned around and sat on the first step, watching the snow fall and collect. Bluish-white all over the lawn, in a calm and empty sound.

I took a deep breath of the cold air and rested my chin in my hands. I thought to myself, *Now this is done.*

Snow fell the next three days and nights. I sat up late on my bedroom floor, with my back pressed to the mattress, smoking the rest of her cigarettes. I tried to read but nothing registered. I didn't even try to play my guitar. Before going to sleep, I turned off the desk lamp. Opened the blinds and pushed up the window. I imagined Josie standing there. Smiling with her arms crossed and her hair tucked behind her ears. Once inside, we'd sit together at the windowsill, in the dark, staring up and watching the snow fall. Shoulders pressed against each other's, I would wonder how all of this begins, how it seemed to appear the moment I looked up at a certain spot. And, after a while, I stopped looking at the way it all drifted down together and focused on the way that one or two flakes fell, as they swayed down to my outstretched hand and disappeared.

ARRANGEMENTS

Wrendon and Loren's fenced-in yard was crowded with pickup trucks and cars. I pulled my Bonneville past the gate and parked in the only open spot, between my mother's Taurus and one of Wrendon's new oak trees. The van sat by the side of the house where he'd left it in March, three months before, when he started on morphine and had to stop driving. Patches of grass had grown around the wheels, where the mower couldn't reach. Sometime later that night, if I got it, I'd need to wash off the dirt from that spring's rain. Casey had agreed to come over that night to help pull out the sink, cabinets, and linoleum. I had already cleaned out my own car. All the empty cigarette boxes, McDonald's sacks, and CDs. Everything now depended on Loren saying yes.

I rolled up my car's windows and cut the engine. Pulling the keys from the ignition, I looked at his white modular house and thought of all the people inside, from the funeral. Maybe two dozen. I considered the things I needed to grab. Two cans of Schlitz and his hidden cigarettes. The keys to the van, if she let me have them.

I got out and felt the humid June air. The moisture on my back and arms. The day felt too bright, the sky too big for a funeral or a wake or this new black suit. Beneath the shade of a magnolia tree sat a green lawn table with blown-over chairs. I considered picking them up but decided to let them be. Instead, I glanced at his backyard garden, with its plants already drying. Three weeks ago it was full of tomatoes, carrots, and peas. Now metal stakes stood with brittle vines wrapped around them.

Three weeks ago I was here for the afternoon, making up on two missed visits. On my knees and pulling weeds in the garden, he was asleep in the hospice bed they had placed beside the living room window. A morphine drip hung off its metal railing, and the console TV sat on top of a cooler, with the volume low. All the curtains were pulled together, and the room smelled like burnt amber. Tossing weeds off to the side, I heard the back door slam and looked up to see him coming. He walked slowly with a glass of tea, wearing jeans, a button-down, and boots. As if he'd gotten dressed up for this. I stood and wiped dirt off my knees, surprised but glad to see him awake. I was always surprised by his face after the surgery. He smelled like a hospital, but he was smiling. An IV needle taped to the crook of his arm. He held the glass out, and I said "Thanks."

He pulled his notepad from his shirt pocket and wrote something down. *You should have woken me when you got here.* Looking over the garden, he set his hands on his hips and dug at the dirt with the toe of his boot. *Thanks for doing this.*

"I should have done it last week," I said. "I'm sorry I didn't come over sooner."

He shrugged and wrote something else. *I've missed you. How are things going?* His eyes stayed on me as I read.

"Keeping busy," I said, avoiding his look and staring off at the line of sunset. "Work and school. Band stuff. How are you? You look good."

I look like shit. I just sleep. No wonder you never come over.

"You need to sleep," I said.

He put his hand on my shoulder, squeezing tight. Laughed to himself, and it made me smile. I was glad to be here, though I dreaded each visit. Every time, he was different. Getting skinnier and more easily confused. But today he seemed his old self. Back in January the doctors had given him four months. But here we were at the end of May and he seemed good. On days like this, there was a weird sort of hope.

Now, with him gone, I needed the van. I needed to go.

Small blades of grass were already sprouting in the garden. By the end of summer, it would be covered.

I kept the keys to the car in my hands. Walking toward the porch, I glanced down at the dirt and noticed imprints from the wheels of the stretcher they had used three nights ago, and I stopped. I looked at the front window with all the people in his living room. I didn't want to go in and make small talk, and I was nervous about Loren saying no.

The night before, when I called to ask for the van, she flat out called me a vulture, saying I was just like my mother with her insurance. The policy no one had known about except her and Wrendon, that they had managed to keep secret until he died at nine p.m., June 23rd. Loren found out when she called my mother to say he was gone, and my mother had to tell her. That she and Wrendon had taken it out two years before, when the cancer went into remission the first time. He had needed to live until June 24th. My mother asked her to hold off until midnight to call the hospital. Just three more hours and there would be enough money to cover his funeral and their mortgage. It was the deal she and Wrendon had made. My mother got to keep the rest. "If we call now," she said, "no one gets anything."

Later that night, as they sat at the dining room table, with Wrendon in the bed a few feet away, Loren asked for the details. The full amount. My mother said that she and Wrendon had decided to keep it between them. Loren said if there was more, she was entitled. As much as half. My mother said it was the funeral and the house. That was the deal.

I didn't know all of the facts and didn't care to hear them. Standing by the porch, I pictured them talking, starting to argue, with him so close. Money and hustle, as it had been all his life. And here we all were making more.

But I needed to get the van. Everything I'd worked for was at stake. Not just for myself, but the other guys. I wasn't sure how hard I could press Loren, and I worried I wouldn't be able to push through. To do what Wrendon would have, to get my way.

I ran my foot over the dirt, smoothed the inch-wide tracks, and went inside.

* * *

The night he died, my band was playing a club called Trees in Dallas, opening the *Dallas Observer* Music Awards. We were all eighteen now and could play wherever we wanted. No more back doors or open mics. Earlier that month we were voted best new act in the alternative weekly's annual "Best of " poll and given the opening slot at the ceremony. After the set we were hanging out backstage with the other bands, sitting on couches and chairs, when Rhett Miller of the Old 97's gathered us up. He asked if we had a reliable van and if we were free throughout July. Another group was lined up to open the shows on their tour, but they had to cancel. Rhett explained they needed someone quick, and they thought we'd work out great. Everyone—Brian, Jerry, and Casey— said yes immediately. No question about it. They all looked at me, and I said I was sorry but couldn't say yes for sure. Not with Wrendon. Rhett said he understood, but he needed an answer soon, otherwise they had to move. After that, everyone in the band stayed distant, not even talking to each other. Just one more instance of me holding them up.

A few minutes later, the club's manager, Steven, popped backstage. "I've got a call for Chris in my office. She says it's important."

The room quieted down. Most of the people in the bands knew each other, and most of them knew about my father. I stood and told Casey I'd catch up later, and I followed Steven out. Walking behind him along the crowded balcony, people were lined along the railing, saying hello as I passed by. I smiled and said hey, but kept my head down to avoid conversation. We reached his office, with its beige soundproof walls and a thick window that looked out over the crowd and the stage. He pointed to the phone on the desk and said to lock up when I finished. I picked it up and said, "Hello?"

My mother said, "I've been trying to reach you."

I looked through the window, out over the crowd. "Is he gone?"

"A little while ago," she said. "I'm over at Loren's."

A clock on the desk read 11:45. "Did you call the hospital?"

She said, "Not yet. But you need to hurry because I've got to call them soon."

"I'm leaving right now," I said. I figured she would wait so I could see him one last time before the paramedics took him away. The hour-long drive took forty minutes. I got to the house and saw the ambulance already backed up to the porch. Its red lights spinning and the headlights shining across the yard into the street. Loren and my mother stood beside it. "Where's he at?" I said. "I thought you were waiting."

A paramedic appeared in the doorway, walking backward and carrying the sheet-covered gurney. I felt a huge punch to my chest.

Loren said, "She wasn't waiting for you. It turns out they had some deal going, and he needed to last until twelve. Otherwise she wouldn't get paid. As soon as that time came, she called. He's been dead for a while."

Confused, I turned to my mom. "What's going on?"

She rolled her eyes and crossed her arms tighter, staring at the door. "I tried to reach you sooner," she said. "But I couldn't wait any longer."

"Otherwise they might have figured her out," Loren said.

The paramedics carried him down the steps. I wanted to see him but couldn't imagine how to ask. They wheeled him around to the back of the truck, pushed the gurney in, and slammed the doors shut.

The engine turned and the truck dropped into gear. I glanced up at the porch light where gnats twisted around and heard gravel turn as the truck pulled away. The sound of the engine disappeared around the corner. Just the chirping of crickets and half of me gone. Nobody spoke. I looked around as though for something, and I remembered there was the letter. He'd told me about it that afternoon in May, when we talked in the garden. It was inside his desk, sealed in a manila envelope. One last time to be near his voice. I climbed the steps and went inside.

The living room was loud with people. Men in old suits and women in dresses, holding cans of beer and red cups full of liquor. I braced the screen door to keep it from slamming so people wouldn't look up. Out of habit, I looked where his bed had been, expecting him there. But everything was back to normal. The console TV on the floor. The couch by the window, full of people talking.

I let the door close and stared through the crowd toward the kitchen. I needed to get to the refrigerator and grab the cans of Schlitz. I kept my head down and started moving, hoping no one would stop me. But someone said my name, and everyone turned. Wrinkled faces, bloodshot eyes. Their heavy smiles. I waved hello, thinking that might suffice and they'd let me pass through. But every man there wrapped his hand around mine, and every woman leaned in with dried red lipstick to kiss my cheek. Alcohol wet on their breath, each step was into someone new. "He was a good man," they kept saying. "He's at rest now." "At peace." As I moved, I said, "Thank you." And with each person, I waited for someone to grip my shoulders, stop me solid, eyes on mine, and say the truth. "He sat alone here, waiting for you. Watching the door." But no one did, and I kept pressing forward.

At the doorway to the kitchen, my mother came out, holding a plastic cup and a piece of sheet cake wrapped in a napkin. We hadn't spoken since the morning after he died, when she tried to explain the policy. She sat on the couch then, trying to stop me as I walked to my room. I'd waved her off, saying to save it, as I intended to do now. I nodded and tried to step past, but she blocked me.

"You're not still upset?" she said.

"I'm thirsty," I said, and tried to get around.

"Out of everyone, I thought you'd understand."

I looked at the sheet cake. "Of course I get it. I just wish it wasn't all that you and Loren wanted to talk about."

"She's the one making an issue out of it."

I was already annoyed with the conversation. The anxious look on her face. "She wouldn't be making an issue out of this if you'd been smarter about the policy."

"What's that supposed to mean?"

"There were a million ways to go about this," I said. I checked to make sure no one was listening. "When you told her about it that night, you could have pretended you thought she knew, that you thought Wrendon had told her you were going to pay off the funeral and the house."

My mother considered this.

"You should have known she would ask how much it paid. That she'd want more. And you should have had some amount figured." I let this settle, realizing none of this had ever crossed her mind. Of course it hadn't. "Before he died, you could have asked what he and Loren owed on the house, got an estimate on the funeral. Doubled that, and told her that's how much the policy paid. That would have sufficed. Or at least guessed the balance they owed on the mortgage sometime before coming over here that night. It would have been easy."

She wrapped the cake up in the napkin. Put it in the garbage and wiped her hands, like she was ready to do business. "Do you think it's too late to try that now? What you just said?"

"Of course it's too late. But you need to do something. Otherwise, she'll never leave you alone."

She took a drink. "And now she wants me to cut her a check, instead of paying the mortgage myself."

"Why do you care how she spends the money? Just cut it and be done, if that will make her happy. After that you'll never have to talk to her again."

"That's not what I agreed to. He said specifically, 'Write the check to the bank. So she won't spend it on something else.' You have no idea how much this policy cost me. I'm not just going to hand over the money so she can use it however she likes."

I said, "No wonder she won't let me take the van."

"I spoke with her about that this morning."

I looked up, hopeful, but she frowned. "Turns out, she's already got someone interested."

I said, "How much?"

She said, "Five thousand."

I said, "You're kidding." No way I could come up with that amount, and no way Loren would let it go for nothing.

"Who knew it was worth so much? I told her, 'Surely, you understand what this means to Chris, and what it would have meant to Wrendon.' But of course she started in, saying he would have given it to you himself if he really wanted you to have it."

I thought of his letter and all he'd written, and I wondered if he actually felt this way. "Isn't there *any* way you could buy it?"

"It doesn't make sense to pay for something you should get for free," she said. "Besides, if I tell her I'm splitting the money in half, it wouldn't look right to say I've got this extra."

I said, "All right." Just so I could go.

"I'm sorry I can't do more," she said. "But good luck."

You could do more, I thought, moving toward the kitchen. There were a million things she could do, particularly now with the money in hand. But she didn't have it in her to threaten Loren. To tell her she'd get nothing if she didn't give me the van. It would have never crossed my mother's mind, and she wouldn't be able to see it through. This was something only Wrendon or I would have thought of. But he would have done it without thinking, and I would think about it too much. I didn't want to guilt Loren, as he would have, right after such a loss. He would have seen this as an opportunity, with her upset. I wasn't sure I could and hoped I wouldn't have to try.

Cookies, chips, and sandwiches sat on the kitchen counter, next to bouquets of flowers. Half a dozen they'd brought from the service. Plastic bottles of whiskey and vodka lined the sink, and one of our old coolers sat on the floor, full of soda, beer, and ice. People came and went, pouring drinks and grabbing handfuls of food. But Loren was nowhere.

Wrendon's mother, a woman I'd only met that morning, stood by the refrigerator, close to the zinfandel. Even in the June heat, she wore a thin sweater and pink slacks. She and her husband were staying at a Hilton outside of Burleson. I reached for the handle, and she stepped aside. "How are you doing, Chris?" she said. "You hanging in there?"

I said, "I'm fine," and bent down inside the door.

"Your grandpa and I were wondering whether you might let us treat you to dinner tonight. Maybe catch up."

Looking over the near-empty shelves inside the refrigerator, I pictured the three of us at some restaurant talking about my life and Wrendon's. She hadn't seen him in all these years. I opened the crisper where he kept the Schlitz and tried to think of a lie. "We have a show tonight," I said. I grabbed two cans and tucked them through a hole I'd made in my jacket lining.

"I understand," she said.

I pushed the drawer back in, grabbed a Coke, and stood, shutting the refrigerator door. From the look on her face, I could tell she didn't.

In that same voice, she said, "Your mother mentioned you were playing a show the night he died."

I popped the can and leaned against the counter. "There's more to it than that."

"She said you'd won some sort of contest with the local paper. That you absolutely had to be there."

"It wasn't exactly a local paper," I said. "And it wasn't a small contest."

"I guess in a way, I am surprised, knowing he was sick, you'd schedule something like that."

I swallowed hard. Of course she was surprised. She hadn't known what it was like these past few months. Particularly the last few weeks. He had insisted on trying to stay awake, although he couldn't because of the pain and the morphine. I sat useless on the couch as he slept. Feeling bad for wanting to leave and making up excuses not to come. "It wasn't just me," I said. "I had the other guys to consider."

"Oh well," she said, patting my hand. "I'm sure your father would have told you to go. You know your dad. He would have said that life is precious and should be lived."

I knew my father would have never used *precious* to describe anything. But I got it. This had been happening all day. People talking about Wrendon, reciting lines from Hallmark cards and movies. How he lived by his own rules, and the charm that sort of life entailed. Everybody tried to outdo each other. He was a ladies' man, chasing skirt at church picnics when he was five. He could do anything. He had once been a mechanic and worked on a ranch. Stories he told me in the van, on those trips back and forth from the coast. But nobody mentioned the running around on my mother or how he couldn't hold a steady job. With each new story, he was becoming a different person, someone better, and this woman didn't know him at all.

She didn't know about the call on the afternoon he died, how I almost missed the show. I was in the driveway at my mom's house, loading my guitar and amp in the trunk, when the phone rang. Standing there, I knew it was him. He had started speaking again when his morphine dosage jumped. He called the house every few days, saying he needed me to rush over, that he was alone and coughing up blood. The first few times I drove ninety miles per hour, rushed through his door, and found him asleep. I stood in his living room, covered in sweat, unsure whether to be happy or mad. Since then, I let the phone ring out and waited ten minutes to call his house. Loren would answer and say he was fine.

I stood by the Bonneville that afternoon and stared at the house, letting the phone go. It was four, and I had to be at soundcheck by six. The ringing stopped, I slammed the trunk shut, and the ringing started again. He never called twice. I ran inside and picked up the phone.

"Chris, is that you?" His voice was gravelly and forced. Coughing hard.

"Are you all right?"

"It's on the sheets, and I can't stop it."

I said, "Where's Loren?"

"She's not here," he said. "Please, Chris. Come over."

I stared at my car. I wasn't sure if I could even reach him in time. "Maybe I should call an ambulance."

"No ambulance," he said. "Just come."

I considered having to cancel the show. The *Observer* would call the runners-up for our slot. The winners were being announced that night. I said, "Wrendon, I need to know if this is happening. You have to promise." I wiped my cheek but couldn't finish. Promise what?

He hung up.

I was about to call Casey when the phone rang again. I said, "Hello?"

"Hey, it's me," my mother said. "Are you all right?"

"Wrendon just called," I said. "Nobody's there, and he's coughing up blood. So I'm about to head over."

"Don't you need to get to Dallas?"

"I can't just leave him."

"I'll go," she said, "and you can call me from the club."

"But what if this is it?"

"You can't think of that," she said. "Just go. I will take care of this."

So I went.

Two hours later, I reached her. She'd driven to his house, knocked on the door, and nobody answered. It was unlocked, and she pushed it open to find him sleeping on the bed. Loren sat in a chair, asleep beside him, with her head resting on his stomach. My mother watched as his chest rose and fell, then went back to her car.

I looked at my grandmother. She finished her wine and said, "Maybe tomorrow. Or even better, you should visit us sometime this summer out in Pensacola."

The cans were soaking through my jacket. I said, "You bet. But right now I need to get to the bathroom, if you'll excuse me."

"Of course," she said. "But come and say bye before you leave."

I said okay and made my way out of the kitchen, down the hall, and to the bathroom. Once I was inside I turned the lock and looked over the room. The counter, the sink, the mirror, the bathtub with the yellow shower curtain. All of the cabinets. Above the toilet hung a framed watercolor of an umbrella on a sunny beach. I pulled the painting off the wall and turned it over. On the inside of the frame, I found the Merits that Wrendon stashed, and I stuffed them in my jacket pocket. Almost everything. The beer, the cigarettes. I just needed to talk to Loren. But it seemed there was something else I needed to get or do, though I couldn't say exactly what. I looked around the bathroom, turning on the water so no one would hear me digging through the cabinets.

Beneath the sink were Loren's tampons, hair color, and moisturizers. A blue disposable razor with his flecks of skin, a black comb with his hair. There was an empty morphine bottle that read in faded green letters: *Wrendon Saxton*. I considered taking this because it had his name.

Someone knocked, and Loren said, "Is anybody in there?"

I said, "Hold on," turned off the water and opened the door. Stepping out into the hall, I held the inside knob. Her hair was pulled back from her face. She said, "I didn't realize it was you." Her eyes were glassy from all the drinking, and I knew if I was going to push, to do it now.

As she started to go in, I kept my arm straight and held the door. "Do you have a second?"

She held up her hand. "You already got my answer," she said, and tried to move past me. But I kept my arm stiff, and she stepped back.

"I know you've already agreed to sell it," I said. "And last night you said he wouldn't have given it to me. But I know he would have said yes, if he were alive."

"But he's not," Loren said. "He gave you the chance to list some things you wanted, and you couldn't even be bothered with that. So now it's mine, and I'm going to sell it."

"Don't you understand what I'd be losing?" I said. "I won't get this chance again. All I'm asking is you let me borrow it for the summer, and you can sell it when I'm done."

"After you've driven it across the country? With all the miles?" she said. "No way."

I couldn't picture taking the Bonneville home, calling everyone in the band to say we couldn't go. The thought made me sick to my stomach. As she tried for the door again, I said, "I'm going to talk to Mom."

"Talk to your mother all you like, and I'll give her the exact same answer."

"I'm going to talk to her about the insurance," I said. "And I'm going to tell her not to give you anything."

Loren stepped back. "You can't do that."

"She and Wrendon never put it in writing. No formal agreement saying she would pay off this house. The whole policy is in her name, and she isn't obligated to give you a cent."

Loren said, "Your mom would never do that."

"Don't you think it's crossed her mind?" I said. "All she needs is someone else to say it. I'll tell her she's crazy to give you anything. Especially when she made the payments, and to the woman her husband was cheating with when they split up. She'll be relieved."

"I don't believe you," Loren said. "Not for a second."

"You should find out what I'd do," I said. "Just imagine losing your house over five thousand dollars. For a van you know is more mine than yours. I sold shrimp from it before you met Wrendon. I ran his business from it when he couldn't. I paid your bills when he was sick, and while you two sat at the bar. I've got nothing to lose by talking to her. She'll probably buy me a new van." I let go of the bathroom door, so Loren could move past me if she wanted.

"The keys are in his desk," she said. "Just take it."

I almost asked if she was serious.

She said, "You know the real reason your mom doesn't want to give me the money? It's because he came to me, and he never once cheated on me. I could have left him years ago, when he first got sick, but I didn't. I wasn't like you, constantly making up excuses. And now I'm stuck inside this house that your mother is paying for. Standing in the hallway, with you saying this. When a simple thank you would have sufficed. 'Thank you, Loren, for looking out for him. For not leaving him alone.' Because you practically did, there at the end."

I stepped aside, and the hallway went dark as she shut the door. I could now feel the sweat on my back, and my hands were shaking as her words sunk in. I could go. But she had finally said it, that I left him there alone, and the shame from earlier returned.

In half a daze and almost numb, I walked down the hall. Turning the knob, I went inside the den and pressed my back to the door. The air was cooler. Finally, no one was talking to me, and no one expected anything. I gazed over the blue carpet and the wood paneling. Dusty sunlight came through two cotton curtains. A vinyl couch sat to my left, and a television was on the floor. I walked to his large metal desk in the corner, remembering now another thing I needed to do, what he had asked of me in his letter.

* * *

He first mentioned it that afternoon three weeks before, as I followed him from the garden to the plastic table by the magnolia tree.

"What can you write that you can't tell me now?"

People forget.

"I won't forget," I said.

Sometimes wisdom only gets me in the dark. About the only time—ha ha. Besides I want to hear you talk. Your mom mentioned some contest.

"She did?" I said. I'd asked her not to tell him. The chance he would make it to that date was slim, and I kept it a secret in case he didn't. Besides, he never talked about the band. When I was younger, he thought it was silly. And these days he saw it as my excuse not to visit.

"Every year the *Dallas Observer* does this poll," I said. "And we were nominated best new act. Turns out we won, and now we're opening the ceremony. There will be about two thousand people in the audience, including label scouts. The other bands are sort of huge. Some are already signed."

He looked at the setting sun, squinted against it. He closed his hand into a fist and rapped the table, a smile at the corners of his mouth. He wrote something down and pushed his notepad across the table. *Don't forget who got you started.*

I looked up at him and laughed.

Standing next to his gray metal desk, I pulled out the chair and sat down, looking it over. On the left corner sat a framed picture of his old seafood store, a square white building, with him in front of it. Hands on his hips, he was tan and wearing a cap. Across the desk, on the right-hand corner, stood a picture of him with Loren on the wooden front steps of Greener Acres. He wore a cowboy hat, snap-button shirt, and boots. In the center, there was a picture of him, Buddy, and me in front of the van. The same picture I had on my desk in my room. I heard Loren and my mother on the other side of the door. My mother saying, "Have you seen him?"

"A while ago," Loren said.

My mother said, "About the policy. I'll be honest. It was $75,000. I'm going to give you thirty-seven. Enough to cover this house and some extra. We're going to pay off our house too. And that's it. All of the money. But here's the deal. I'm only willing to cut you a check if you'll agree to give Chris the van for the summer."

Loren said, "I appreciate it."

"Well, good," my mother said, surprised that Loren had caved so easily.

"When does he leave?"

"The day after tomorrow. I can't believe he got this break. It's unbelievable. He'll be playing to hundreds of people every night. Sometimes thousands."

"Well, I'm glad," Loren said.

With every second, it was getting more real, that I would be going out on tour. Playing to people every night, all over the country. First across the south, up the Atlantic, and to New York. West to Chicago, and further west. Places I had never seen, sometimes in huge clubs. But I wanted to wait to think about it. There was still this, being in his house. I focused on the top of his desk and considered three nights ago, when I came inside this room in the dark, turned on the desk lamp, and found the manila envelope. In the side drawer, on the bottom, tucked away where no one could find it. The cover read in black ballpoint, *For Chris Only*. I wanted to read it there but thought someone might walk in. He had said that no one knew. I finally opened it when I got home, sitting at my own desk. The letter itself consisted of different dated entries, written over two weeks, in different pens and types of handwriting, on spiral notebook paper. You could tell when his mind was foggier by the slant of the lines and misspelled words. It started out talking about how happy he was for me, and proud. His hopes for my future, giving advice. It started out as I had expected but changed with the last entry, a few days before.

Now sitting in his office chair, I tried to tune out all of the talking from the other rooms and consider what he'd written. *Once again, you have broken a promise. Just for a visit.* Moving along, he spoke of the loneliness in dying. Saying he knew he hadn't been the greatest father but wondered whether he deserved this.

On the last page he said to put myself in his place and think of how it felt there at the end, to be so alone. He said to someday come to the den all by myself and lay my head on the desk, where he laid his head himself as he wrote. Imagine waking up from all the drugs, just before the pain set in, hoping I would be around. Putting off the morphine on those days that I had promised to show, to be clearheaded just in case. Then Loren saying I'd called to cancel. I now knew why he called so often, saying he was sick and asking me to come over.

There at the desk, I remembered the story about Buddy's ghost. Wrendon saying he still talked to his father after he had died. I laid my forehead on the cold metal and closed my eyes, wanting to see Wrendon and say I was sorry. A moment passed, and the doorknob clicked. I opened my eyes and saw my breath collect on the desk. I felt a hand on my shoulder, and my mother said, "Are you all right?"

I said, "Just resting," and lifted my head.

She sat on the couch. "I talked to Loren, like you suggested, and she's agreed to give you the van."

I turned around. "I've got a question."

"I told her the policy was $75,000. But that's a lie. I got a hundred and fifty."

I almost choked. "Are you fucking kidding?"

"I haven't told anyone," she said. "Not even Davis."

"How'd you work this out?"

She threw up her hands. "Your father arranged everything. It's called a high-risk insurance policy, designed for people with life-threatening illnesses. I'd never heard of it until one day when he called me at work to ask if I was interested. Later that week he came to the house, on an afternoon while Davis was gone. Your father explained everything at the kitchen table. For it to pay out, he had to live two more years. If he didn't, all I'd get was what I'd spent. Of course, we hoped that he would live, and if he did, the payments dropped significantly and it converted to a normal policy. But I think Wrendon knew he couldn't change. He said he couldn't afford it himself, but if I agreed to pay off the house for Loren, I could keep the rest."

I pictured the two of them at the table, across from each other, making plans. As they must have years before. I said, "Why didn't he set it up with Loren?"

"She couldn't afford it. And he felt he owed me, for all those years."

"Like some kind of gift?"

"I told him that wasn't necessary, but he wouldn't hear it." She stared across the room. "I still wonder if he hung around so it would pay out. A lot of times, people just keep pushing the morphine button. I can't imagine all that pain."

He had mentioned this in the letter and talked about holding out for me. "He left me a letter," I said. "In this desk. He wrote it out in those last few weeks."

She sat up. "Really?" Almost smiling.

I thought of his handwriting, across the last page. Words scrawled and desperate. Trying to make me understand. "It's not what you're thinking," I said. "Or at least not entirely. At the end he says I should have come by more often, after I moved back to your place. Especially this past year." I looked up at her, surprised that I was almost crying. "That's what I was going to ask you about. Not the money. And it's a stupid question, maybe. But do you think I was mean to him, there in the end, by not coming over more often?"

She pinched her lips and cocked her head to the side, like she felt sorry for me. She said, "I can't believe he did that." She took a deep breath and tried to decide what to say. "My honest answer is this. I definitely think you could have visited more often, and I understand why he was upset." She focused on me, to make sure this set. "But I also believe you shouldn't beat yourself up. I mean, let's face it. I hope he's in a better place, and all those things we're supposed to say at times like these, but I can't count how many times your father left you waiting and never showed. *I* never knew where he was half the time."

"That's the thing," I said. "I go back and forth between justifying what I did and feeling like hell. All my life, I hoped to not be like him. But there in the end, when he needed me most, I was gone. Just like him."

"You may have acted like him," she said, "but you are not him. I mean, he's your dad, so you're going to be similar. And, like him, you can be selfish. But we all have to take care of our wants. You just have to understand the consequences, and, if you follow through, be willing to accept them. Now you have to deal with this letter. But understand your situation, why you acted the way you did. You never hurt people like Wrendon. You knew you needed to take care of yourself, and you felt you'd done all you could for him."

"I think I could have cut back on some shows, though, like he said."

"Sure," she said. "And if you had, you wouldn't have gotten the exposure you needed to win the award. Then you wouldn't have been asked by this band to go out on tour, and who knows what could come of this."

I felt slightly better.

"This thing will haunt you if you let it," she said. "But only if you let it." She patted her hand on the arm of the couch. "What time is Casey coming by tonight?"

"Around seven," I said. "I just have to call him, to let him know what's going on. Can you believe this is happening?"

She said, "Yes," and checked her watch. "It's around five right now. You'd better get moving. Do you have anything else you need to do to the van, or are you guys just going to pull out the cabinets and sink?"

"We have to build a drum riser to put in the back," I said. "All the instruments go underneath, and a mattress goes on top. That's where we'll sleep. There and the floor."

"In the van?" she said. "Don't you get motel rooms?"

"The opening act doesn't get much money," I said. "Sometimes we'll get rooms, but most of the time we'll sleep in Walmart parking lots and places like that. We want to save as much as possible, to try and stay out on tour all summer, even after we split with those guys. At that point, we'll start playing smaller clubs, and it will be more hand to mouth. But we're all excited."

She motioned for me to get up. "Are you about ready?"

I said, "Yes."

"I'm going to write out Loren's check and meet you at the house."

I opened the desk drawer and got the keys. "I need to stop off and do a couple of things before heading back."

She said, "All right. I'll see you there."

Outside, the sky was a darker blue. I climbed in the van and tossed the beers and Merits on the passenger's seat. Moving the driver's side forward, I slipped the key in the ignition. Through the windshield, I saw the chairs by the table, turned on their sides, and knew I should fix them before leaving. I hopped out and walked over. Magnolia flowers lay scattered across the grass. I picked up the chairs and, while brushing one of them off, saw Wrendon's little black notebook on the ground.

Flipping through the pages, I walked into the garden, just in case someone came out and wanted to talk. In his handwriting, there it was. All he'd said in those last few weeks, scribbled down in thin black lines. All the way up to the afternoon we sat out here together.

I'd told him I needed to leave, that I had practice. He said he wanted to stretch his legs, that it felt good to be outside, and asked if I could stay a while longer. We went through the garden, up and down the rows, talking until he was tired and could hardly walk. I said I should go, and he nodded, saying, "Okay." I figured he would head inside, change his clothes and go to sleep. But after I left, he must have come back to the lawn table and sat here looking over his yard. On the last page at the bottom he had written, *Have a good time*. I could not recall him writing that before I left. There was no reason.

I closed the notebook and looked around, remembered what I needed to do. Now that the cemetery was empty, I wanted to go by myself and sit at his gravesite with no one else around. Beside the tree where he was buried, I was going to kneel at the plot, set a cigarette to my lips and one in the ground. I'd drink one Schlitz and empty the other. I hadn't cried yet. Not after he died, and not after I'd read the letter. Not once. But I wanted to be alone when it hit me, when I let myself consider the moment at nine o'clock, three nights before. I'd been onstage, in front of two thousand people, just before the set, with the lights shining down and joking with Casey, trying to shake out my nerves, when Wrendon sat up, looked around at the window, and fell hard against the metal corner of the bed. People were clapping as I walked up to the microphone and closed my eyes while Loren ran across the room to him. Standing there, I started strumming through chords and recognized what I was playing and, without having planned it, started the first words of a Dwight Yoakam song while everyone quieted, letting me go through it, until I finished the last note and opened my eyes. Remembered the stage. Saw the lights. Looked down at the crowd as cheers erupted, and I knew that he was gone.

I turned around in the garden and slipped the notebook in my pocket, making my way across the yard. Past all the magnolia flowers scattered on the lawn, to the van. After climbing in, I turned the ignition and revved the engine as I looked around. The tank was full. The seat was mine, the steering wheel mine, now in my hands. I looked through the windows behind me as I backed out, past the cars of the people still inside. Past the Bonneville and my mother's car, past Davis's pickup. I wheeled it around and shifted into drive, felt the gravel turn and reached the street. I stopped a moment to look both ways, pressed on the gas, and left his wake.

ACKNOWLEDGMENTS

Thank you,

Jen: first and foremost.

Brad Land, Kathleen Rooney, Evan Kuhlman, Joe Oestreich, Courtney Brkic: for reading this in earlier drafts and pushing it and me.

Robin Miura: for being a wonderful editor. For the belief, the kindness, and the supreme conscientiousness.

Kevin Morgan Watson: for championing not just this book but so many.

Everyone at Press 53.

Leonidas Patterson, Austin Hummell, Lee Martin, Charles Baxter, Eric Goodman, Kay Sloan, David Schloss, Jim Reiss, Keith Tuma, Keith Banner, Mary Jean Corbett, Steve Bauer, Tim Melley, Michelle Boyajian, Peter Orner, Debbie Kennedy, Stuart Dybek, Adin Bookbinder, J.D. Dolan, Larry ten Harmsel, Jaimy Gordon, John Dufresne, Cody Todd, Andrea Bussell, Isaac Turner, Melanie Crow, Jim Skipper, Lisa Gullick-Skipper, Kathy Skipper, Roger McDonald, Jane and Terry Smith, Christy Gerdts, April Smith, J.P. Avila, Kyle Minor, Ann Pancake, the Martinsens, the LaRoses, my colleagues at Pacific Lutheran University, and everyone from the Miami and Western Michigan University workshops: for the encouragement and the individual forms of help along the way.

Jason Skipper grew up in Texas and has worked as a bartender, snowboard instructor, and freelance journalist. He studied in the master's program at Miami University and earned a PhD from the creative writing program at Western Michigan University. His stories have appeared in numerous literary journals, including *Hotel Amerika* and *Mid-American Review*, with awards and recognition from *Zoetrope: All-Story*, *Glimmer Train*, and *Crab Orchard Review*. In addition, he is the recipient of grants from Artist Trust and the Vermont Studio Center. He teaches at Pacific Lutheran University and lives in Tacoma, Washington.

Cover artist **BEAT EISELE** is a self-taught, semi-professional photographer from Switzerland near Zurich. His body of work incorporates people-, portrait- and lifestyle-photography. His pictures have been exhibited in shows in Switzerland and may be seen in books and magazines. You can see more of his fine photography at www.beat-eisele.com.

CPSIA information can be obtained at www.ICGtesting.com
Printed in the USA
BVOW051703110911

270955BV00002B/4/P